LOVE AND LECHERY AT ALBERT ACADEMY

LOVE AND LECHERY AT ALBERT ACADEMY

DOLORES MAGGIORE

SAPPHIRE BOOKS

SALINAS, CALIFORNIA

Dedication

To my wife Terrie, for her belief in me and in this work...and for her enduring patience.

Acknowledgments

To Chris Svendsen and Schileen of Sapphire Books, for championing this project and to all the warm, beautiful women writers in the Sapphire family. And to my editor, Kaycee Hawn, my book designer, Lori Reynolds, and my cover designer, Ann McMan.

To Emily Whitman for her inspiration and to the women in our class who evolved into my fantastic critique group. Thank you Leann Elwood McLellan, Kylie Schachte, Elena Wiesenthal, Mary Rose, Suzanne Frank, and Lori Ubell. And another shout out to my Borrego Springs critique group. Thank you, all.

I owe a debt of gratitude for this book, my story, to my sweetheart Katie and her parents, Doc McGuilvry and Joe Gallo. Thank you for your love and belief in me.

And especially to my parents, Giusy and Sebastian Mazzini, for having the courage to stand tall for things they never thought they'd believe in. Well, the newspaper article by me, Pina Mazzini, and Joe Gallo already told so much: about the threats and the fear, the stalking and the spying. It had all happened before and was about to happen to me.

I wasn't always who I am now. So she could have taken me, she who will be nameless here. Shame could have cowed me into her clutches.

And so, I finally dedicate this book to any among you who did succumb and as a warning to others: may courage and goodness guide you to love yourself and the ones you choose.

PINA MAZZINI, December 1959.

Chapter One

Scout's Honor?

*H*omosexuals in Scouts Uniforms!
"Crap, Katie, did you see this headline?" I whispered as we slid into our row.

"Shush, that lady just threw you a look."

It stared up at us from our newfound seat—a full-page, black and white picture of a purposely limp-wristed Boy Scout leader in the New York Daily News dated September 20, 1959. I checked out our fellow passengers. Was anyone looking at us funny? Katie and I quietly swept the paper onto the floor and sank low in our phony leather seats aboard the plane for Andover, our future home at Albert Academy.

The pilot came on the loudspeaker to tell us we were next in line for takeoff. We did a slow pan of our immediate surroundings. By now, we were convinced no one had noticed us and we didn't have a neon "queer" sign on our foreheads. We snatched the small newspaper from the floor, and stashed it in the seatback pocket before anyone could spot it, even the stewardess. Katie and I felt more invisible now and even dared to hold hands under the thin blanket the stewardess had just given us, excited over our first takeoff together.

The propjet picked up speed. As it lunged forward, we were thrown back, pinned against the backrests, while our insides were sucked forward. I squeezed Katie's hand when it seemed the plane and our insides had to burst. Katie's languid look matched the feelings in my girl parts, a feeling I hadn't known until now. I thought I'd scream with the exhilarating thrust of the plane taking flight.

Going faster or further was no longer possible. How long could it be? My flesh was being stripped away. My mind's eye, my "me," we were bursting forth from flesh and bones. One final breath, and then, no more…

Was I still alive? I needed to see and opened my eyes. We were aloft. I sighed as I tried to catch my breath.

I stared at Katie, my mouth open. She flushed, giving me a look that hinted I had just seen her naked and learned her secret. She moved her hand to my thigh, and we both sobbed with joy in silence.

"Remember," she whispered, "what I told you about church, about communion? Like being with you, well, it was like being 'one' in communion. Now…it was like that now."

"Mmm. Like leaving my body—a holy feeling. Like I just took off and travelled in your eyes and with your eyes." I closed mine to hold onto the feeling of so much light and lightness inside of me.

Katie's head found my waiting shoulder. I let myself melt into her. I felt joined to her in a way I never knew. The silence between us was almost sacred.

We had travelled a long way since the beginning of summer 1959. We had aged well beyond our sixteen years. Well, I was almost sixteen. Our story, the one about me—Pina Mazzini—and Katie McGuilvry went back seven summers, seven playful summers in Maine.

And then, a month ago, we crossed over a bridge, a kind of love suspension bridge.

We held our breaths a long, scary time. And finally, here we were, in love, heading off to four years rooming together at Albert. Here in the very real present, feeling like we had just made love, although we hadn't—yet. There would be plenty of time for that. And we had to remind ourselves of the ugliness in that newspaper article. In lots of people. And be careful.

Katie broke the silence first. She whispered, "I felt like you were touching me all over."

"Shush," I said. "I just want the moment to go on and on." She lifted her head off my shoulder. Her gaze just lingered on me. I smiled and pushed her stray dark hairs behind her ear. She caught my hand, checked and double-checked for wandering glances, and pulled the blanket over it as she touched her lips to each fingertip.

"I'm so happy," she said.

I was still too excited, and I knew I couldn't say and do to Katie what I wanted, so I pulled out the News and folded it within the pages of my book. Flashing it just an instant at Katie, I scrunched up my face and, just above a whisper, asked, "Did you really think all homosexuals abused children? That newspaper is so wrong."

"I don't know," said Katie, frowning and switching gears. "Not my father and Joe, but I went bonkers when we first saw them kiss. I imagined all sorts of stuff, like they'd fire him as a doctor, like we'd be poor. I was just so ashamed of him. You know, I had to figure out a bunch of things this summer."

I patted her on the hand. "Jeez! I almost forgot. It was so sudden, losing your mom and then finding out about your dad. About the rest, about us, that was strange. If I was a queer, did that mean I was a lecher? I didn't want to be arrested or sent for shock treatments. You know they do that."

I made a face as if I was drooling. Katie smiled as she shook her head. I got even quieter, "I was petrified you'd reject me."

"Glad you got up the courage to tell me," she said. "I didn't make it easy for you. I mean, I was so confused, and scared. Would I look different, and what if other kids found out?"

"Hey, c'mere." I pulled her over to me discretely. "You're my dream girl, but for real."

Katie's eyes lit up with her excitement, heightened by the early afternoon sun refracted by the porthole.

"You know, Pina, you could take a short nap and maybe dream one of your special dreams. Just look into your crystal dream to see what's waiting for us at Albert," she teased.

Wow. I hadn't thought about the gift of psychic dreaming I inherited from my grandmother. What would those visions tell me now? Didn't even know if I wanted them anymore—my special powers to see the future. Well, maybe they would come in handy in the beginning of Albert. Everything would be new to me at this old, fancy school. I could feel myself wrinkling up my face. "Do you think they'll be snobby?" I asked Katie.

Katie looked as if she was reading a mystery on my face. "You nervous?"

"I guess."

"You used to think I'd be stuck-up too." Katie gave me a soft nudge. "And, you were right!" She giggled.

The pilot announced over the somewhat scratchy PA system that we would be landing in ten minutes.

We cleared cookie crumbs off our laps, smoothed our cadet blue crew necks, and shifted around in our semi-flare skirts. Leaning over, Katie whispered in my ear, "This is it. Remember I love you."

I didn't know if landing in a propjet would be as stimulating as taking off, but I prepared. I fixed my sexiest look on Katie. At first, her deep blue eyes seemed like big ocean waves of question marks. Then, her lips turned upwards in an all-too-knowing smile. She mumbled, "You devil, you!"

I grabbed her hand and said, "Wait till we have our own room..."

After a few unexpected bumps, we came to an abrupt halt. The landing had come and gone. Both of us flared our noses. "That's it?" We had been hoping for something more rousing, like our takeoff. I whispered to Katie that I was still excited that way. Our giggles seemed complicit.

After walking down a set of rickety metal steps, we spotted a man on the ground in a shiny black cotton suit jacket holding a sign. He escorted us to a limousine marked Albert Academy, white with bold, black lettering, "Where today's girls become tomorrow's women."

Sealed in our glassed-in back seat, we rode mostly in silence through the farmland dotted with hints of green going burnt sienna. My comment about the fall foliage got a quiet nod from Katie. Each of us seemed to be preparing for the next step in our schooling and our relationship.

Wow! Every day, every night with Katie in our own room. I wondered if Katie was thinking the way I was. Would we be found out? Could we make our friendship last? I'd die if we lost that. Would she still think I was cool? Man, I had to stop and just focus on the scenery and Katie's closeness.

The landscape mesmerized me and formed an impressionistic painting of Katie's features in greens and rusts. Her dark, Breck-girl hair became wavy hills; her watery dark blue eyes, starry nights.

Who would know I was a charity case? Well, I wasn't, but Katie's dad, Doc, was paying my way. Everyone reassured me he had the money, and anyway, I'd be good for Katie. My mother made sure my clothes were up to snuff, and my aunts and Joe's father had started a special bank account for me. Hmm! Who would we say Joe Gallo was at parent weekends?

My parents, Barney and Giusy Mazzini, could dress up nicely, and my father was good at hi-brow stuff. Katie's dad, Dr. Ron McGuilvry, well, he was Doc—well connected and influential in the Ivy League world. So, how to explain Joe? We couldn't very well say, "Oh yeah, Joe Gallo, Doc's boyfriend."

Almost on cue, Katie patted my arm and said, "We'll be just fine." Easy for her to say. I was so glad I could take refuge in our room together. I could handle most things for a time, but then I needed a good, familiar hiding place.

Was Katie hiding now? "Hey, Katie!" I broke through her mirror-like gaze. "What'cha thinking?" I poked her with my elbow.

"Huh? Oh, nothing. Well, these are really, really smart girls and *rich*, really rich."

"And you're not? Rich, I mean."

"Thanks," she said. "Notice you didn't say 'smart.'"

"Katie." I tried to be quiet. "Cool it! You know you're smart."

"Yeah, yeah. I know, 'smart, just distracted.'"

I reminded her of times she was more focused than I was when we were figuring out the mystery at Camp Minnetonka this summer. I went on to praise her scientific mind and her determination. Then, I stopped and said, "You know this is bull—! Oops! Can I curse at school?"

Katie pulled an exasperated face. "They'll probably be so sophisticated and use fancy curses like…I don't know."

"Like drat and bloody," I said.

She sighed and admitted that she had *some* intelligence, but that she was a bit intimidated too.

"Aha!" I said. "We're in good company."

We saw that we were approaching the Academy grounds. An imposing, red brick building, maybe from the last century, and a huge gate loomed up almost out of nowhere, Marmot Memorial Gate, according to our 1959-1960 Manual. We had also seen photos of Albert's beautiful architecture, but now the heaviness of the buildings towered over the otherwise inviting short-mowed, circular green lawns in their midst.

As the plush limousine inched forward, crunching the gravel between the gate, these main halls, Damper, Albert, McKuen, made their full appearance. They were a complex of medieval-military-like fortresses—for our protection or our confinement? My rush to explore my relationship with Katie, more intimately, and in our own room, momentarily shielded me from sensing any deeper secrets held in the interiors of these brick and mortar giants.

"Wow!" was Katie's only comment as she turned to focus on me. Her earlier, lurid look still undressed me, but there was a new wonderment to it. I held the look for an instant, mumbling, "You said we'd be fine, right?" and pulled her out of the car as we exited in front of our dorm.

A figure cloaked in a black academic gown pointed in silence a long, arthritic finger to the name Smythe Hall cut into the stone above the formal entrance. We turned to thank him? Her? It had disappeared.

Chapter Two

The Dorm

With suitcases bumping and bluing our knees, we struggled up two flights of stairs to our room. We could hardly walk straight on the waxed oak floors. Our leaden Samsonites, and our dizzying anticipation of promised sexual rapture, made for a wild sashay down the hall.

The corridor was long and dark, too long, too dark—and silent. I realized most everyone would arrive the next day, and our excitement effervesced. Katie and I slid and toppled over on each other. We kissed and giggled, pulling each other up only to tumble again.

A light came on. Not a sound. We must have accidentally touched a button. Feeling as if we were the only beings on this bridge to heaven, our soon-to-be ecstasy, all precaution vanished.

As if by magic, our room number appeared before a third or fourth tumble. Our final tumble would certainly be magical.

I let Katie open the paneled door. We almost fell in. I dropped the suitcase and wrapped my arms around her. As we fell onto the bed, coats hardly unbuttoned, Katie screamed. This was no cry of ecstatic passion. I watched as she pulled a travel iron out from under her back.

Our eyes met as if we had just encountered the

equation for relativity. What happened to our energy? What was the matter? It was only then we also noticed the suitcase lying open on the other side of the bed. Not one of ours.

Could it be? I quickly checked the door. Katie's name was definitely there. Beneath it, my blurred vision took in another bit of foreign matter: a name, not a Sicilian-American name, not mine. The ugly truth slapped me in the face: Katie and I were not roommates.

Holding the iron and tripping over the alien suitcase, Katie ran to join me at the door. Once again, we attempted to decipher what now appeared to be hieroglyphics on the nameplate: Dorotea Cabanus.

Katie's usual gentle and caressing touch met the door in a tight-fisted slam. I caught the other fist before Katie did serious damage to herself or the door, or woke the dead, or the living. I whispered, "There's got to be some mistake."

Just as quickly Katie blurted out, "Dorothy Cabanus, she's the mistake!"

As if on cue, a closet door in the room burst open and a black-headed, frizzy-coiffed giant-like creature holding huge bras and underpants projected herself mid-room, almost singing in her un-American accent, "Mistake? No. I'm Dorotea. So pleased to make your acquaintance! Wait, please, I must turn up my hearing aid."

Our manners, or rather, our curiosity took precedence over our dismay and disgust. Who the heck was this, and what had she been doing in the closet? I shot Katie a look. My raised eyebrow silently asked, "How much did she hear or see?"

Katie recovered more graciously than I did. I still

wore a knitted brow. Katie would read it as, "Later, we'll sort this out later." For now, Katie was effusive in response to Dorotea's *"Ach! Wunderbar!* We will be, how does one say, room companions? And such a wonderful room, mit two big beds, each with big window."

Dorotea spoke even louder and waved her flesh-dangling arm in a wide arc, showcasing the room.

Katie sailed over toward Dorotea, pumped her hand enthusiastically, patted the plush, chenille-covered beds, and admired Dorotea's scenic posters of Heidelberg's castle. Tilting her head and smiling a broad, open smile, she added more soberly, "How exciting to be your roommate, but there may be some mistake. My father arranged for my, uh…my old friend Pina Mazzini to room with me."

Dorotea now attempted to kiss both my cheeks, mistaking me for a native-born Italian. Of course, she spoke Italian too and almost crooned, *"Auguri,* greetings, *benvenuta!* Welcome!"

I squared my five-foot frame, and pushed her away with my extended robot-like hand. I almost clicked my heels and with my best Queens, New York accent said, "Yeah. I'm Pina Mazzini. Howsitgoin?"

"I beg pardon. What do you say?" Dorotea said.

That put her in her place. But shoot! What was her place? Here with Katie?

Katie politely answered for me. "Oh, Pina was just giving you a taste of another American accent." Hand behind my back, Katie twisted a piece of my sweater along with my flesh, nodding at me, "Right, Pina?"

I smiled my best cheerleader smile, pulling out of Katie's pinch.

"Yes, Dorotea, but now, Katie has to help me find my room, don't you, Katie?" I returned Katie's pinch, pushing her at the same time in the direction of the open door.

"Jeez!" I burst out once we were in the hall. Katie slipped her hand around my waist after checking the long hallway for others' eyes.

"Shush," said Katie. "Come closer. I just wanted to hold you and hold you. And now…"

"We can't. Not here," I said. Yet just as soon, I looked around and held her face, pressed her lips to mine, and jerked back as if I had just pulled a fire alarm, which I think I did, judging from Katie's sigh, collapsed shoulders, and flush. My kiss had set off a spark.

"Let's find your room." Her almost-swooning body said why.

"Swithins-Jones, Ogilvie-Brown…" I read the nameplates as we passed by successive doorways and then stopped short. I wheeled around to the room on the left.

"Wolf's kiss," I snarled.

"What?" said Katie.

"Wolf's kiss—Baciadalupo—wolf's kiss in English."

"What are you talking about?" Katie was still staring in the direction of the very long high-ceilinged corridor.

"Crud!" I pointed to the door, to the nameplate, Alda Baciadalupo, and now the gorgeous face appearing at the opened door.

Gorgeous: rich, dark skin, dark eyes, long lashes, longish, wavy, silk-black hair falling onto broad shoulders and breasts, gorgeous, big breasts in a lime green angora, clingy sweater.

"*Santo cielo!*" English escaped me at such an exotic moment.

"*Benvenuta. Avanti, avanti!*" sang the beautiful creature.

"Oh, I don't really speak Ital—" I puffed each word out with what little bit of breath I had.

"Huh?" said Katie, pulling on my sleeves.

"Oh! This is Katie, your roommate. No. I mean, I am, your roommate, that is. And Katie, Katie McGuilvry, she's...she's my best friend. Pina Mazzini." I extended my hand to Alda. Alda. Gorgeous!

I was aware of only two things, besides Gorgeous: Katie's somewhat quiet "hmph!" and a wink as Alda said, "Best friend, Katie, huh?"

She gave Katie the once-over and pulled us both into her room, displaying with a dramatic flourish a tray of cannolis and a tiny bottle of Vin Santo, which she tilted back and forth in a gesture of "Now you see it; now you don't."

Maybe this could be next to heaven; I was almost dreaming. Katie relaxed and pulled me down next to her, sitting on one of the beds. I breathed in Katie's cologne Canoe, once, twice, three times to break the spell and smell of Alda.

We started to laugh about Alda's last name Baciadalupo, wolf's kiss. She said she was really an Italo-American sheep underneath this disguise. We sampled the silky, ricotta cream filling and the just right, sweet, crispy cannoli shells. Alda said her father's friend, Frank, sent them from Maine and that, devil that he was, he also included the sweet liqueur.

Alda came from Queens too, but she was definitely not a charity case like me. She said she was glad not to be the only Italo-American here at Albert, breaking the waspy mold. Katie's leg started to twitch next to mine. Her cough interrupted our reminiscing of Queens, New York, and her hand on my shoulder screamed, "Mine!"

"There's been a mistake," she said. "We're supposed to be rooming together."

Alda raised her eyebrows, tilted her head, and pseudo-pouted. "Oh, we should all three be together. We could have a lot of fun." She laughed a make-believe diabolical laugh. We all had had a teeny-tiny sip of the Vin Santo.

Katie and I also laughed as we exited, excusing ourselves to go call Katie's dad to fix the mix-up.

Chapter Three

The Phone Call

Alda's door had just closed. And with it, Katie's laughter died. An immediate glare covered Katie's face, accompanied by Katie's unexpected shove to my back. We were very much alone in the darkened hallway.

"Hey, Katie, you're hurting me. What's the hurry?"

Releasing her grip on my elbow, Katie pushed me towards the shaft of late afternoon light peeking in from the corner window. She held me at arm's length and stared, just stared. She snarled, "Thank God my father will save us from that!"

"Wha?" I was totally confused and still under Katie's intense scrutiny. She seemed to be looking for familiar features on my face. Her gaze narrowed, squinting as if to recognize me.

During this inspection, it struck me how different Katie was, different from the girl who had just entertained us, for Alda did entertain, what with the pastries and wine and humor. The translucence of Katie's white Irish skin, even in this dimming light, made her almost glow in the dark, and her blue eyes riveting through me were vampire-like. She was devouring me with her eyes.

"So you liked what you saw?" Katie broke her silence and her stare.

"Ah man! Jealous, you?"

"You couldn't keep your eyes off her."

"You have to admit she was larger than life."

"What's that supposed to mean?" Katie spat the words back at me.

"Katie, stop. She liked us, both of us. She winked because she saw who we were."

"Hmph. I notice you said, 'were.'"

"Je-sus! It's correct English."

"Yeah. And your 'howsitgoin' to Dorotea? Good English?"

"Oh, Katie. Stop! Your roommate, I mean Dorotea, the Mistake, she's something else."

"And Miss Alda isn't?"

"Sweetie, don't be a doufus. I love you. We'll get this all worked out, and then we can make mad, passionate love all the time. Let's go call your dad."

"You mean it? You'd rather be with me?"

"Dangit, Katie, while we're still not officially registered at Albert..."

"Right, we can go anywhere and call whoever we want until then."

"Hmph! Did you know Albert was so strict?" I said.

"No. I guess we'll have a few surprises."

"Yeah. Like we haven't already had some."

We found the public telephone booth on School Street just outside campus. While Katie dialed her dad and inserted the correct number of nickels, I admired the maples beginning to color against the whites and greys of the sturdy eighteenth century buildings on Andover Hill. I was beginning to feel calmed by the foliage and the orderliness of the village green after the heated conversation with Katie. Then her usually calm demeanor flared up again.

"What? No. I refuse. Absolutely." Katie said to her father.

I couldn't imagine what she would refuse her father, but I knew I was about to get an earful. For now, the door to the booth remained closed, and Katie was sobbing and shouting, "No, no, no!" Finally, she screamed, "Well, find out!" and slammed the receiver down.

"I'm not going back," said Katie.

I tried my best to spin her around to face me, but when I succeeded, she pounded both fists on my shoulders and shrieked at me, "You can have your new Gina Lollobrigida."

"Hold on," I said. "What did he say?"

"They did it on purpose, and he didn't think to tell us." Katie continued to cry, and slumped to the edge of the sidewalk. We sat down, cloaked by the dusk. I pulled Katie close to me and slid my hand up and down her arm, soothing her and myself with the silkiness of her arm's dark, downy hairs.

"Katie, explain," I whispered, brushing my lips against her ear.

"My father knew about the rooms. Before we left, he got a call from the residence dean who said the administration always finds it best to 'expose those of more modest means to those more fortunate.'"

"What!" I almost screamed, "And you're not fortunate enough for me?"

"No. It has to be someone 'unfamiliar'. So Alda is your 'unfamiliar' more fortunate roommate. I guess in more than one way!"

"She-it!" Oops. "What are we going to do? We can't just sit here. Can your father do anything?"

"He said no. I just want to go home."

"We can't do that either," I said.

"I know."

"Pain in the bottom! We've got to register. They're expecting us tonight. Then should we trust Alda?" I held my breath as I spoke her name, expecting another eruption of Katie's jealousy.

"Pin, we can't tell anybody anything yet, but maybe we could hang out together with Alda until ten, that's 'lights out,' right? And then I'll go sleep with Dorotea, the Mistake!"

"Mistake? Hey. We can call her that. Whoa. What do you mean 'sleep with her?' Gross."

"Yuck! I'll wear a coat to bed." Katie bundled her sweater around her.

"Sweetie, we'll figure this out in the morning. Let's go before we get in trouble even though we're not official Albert girls yet."

"Barf!" Katie said as she grabbed my arm. We walked off to find Marmot Memorial Gate. Creepy.

Chapter Four

Registration

We knew the Registrar's office was located in Damper Hall, the place that had filled our eyes with awe upon our arrival. Now in this New England early evening gloom, Damper seemed to give off an ominous heaviness, starting with the dungeon-like turret on the left, to the dark, receding arches across the front of the building.

Posted on the frosted glass door, the sign read, "1959 Albert Boarders." Katie signed a fancy signature with flourishes not typical of Catholic school penmanship, and handed me the pen, smirking. "We're 'Albert girls' now." She twirled her index finger into her cheek by the side of her mouth and pasted on a great big cheerleader smile. I used my newfound block signature, which I thought made me seem 'artsy.'

Slapping each other on the back and rubbing noses, we skipped down the hall towards the exit. "We're going to be fine." I spun Katie around and leaned in to kiss her on the nose, there in the dark lit by the reproduction nineteenth-century electric candle lantern, our footsteps padded by the narrow Afghan runner escorting us to the massive exit door.

"Ahem!"

A dry cough, echoed and reverberated through the alcoves off this main corridor. We immediately jumped apart. Where it came from, we didn't have a clue.

"Ahem!" And then a voice so thin and brittle, a high note could shatter it. "Girls! Albert girls!"

We stopped as frozen as the Carrara marble we walked on, squeaking and almost sliding directly into the glacial gaze of a tall, bony person, a woman, we thought, but hard to tell. Cold like the marble, cold like the blood running through our veins. Who was this creature?

As if reading the look on our faces as confusion, she said, "Head Mistress Craney—ahem!—I am your Head Mistress, Katie." She spoke directly to Katie as she forced a frigid smile back from clenched teeth. She extended a pointed finger in Katie's direction, not to shake her hand, but to indicate she was acknowledging her and not me.

"Giuseppina Mazzini." She pulled her head back in a bird-like movement and peered over her half-glasses, down her long, bony nose. Her nostrils flared.

"Ah yes. Miss Mazzini." Her lips seemed to curl. "*Do* tread lightly!"

I thought I died. There was no mistaking her warning for a kindly request to be careful exiting in the dark. I had already seen the apparition of my first real enemy. Well, then again, there was Dorotea, but I had a feeling I could handle her.

We were about to respectfully say "good night," but the velvet tapestries covering an alcove swayed in a lazy wave, and then stillness, utter stillness covered the chilly hall. The Head Mistress slipped away as she had slithered in.

"Oh, Jesus," I said. "Let's get out of here."

"Pin. Hey! Calm down. I heard she was weird."

"Weird? God, she stabbed me through and through. One look and she got me."

Chapter Five

Back to Alda

We hurried back through the grove of trees, constantly turning around to check out each cricket chirp and frog croak. Katie looked as sick as I felt. I could still feel the Head Mistress's glare.

I only vaguely heard Katie mumble, "Remember, no flirting."

It took me a few seconds to realize Katie was more worried about Alda seducing me than the Head Mistress penetrating me with her x-ray vision. I had to convince Katie I did not intend to fool around with Alda; I had to convince myself too.

"Hey, stop it!" I said. I pulled Katie as close as I dared, almost a foot away. "Listen, I'll set her straight."

"I doubt it." Katie sighed.

We had arrived at my room. Alda opened as soon as I knocked. Not only was she gorgeous, still, but she was smart. She read our faces immediately. Her eyes filled with concern. Her tone softened. As she pulled both of us into the room, she thrust her head out in the hall. She let it swivel mechanically in both directions. I sensed she had some experience doing this.

Katie sat close to me on the chenille-covered bed that Alda hadn't claimed. Alda placed herself on the bed opposite us. She leaned forward, almost wedging herself between Katie and me. Katie and I explained the horror of the phone call. I added the details according to Dr. McGuilvry: Alda came from fortunate means, but she was not familiar like Katie; the ugly words used by Katie's dad almost gagged me as I said them.

Alda waved her finger at my rising anger and laughed. "Honeys," she said. "I hope to become familiar!"

Katie bristled. Alda noticed, saying, "I don't mean to shock you." She almost hummed. "I just hate all that stuck-up stuff." Alda gently rubbed Katie's arm.

I could see Katie soften. We all laughed in agreement.

Alda sat up straight, studying our faces. "There's something else going on."

Katie looked away, blushing. I knew what was on her mind. I still felt the tightness carved into my face from my bone-chilling encounter with the Head Mistress. I said one word: "*Craney.*"

"O Madonna! Sorry, I learned my curses in Italian. Be careful!" Alda stiffened.

I explained briefly. "It felt like she saw through me. She flicked her eyes back and forth between Katie and me, and it's like...well, maybe I imagined..." I didn't know how much I could say about Katie and me.

"Imagined, nothing," said Alda. "They say she seduced a youngish lady instructor and then had her fired. Accused the instructor of *molesting children!* You've got to watch yourself. She's evil!"

I groaned. More battles and one I had no power to win. Maybe with my grandmother's help, with the dreams. I felt Katie's fingers tiptoe into the crook of my arm. They were ice cold; her face was ashen.

"Aw crap!" I mumbled, "Enough for one day."

Alda patted Katie on the shoulder. "Want to stay

here tonight?"

Katie's grip tightened. Her eyes welled up. "I don't dare do anything wrong."

I hugged her at arm's length, telling her to come back if anything was too weird with Dorotea. Alda said, "Don't worry. I'll take care of her."

I didn't know whether Alda meant Dorotea or me. Katie blushed and left, hardly closing the door.

I hated to see Katie leave, but I sensed this longing for Katie also masked a floating fear and curiosity about what might happen with Alda. No sooner had this thought crossed my mind, than I threw myself under the covers, chenille up to my nose and beyond.

As if a switch had been thrown, Alda stirred, ambled, and sashayed over to my side. "Here, give me a goodnight hug."

Lord! What to do? My mind told me one thing; my body was yelling over my mind, screaming something entirely different. As Alda leaned over me, my mind managed to find the direct circuit to my hand, shooting it up almost at Alda's throat. "No," I whispered. "No. I can't."

Just as quickly as she had come to my side, she pulled back, almost mechanically, and winked. "I know." She smiled. "I like you. And you're real."

She blew me a virginal kiss and laughed a hearty laugh. "We're going to be fast friends. You watch."

Alda snapped out the light and ever so gently began to snore.

I thought the rhythm of Alda's snore would carry me away to dreamland—and oh how I needed a good Grandma Francesca dream, the kind that helped me see where to go with my life, but I couldn't stop worrying about Katie. What if she had been there when

Alda wanted to hug me?

Well, I really only wanted Katie, didn't I? Alda was…yeah, she was something, but I was in love with Katie. She got me, really got me like no one else, in a real, deep down place. I'd just have to keep reminding myself.

I decided to go say goodnight to Katie, Dorotea or no. The Mistake, I mean.

Chapter Six

Dorotea and The Dream Machine

I was on the point of sneaking into Katie's room on tiptoes when I heard voices. Although I remembered to knock out of respect for Fraulein Mistake, my fist froze mid-air when I heard Mistake's voice, raised louder and louder as if her words swam on spittle through her clenched teeth. I, Pina, was the subject of her rant.

"She's rough, how you say, rough around her edges. What, she is ein boy-tom, mannish. *Ja, javohl,* das ist it: she comes here, hair all wired crazy, eyes like torches; she barks orders to you and me, who only wants to make nice, keep clean, offer hospitality. But no, this Pina has no grace; she probably will clank her teacup and will call my strudel 'shoe dull!' Was ist loss with her? What's her problem?

"She is so small, dark brown too, but she puffs up her teeny breasts as if she is Amazonian. I know. I will fix her. I am sorry, Katie. You say you like her, but she is *evil.* There is a name for girls like that, 'lesbisch.' Ja. That's it. This is all wrong—must not be. You see. I will fix her."

Hmm! Evil? She'd show me? And Katie? Why wasn't she saying anything besides, "Yeah, yeah" and "Tomorrow, Dorothy, tomorrow?"

The last thing I heard was "Dorotea, Dorotea! I

am not your Dorothy!"

Well, she wasn't even that! She was our Mistake! But Katie was right. "Tomorrow." We'd fix her tomorrow. For now, I desperately needed sleep.

Back in bed, I rubbed and rubbed my eyes until I saw the oranges and purples and magentas, and coils and stars. They drew me into a full spectrum spiral, deeper and deeper into my mind, where the waves of color pulsed me into sleep's soft arms: dreamland.

Circus music, drumbeats, and barkers' cries lured me into the dirty-white canvas tent. Fresh straw and manure warned me to look out for animals—or was I in the ring? I paced, tight and panicked. The dry crack of the whip spun my head around; my eyes narrowed, my upper lip pulled back, and my mouth made a hissing sound.

There on a stand, whip in hand, was my tamer squeezed into a tight blue-gray uniform, high, tight, shiny black boots, golden medals and epaulettes flashing. She wore a monocle and spat out the words "tief und hoh." That could only mean up and down since that's what my haunches were doing. My head snapped back, and my right paw flailed up as I screeched. The flick of the whip had landed on my prized tail. A bead of blood began to take solid form. "Gutes katzchen!" Good little kitty! The tamer—or was she something more sadistic— cooed as she descended from the stand and inserted a thin cigarette holder in her mouth. The rolls of flesh protruded from her high stiff collar, wattle-like, as she inhaled deeply and goose-stepped into the shadows.

A crackle, more like a shriek, announced a

presence. An enormous presence filled my eyes: tall, pencil-thin, its black gown swishing across the floor, its hood falling forward, lower and lower on its head. The apparition held a book in one hand and a scythe in the other. Where the face should have been, an ashen oval glowed and shrieked, "Down! I will lay you down!"

I rolled over and played dead. I felt every strand of fur fall into a stiff place. Was I dead? Which of my nine lives did I just give up?

In another life, I opened my eyes. I was warm, and my body lolled on a soft, fleshy lap smelling of old lady. My belly vibrated in a loud purr. Grandmother's short, plump fingers chucked me under the chin. I caught sight of a mouse, but the word pazienza, patience in Italian, gently teased my attention away.

I lifted and rolled my head in her caressing hands and allowed her to brush the mouse away. She nodded her head, ringed with gentle white curls, up and down and smiled at me. She placed a miniscule life preserver over my head and set a box of Wheaties and a jar of caviar in front of me, repeating "campione!"— champion—over and over and over.

⚶⚶⚶⚶

I never got to sample that caviar in my dream. When I heard three loud knocks—customarily used to announce the beginning of the Shakespearean plays they took us to see at Stratford, Connecticut—I thought the next dream-reel had started to roll.

I yawned and opened one eye and then the second. I had no fur. Chenille was the closest thing, but I knew my grandmother had sent me a dream.

The door burst open. Katie threw herself at me.

"Thank God!"

I was beginning to come to. "Yeah, thank God," I answered.

"You won't believe what Mistake said. Prussian Cow!"

In a rush of words, Katie allowed herself to explode about Mistake's speech. I tried really hard to focus after my eventful night. I nodded as Katie went on and on.

"Katie, sweetie, I was there, right outside your door. I heard everything."

"What are we going to do?" Katie asked as she started to creep into my bed. She looked over towards Alda's bed and probably decided Alda was the least of her worries.

Alda yawned and answered right back, "Yeah!"

I had no idea what she was agreeing to. Before I could figure it out, Alda piled onto my bed too.

"Uh…" I felt like I was supposed to have answers. I mumbled, "Maybe I'm chickening out, but if Dorotea doesn't insult me to my face…"

"Pina!" Katie gaped at me.

Since when was Katie so belligerent? I needed time to think; today was our first day. Katie was studying my face. Did I look like a coward?

"Hold on, you two." Alda seemed to be reading our minds as well as our faces. She looked from Katie to me, and back again.

We were all business now, no hint of love and mushiness or sex.

"I mean, I have to play it cool and see if Dorotea is going to rat on me," I said.

I leaned over to reach for Katie's hand. She gave a half-hearted squeeze back.

"Katie, listen. You too, Pina. I'm going to investigate." Alda seemed to rifle through files in her head. "I've got my ways."

Alda snapped her fingers like it would be a breeze. "I'll take care of Mistake."

I smiled at Alda, carefully, so Katie wouldn't worry about my intentions.

"I've got an idea too." I hesitated to say more. "I had a dream last night."

Katie, who knew all about my intuitive dreams from the previous summer, encouraged me, her eyes wide. "Sorry I snapped, Pin. Tell us about the dream."

"I don't know what to think about it, but I have a feeling it's got some answers."

Seeing Alda's wrinkled forehead, Katie said, "It's Pina's dead Sicilian grandma, Francesca."

Alda started rubbing her hands together. "Meno male! You've got an old one on your side! Does she really come to you in your dreams? Neat!"

I sighed. "Well, she kind of tells me things, but I don't really see her. I mean—" I stopped short. I didn't know how much I should say. Besides, it was time to get ready.

We had to go to some orientation thing in a little while and made plans to get together alone after lunch. We worked out some winks and gestures like an index finger to the temple to signal a getaway, with eyes cast left, right, up or down to indicate direction.

For now, we decided that I would get dressed right away and go back to Katie's room with her so she could get ready. She couldn't bear the thought of facing Mistake alone, not this morning.

While I was dressing, Katie and Alda stayed propped up on pillows in my bed. Katie toned down the melodrama as she told Alda more details about Mistake's speech. I caught glimpses of Katie leaning her head back on her pillow to smile at Alda, who listened and "oohed and aahed" in all the right places.

By the time I was finished, they seemed to be old friends, laughing about the Mistake's "flatulence" and Pina, the "dreamgirl."

Chapter Seven

Dressed for Battle

Katie and I were on our way to face the Mistake together. As we crossed the hallway, Katie took my arm. "Pina, this is all screwed up. It wasn't supposed to be like this."

"Hey! We're in this together. Alda's going to help, and the Mistake, well, she's just a mistake."

Katie slowed her steps in her big, padded Indian moccasins, checked for our faculty hall monitor, and rubbed my back.

"You know," she said. "Maybe it's just first day nerves. Huh? Just maybe."

I wanted to believe that too. After all, my grandmother gave me a life preserver and Wheaties! I told that part of my dream to Katie but held onto the rest. I was busy pushing it back, way back into my head as we approached Katie's door.

"Ready?" I asked.

"I guess." Katie sighed and rolled her deep blue eyes. I was beginning to lose myself again. I didn't dare glance at her full red lips.

We entered on tiptoes. The Mistake was nowhere to be seen. We remembered her previous closet act and nodded agreement not to speak.

I sat on the edge of Katie's bed. Katie sort of hummed while she put on her clothes, turning to throw me a nervous smile now and then. I stood up to stretch my neck and yawn when the Mistake appeared less than four feet away from me.

Dorotea towered over me, large and fleshy with her massive cleavage in her European chiffon plunge-neck blouse. Beads of perspiration mottled her ecru complexion. She could have been Brunhilde in the Niebelungelied. (My aunt had taken me to see the Opera at the Met.) She was, without a doubt, the quintessential Nazi Fraulein, and she longed to conquer the room.

She spread her legs, planted steadfast at the foot of the bed, and thrust out her powerful arm. Her underarm flab shimmied in rhythm to her flexed hand grabbing for Katie. She seemed to say, "This too is mine!" She actually quoted in Latin, "veni, vidi, vici." I came, I saw, I conquered.

I remained dumbfounded, stunned into silence. I felt like I had to be the Flag Bearer for the Allied Forces. This had to be the Normandy Invasion.

I snapped out of my fantasy. Katie threw me a look that I read as "Stay cool!" I started to say "guten morgen" and decided against it. I merely nodded. "Good morning to you, Dorotea!"

Nothing followed; no words, no fanfares, no dramatics.

Chapter Eight

First Day

After my encounter with Mistake, everything seemed easy. Katie, Alda, and I walked arm-in-arm down the hall of Smythe to the iron circular stairs to Albert Hall. Alda winked, saying this way no one would ever suspect. Easy too, our academic gowns seemed to float over our black dresses while the junior girls attached tassels to our caps before the solemn march into the auditorium. Even the recitation of the awful religious invocation and the singing of "Halls of Albert" flew by. The rest was blah-blah about how we were now Albert material and would always remain Albert material. The elitism wasn't even subtle.

Once outside, the three of us joined hands a moment under the copious folds of our black gowns and wished each other luck for our morning classes. Katie and Alda were off to gym and I to French.

Upon entering Salle Simone de Beauvoir classroom, I started to drag my feet. I realized I was now on my own. An icy mask crept over my face when I heard the instructor say a whole bunch of musical sounds in French. Some of the girls must have understood since they giggled. I didn't have a clue outside of the few words I knew in European languages from my sampling foreign languages lessons in grade school. Yet, as Mademoiselle Lesage continued to chirp away, I found myself laughing. The others had stopped, in surprise.

My hand shot up. In perfect French, I said, "Merci de votre gentillesse, Mademoiselle." Thank you for being so kind, Miss. Well-coiffed heads turned in my direction; a pixie-ish head in a beret whispered, "O, toi aussi!" And I collapsed inside myself to marvel at the mystery of how I knew those words in French. My grandmother must have been at it again, giving me visions and words I didn't really know.

I tried to make myself small when I sensed a whoosh. The whole class rose to announce the entrance of *La Maitresse*, the Head Mistress Craney, her black gown in a fantastical swirl around her meager body. Her aura was huge, her pale, bony nose the only thing protruding from her blackness.

We seated ourselves again. Miss Craney had her back to us. Her presence swallowed up Mademoiselle standing in the very front of the room. The waves of Craney's gown's sleeves seemed to be flagging down vehicles in a race, imaginary spirits whizzing through on both sides.

When she spat out the words *attention à la petite,* watch the little one, a bony finger shot out from her academic gown, revolved around, fell upon me, and whirled back all in one unbroken gesture. It had happened so quickly, I wondered if I had imagined it.

Everything I had previously believed as real changed as Craney streaked towards the door. Mademoiselle raised her once honeyed voice to say, "Oui, je sais déjà." Yes, I already know.

Either I passed out or the classes were short, just minutes, that day. The door opened, and everyone filed out. It was then I noticed Dorotea, our Mistake.

She looked down at the sweat forming on my brow and smirked. "*Attention!*"

My next two classes, Latin and math, were similar; I somehow already knew translations for the Punic Wars and trig equations. The grand entrance of the Head Mistress marked each class and each class sped by. Each time the finger sighted me. How long before I'd be executed?

I almost fell upon Katie and Alda in the refectory. If we had been wearing our academic gowns, this would have felt like a monastery. Small rectangular windows high up by the cornice just under the rounded arch were the only things that pierced the high white walls; the wooden beams seemed to bear down on us. Thank goodness we didn't have to eat in silence. There was so much lively chatter, stilted, snobby accented drivel, that it covered my drastic ravings to Katie and Alda.

I explained briefly that the Head Mistress was dogging me. Alda told us to eat quickly, and we'd go outside to talk more freely. Better, she said she would cover for Katie and me a bit so Katie could hold me in the grove of birches. She said I looked like I needed it.

We did just that, with Alda standing guard right in front of the breech between the trees. Katie held me while I whined, "She's got it out for me, the Head Mistress. I can feel it. That's not all, Katie. I know things again. My grandmother's back!"

Katie kissed my eyes quickly and wiped them with a gentle sweep of her thumb. "Just be cool for now. Only two more hours today, and then we'll be together with Alda."

We had no sooner come out of the camouflage of the yellowing, flickering birch leaves than Alda sailed up between Katie and myself, pulling us forward by our elbows. Dorotea, the Mistake, stood rigid under a nearby arch and craned her flabby neck in our direction, saying, "Pity, not even mistel in those trees."

"I think it means mistletoe," said Alda, whose aunt had married a German.

"Shoot!" said Katie. "Mistletoe? Like for kissing at Christmas?'

"Stop worrying." said Alda. "No one could see you two kissing."

I was about to turn around and stare down Mistake when a long, skinny leg protruding from a draped black cloth flashed by. Craney again. Neither Katie nor Alda noticed.

When she saw me blanch, Alda pulled me down onto a stone bench in the loggia connecting the refectory and the library. She threw an arm around my shoulders and cheerily spouted off about rituals, birthdays, and celebrations. She said she knew when my birthday was and that she was going to be my fairy godmother, to me and to Katie. She would grant us our fondest wish.

Her sheer exuberance, not to say her craziness, totally grabbed my attention. Color was back in my cheeks, which she was pinching while slapping me on the back. Katie shrugged her shoulders at first, but gave in and laughed at Alda's antics.

Just as abruptly as this zaniness had come on, a seriousness took hold of Alda as she sucked her lower lip and sat up straight. "I told you I would investigate, and I will. I'm making a plan, but first, the library!"

We found our way to the library orientation, after which we had two more short classes. I was prepared for looney tunes, but my English and history classes went smoothly. The best was to discover Katie and Alda in the same history class.

Chapter Nine

Strategy

Dinner came and went without major incident. Actually, we were able to sit together, Alda, Katie, and I, since formal dinners with assigned 'fortunate-less fortunate student' seating only took place on Wednesdays and Sundays. Tonight, Monday, we were free to be "birds of a feather" or "flit about," according to our manual, which described in minute detail these Neanderthal practices in soon-to-be 1960.

Alda, Katie, and I met some other girls we liked and who liked us. That amazed me, that I seemed popular with some of these girls, girls like Jeanne from the South End of Boston. That, she said, meant she wasn't Irish even though she had freckles and her name was Scottish. She wanted us to know she was and still is Negro and a scholarship case! She even sucked her teeth and said, "My friends." We definitely liked her. She was the first Negro friend we would have.

Another girl introduced herself as "Mortified", explaining that she was embarrassed to go to Albert because of the price tag stuck all over it. That's what sold her father, she informed us, rolling her eyes at the other debutantes. I received my first lesson in "money talk."

After dinner, Alda, Katie, and I decided to plan.

Alda was big on strategizing. "Butter," she announced, raising a finger to her mouth and nodding to me to open the door to our room since her hands were occupied with plotting. She pulled the red, green, and black striped Hudson Bay blanket to the floor and said, "Sit!" and repeated, "*butter*. The answer is butter."

Katie sighed a big sigh, becoming familiar with Alda's flamboyance. "Okay," said Katie. "I'll bite: butter, what or who is it?"

Alda apologized and said, "Mistake, of course. We'll butter her up. She probably wants friends desperately; we'll give her friends."

"Oh Lord!" I said.

"No, Pina," she answered. "I've got a plan. Watch! *And* I will personally take her off your hands so you two can have your birthday wish, your fondest wish. *Your private sweet sixteen!*"

"Wha? No? You could find a way?" I didn't quite understand how she knew we needed that kind of privacy or how she could arrange it. Was she counting on kidnapping Mistake?

For now, she wanted Katie to go back to her room and chat up Mistake. Katie would tell Mistake that she planned to have a little get-together the following night so Dorotea—we had to be careful now during this stage of the plan not to risk calling her Mistake—could really get to know Alda and Pina who, of course, wanted to apologize for being brusque the other day. Katie would add that Pina is really a sweetheart; she just had a toothache, that's all.

Katie said she got all that and that she would lay it on thick. I almost gagged.

"*Next,*" commanded Alda. "Katie, you tell Dorotea you need a little walk by yourself, and you leave. Once I see you in the hall, out of the room, I go and knock on Dorotea's door and pretend I'm looking for you."

Alda then turned to the both of us, clasped our hands together and tinker-belle-style, pranced around, saying, "And that, my dears, is lesson number one in how to get you some privacy. Enjoy! You'll have ten minutes alone in the room."

She explained that during this "chance meeting" with Dorotea, she would begin "Mission Friendship." We were all going to befriend Dorotea. Yeah! I was on board if it meant Katie and I could be alone together. I couldn't believe we would get a good ten minutes alone. *Alone*! I couldn't wait to feel her next to me, in bed, like in Maine. Yes! And how did Alda know what our fondest wish was? Nothing could happen in ten minutes.

The plan was working. Katie came into my room, slithered her way up the door, flipped the key, and burst out half-laughing, half-crying. I ran to her, and we clasped each other, crying for real now. Katie kissed every inch of my tear-stained face and finally found my mouth. Her kiss was not the summer Katie kiss. This was new and greedy, one hand around my hips, pulling me tight to her, the other hand stroking my lips apart as her lips pulled each of my lips into her mouth. She pushed me onto the bed, and I felt her tongue enter my mouth as her hips set off a series of throbbing vibrations from my thighs up to my throat, setting off mini eruptions at all the sites in between.

I started to slip my hand under her shirt and caress the swelling of her breast. I was beginning to lose all touch with the time and the room—evening, dusk, chenille, maple frames. I only knew my craving for Katie, deeper and deeper. Was there any way we could inhabit each other's being?

Bells rang out. Everything froze. Damper Hall's bells were ringing. I had a flash vision of the Head Mistress. I felt a stinging sensation on my bare leg like the whipping flick of a toreador's cape. Only this cape was black.

"Stop!" I pushed Katie.

Stunned as much by her newfound assertiveness as by my thrust, Katie screeched to a sudden stop, perched on the edge of this sensual cliff. She gasped crimson-faced and shook me.

"I'm so scared," I mumbled. "Craney. I know she's here."

Katie stroked my head; her eyes calmed with a new look of caring and concern. "It's okay. We'll be okay." With that, Alda tiptoed in, telling us to shut out even the nightlight. Craney was patrolling the hallway, her black garb swishing from one doorway to the next.

Chapter Ten

Heart to Hearts

Katie slid off the bed, pressing her fingertips to my lips. "Ssh" was all I heard before a dusty whoosh of the door. Katie left on tiptoes.

Alda slipped into her bed and reached across for my hand. Her warm touch calmed me, and after a few moments of silence, I started to tell Alda about the summer, about the first sparks of romance between Katie and me.

"You know, about Katie and me," I started off slowly. "I think I've always been in love with her, for like these past seven years. But, well, I didn't have a clue."

"Not ever?" asked Alda.

"Well, like she'd say these really sweet things to me, and I'd just brush them off. I thought she couldn't really like me."

"So, Katie knew?" In the dark, I saw Alda's eyes grow wide.

"No. She was just herself. Like she's always nice, but I started blushing around her, and…if she accidentally touched me…"

"Katie? No!" Alda put her hand to her forehead in exaggerated shock.

"No, c'mon. I mean like if she brushed against me or grabbed my arm, God, I'd get all tingly, and I was afraid she'd see."

"And? You were chicken? You?"

"I was panicked I'd lean over and kiss her. And then, I thought to myself, 'Holy crap! I'm a lezbo. I can't be. I don't want to be—like they're gross.'"

Alda sat up straight and got real serious. "Really? I don't think you are."

I hoped she wasn't saying more than that. I really didn't want her to touch me, but she was sexy, and sometimes when she touched my hand, I got the tingles. I had to tell her again that Katie was the only one for me. I kind of snapped back at her, "Yeah!"

"I started to get that same ugly feeling I used to get in my stomach, the one when I suspected I was a queer. It was that feeling—and my fear Katie would get that same yucky feeling about me—if I told her how I felt about her.

"I finally made up my mind. Alda, I could never pretend to be someone I'm not. So I told Katie. It took a few days, but in the end..."

"What? Don't stop. C'mon, Pina."

"Well, in the end, she agreed she loved me too."

"And? C'mon, get to the punch line." I had the feeling Alda was hanging on my every word—and maybe getting off on it.

"Alda, stop! Yeah, we made out, but it's like sacred."

"Just made out?"

"Well, some more."

"But you're still...I mean the two of you didn't really do it?"

"Alda!"

"Dio mio! Pina, am I going to give you a birthday present! Wait till you see what I've got in store for you and Katie."

"Oh God, Alda, please don't tell Katie I told you. It's not like swapping guy stories, guys bragging who got to third base. It's really private." I sighed. "C'mon, Alda, can I trust you?"

"Yeah, Pin. Sorry. I'm just so crazy about the two of you. Never been in love. Never had anyone love me."

I think Alda's voice quivered a bit when she admitted that. I still didn't dare hug her. I puffed myself up, saying I'd go to work on finding her an *inamorato*. I asked nonchalantly if she wanted a guy or a girl.

She just laughed and said she would be too busy fanning the flames between Katie and me. We were quiet for a few minutes. I felt safe now. I actually told her more about my dreams and how they helped solve a twenty-year-old murder this past summer.

Then, Alda almost pitched herself out of her bed, trying to grab my arm. She swore me to secrecy to what she was about to tell me. I almost landed on her in a heap on the floor. By now, I expected her to tell me she was a queer too. Instead, she bit her lower lip, whispering, "My father…he's different."

I laughed and said, "That's all? Mine is strange too. And Katie's? Why, he's a queer, and so is Joe Gallo, his boyfriend." I was giggling, quiet belly laughs; it felt good to goof around after all that tension. First my make-out scene with Katie and then? Was it really Craney?

Alda pulled me back from my mini convulsions and wrinkled her brow. Shaking her head, she closed her eyes to say, "Scary." She had begun to tear up. "I'm not sure, but I suspect that he does really scary things. I don't want to believe…"

I blew out and scrunched up my face. All I could

say was, "Is he scary with you?" I   figured it would allow her to say, "No," and she did. Her father, Wolfie, sounded a lot like Fifi, Joe Gallo's dad, an ex-Mafia guy and a real sweetheart. I promised not to say a word and added that loving families and loving friends were what life was all about anyway, wasn't it?

We agreed that making nice-nice with Dorotea the next day was going to take a lot of energy and that we needed our sleep for that. I crawled back to my bed, curled up under the covers, and thanked her for her ten-minute gift to Katie and me, a real gift from the heart.

Chapter Eleven

A Brighter Day

Well, if yesterday was a day of blackness and gloom, today seemed rosy in comparison. When Katie, Alda, and I finished eating in the refectory and lounging in the sun-filled loggia, the three of us went over plans for the party that night. Katie and Alda swapped their versions of Dorotea's swooning for joy, reacting to their invitation to the get-together. Things were not just rosy; they were peachy-keen.

Alda had gone back to her room to gather goodies for the evening's festivities. As we walked towards my French class, Katie started to lecture me on my best manners towards Dorotea.

"Pin, you've got to be sweet. C'mon, you can be nice when you have to."

"Gee thanks." I rolled my eyes.

"You know what I mean. Just smile, chat her up about her strudel, and don't, absolutely do not strut or act butch." After checking to see that no one else was looking, Katie leaned towards me, smiley, cheerleader style to push my hair in place.

"Barf! Butch? Me?" I squared my jaw and clipped my fingers in the waist of my A-line skirt.

Katie tilted her head and smiled at me, a smile that whispered, "Please." I shrugged and smiled back in agreement. I knew I had to win Dorotea over. I also knew I didn't have it in me, not really, to be cruel to someone, but just then, I remembered my dream, the one of Dorotea, the Nazi lion tamer.

I had no sooner described to Katie Dorotea's sadistic Nazi officer character and therefore my doubts about her good will towards me than Dorotea's head popped up in front of us. Topped with a red, white, and blue beret, she waved a mini red, white, and blue French flag at us, and pinned a miniscule Eiffel Tower on the lapel of my navy blue wool blazer. She completed the act with a deep European curtsy, saying in French, "A ce soir. Comme je suis contente! See you tonight. Boy, I'm happy."

Trying to make sense of this latest version of Dorotea, I felt Katie pinch me. She narrowed her eyes, indicating that I needed to respond to Dorotea. I forced myself to smile so the French words I didn't really know could come tumbling, flowing, cascading freely out of my mouth. "Oui, moi aussi, j'en suis ravie!" When I mumbled to myself that I was delighted too, the English words were drenched in sarcasm.

With that, Katie pushed me into the Salle Simone de Beauvoir classroom, huge question marks in her glare as if to say, "Dorotea, sadistic, Nazi officer, complete with whip?"

My glorious French affair did not end there. Mademoiselle Lesage informed me that I was being considered for special placement in the French wing of Albert Hall. This was an honor bestowed on the crème de la crème and never, "*jamais!*" on first year students, she informed me.

Dorotea flashed her most saccharine, Bavarian yodeler smile on me and whispered in German, "Stimmt, of course!" I couldn't tell if she breathed it out in awe or awful jealousy. Her chubby cheeks continued to puff into a cloying smile.

Out in the hall after class, I signaled to Katie. Her smile was solid; I could build a future on it. We were exchanging a quick, upbeat evaluation of our first period class, when the Head Mistress appeared.

Something was definitely in the air today, for there was Miss Craney clad in a simple red wool gabardine suit with a delicate yellow gold crane on her lapel and a pale tan and gold Chanel scarf tied like an ascot, adding volume and élan to Miss Craney's throat and chin. Her cheeks seemed discreetly powdered and rouged and her rosy, smiling lips accented them. Her beaky nose had all but disappeared. She was stunning.

She lowered her eyes upon me in a sidelong glance as she told Katie, "You run along to class, Miss McGuilvry." Before I knew it, her arm was through mine, and she was inclining her head towards mine, three inches away. "I will crane my neck to watch out for you." Her fingers appeared as if by magic from the silk cuffs protruding from her suit sleeve. She tapped me once, ever so lightly on the cheek, which was now two inches away from her. "You will be my little fledgling. Remember cranes in Chinese mythology. We are the symbol of longevity and immortality. Ah! And magical transformation to fly away on journeys." She finally let her breath out as if in ecstasy.

She was gone. I was mummified. Katie was late for class as she emerged from behind the potted snake plant, her lookout onto the latest appearance of Head Mistress Craney.

Later I told Katie about my Craney dream, Craney the reaper whose words were, "I will lay you down." Katie wasn't able to match up these different

Craney apparitions. Neither of us cared to clarify what she might mean by "lay me down." Maybe not a red-letter day after all.

The party later that evening was a success, if the meaning of success was Dorotea's attaching herself to us. Alda was seductive in a food and drink sort of way, actually getting Dorotea *ein bischen blau*—well, more than a little blue or drunk—on the Vin Santo.

Colors. Oh yes, Dorotea had decorated the room with little red garden gnomes. She broke out land jaeger, dried spicy meat, strudel, and even some peppermint Schnapps. Her mother said the peppermint alcohol was for "stomach hurt." So Dorotea was blue-drunk but definitely not blue-sad.

She did say a bit too much. Her father was in Argentina; he was not allowed to go back to Germany; she missed him and only got to see him intermittently between her schooling in Germany, Switzerland, and France. His picture, lovingly presented in a beautiful German porcelain frame with pink cherubs and fuchsia roses, was at least ten years old. He could have been the male version of Dorotea in my dream complete with boots, crop, and Iron Cross. The resemblance was deadly.

I was equally blue, true blue to my promise to be on my best behavior towards Dorotea. I did apologize and actually found myself feeling bad for this lonely girl who tried so hard and had so much to hide. I think I knew what she was feeling.

Alda and Katie were red. The eating and drinking, in addition to the dancing to Elvis as well as to Dorotea's "oom-pa-pah" music blushed their cheeks equally rosy on Katie's china-Irish complexion and Alda's swarthy tan.

As we started to say goodnight and Alda and Dorotea made plans to hang out, I couldn't help noticing a certain grayness. Was the motivation for this "Mission Friendship" clear: merely to butter up Dorotea? Was it still black and white? The end of this day seemed to place us in a gray zone. Maybe black wasn't always bad and white good.

Chapter Twelve

The Morning After

Psst!" I kept on hearing, "Psst!" I imagined a bee buzzing around my head. Or was that just a buzz from the Vin Santo and Schnapps?

What a relief to see Katie's head emerge above the edge of the bed! Her eyes didn't look great, but they were definitely not bees' eyes.

She slithered more like a snail into my bed and suctioned herself onto me under the covers. Her "hi" sounded more like a "moo," and the response of "baa" from Alda's bed told me we were all three somewhat hung over.

It was early yet; we had time to get it together before breakfast.

"Hey, so are you going to sleep with Craney?" Katie asked me. The question would have made sense if Katie had hiccoughed, if she were still really drunk, but now? I just stared at her, her head all shaggy and hanging over the side of the bed, a bit of drool forming in the corner of her mouth. This was a crazy question coming from someone looking rather crazy.

"What the heck?" Alda sat up suddenly and just as quickly held her head and then her mouth. In an instant, she was off the bed and into the bathroom. Gurgling and splashes announced her vomiting.

Back in the room, Alda flopped onto my bed and

said, "Okay, explain."

I repeated Craney's words about keeping me, her fledgling, under her wing. When I added the part about laying me down, Alda began to howl and actually beat the bed as I continued to explain that cranes in Chinese mythology symbolized a person's power to transform into a crane and tele-transport.

Katie shrieked, "God, she could be under the bed right now."

We all laughed, saying we didn't smell a crane, nor did we hear one, but we did, in fact, hear a scratching on the door and a sort of whistle.

Crane or no crane, Alda and Katie both bounded out of the bed, Katie to the bathroom, Alda to her own bed. We breathed a sigh when Dorotea tiptoed in.

"You have too much fun. I can join, yes? What you say?" Her morning German accent aided by a schnapps slur was extra heavy.

"Huh? Oh. What are we talking about?" I said.

Alda began to tell the rumor she had heard about Head Mistress Craney.

"They say she seduced Miss Whitfield, an English instructor."

"Seduced? What is the meaning?" asked Dorotea.

There was a longish silence as Katie, by now out of the bathroom, and Alda and I looked from one to the other. Alda began, "Uh, she flirted with Miss Whitfield. Uh, she sent her poetry, and she snuck into her room at night."

"Ja?" said Dorotea.

Katie and I sat in silence and tried to signal Alda with eye rolls and the pursing of our lips. We wanted her to quit while she was ahead. Yet, Dorotea's enthusiasm to be one of the gang and in on the dirt about Miss Craney appealed to the actress in Alda, who immediately began to mimic a lecherous, vampire about to suck Dorotea's blood and more.

Dorotea made gagging sounds and uttered an equally disgusting word in German, *"Schrechlich!"* Dorotea had taught us a whole lot of German while she was drinking.

"Oh, disgust!" she said. "That is not natural. We must to tell the police or the church. Ya? She is 'lesbe.'"

Realizing her mistake, Alda said that maybe these were just rumors started by angry students because Miss Craney had fired Miss Whitfield, their favorite teacher. Her eyes pleaded forgiveness from us. "Besides," laughed Alda, "You think everyone with short hair is a lesbo, Dorotea."

"Ja. Vielleicht, oh, perhaps, you are correct."

Alda's shoulders dropped back down as she twirled a strand of hair and whistled "The Happy Wanderer" song. Dorotea was smiling and singing along with the German version. Then she grabbed Alda's arm and said they must go early to breakfast to plan her weekend visit to Alda's house. Alda agreed that October 4 would be perfect, and they left arm-in-arm.

Hand on the doorknob, Alda turned and winked at us, repeating, "October fourth, yeah, that's a great date." She closed the door just as Katie leaned over and pinched me. "That's your birthday weekend. Alda's giving us your birthday weekend, *alone*: our fondest wish!"

"Whoopee!" Katie and I fell onto each other, laughing and whooping it up as it sank in what Alda was doing. She would get Dorotea away from Albert for the whole weekend, leaving us the room to really celebrate my sixteenth birthday.

I started to get turned on at the thought of being alone with Katie, finally! And at the sight of her now in her short, ruffled baby doll pajamas coming unbuttoned. She got all serious though, and rushed out to her room to get dressed. We had a lot of planning to do, she said, to really guarantee we would be alone.

A slight crisp breeze welcomed us as we made our way to breakfast. The scent of apples and mushrooms and an air of excitement of colors and of feelings announced early fall as well as my birthday in two weeks.

We walked quickly as Katie rattled off things to do: call the two sets of parents to tell them to celebrate my birthday a week later because of a special student party on the weekend itself; sign out off campus for the day, but sneak back in; buy treats and sexy underwear and creams and massage oil and—she snickered when she asked if we could find a book on s-e-x.

I started to howl as we approached the refectory, but stopped dead. Head Mistress Craney was beaming down on me, a smile that would curdle milk. I cringed at the sight of her kid-gloved hand, which had brushed a wisp of my bangs from my forehead.

"Yes. These are happy fall days," she said. "Hmm. So happy."

I greeted her with a stiff smile, feeling like I should also curtsy.

"Oh," she said with a certain lilt to her voice. "Do come to my office tonight. I have a treat for you." Her eyelashes fluttered. I agreed to go at seven.

Katie's eyes darted sidelong back and forth, as Craney disappeared. "Don't say anything yet," I whispered. After a few seconds, Katie curled her full lip. I no longer felt moved to take it between mine. We entered the refectory and ate almost in silence. Her tone had become business-like by the time we left. "After lunch…we'll call the parents, after lunch."

By now, I was almost leery of going luscious, romantic places, even in my head. The shopping would have to wait until the next day. I began to worry that Craney could read my thoughts the way I could sense others' thoughts in my dreams.

Chapter Thirteen

Birthday Set-Up

Katie and I snuck through the shrubs on the side of Marmot Gate to get to the village phone booth. After postponing birthday plans with Katie's folks, we called my parents, who were delighted to hear from me. I summarized Albert news, the version they wanted to hear; Albert was so wonderful. I was so grateful.

I explained that they would have to put off for a week the trip they were planning for my birthday. My father agreed, and we made plans to include Katie, whom my parents absolutely adored from all our summers together in Maine. We would all go to dinner.

We snuck back onto campus and left for our respective classes. All three of us, Katie, Alda, and I, managed to meet up for a few seconds between classes when Katie and I gave Alda the biggest hug imaginable. I admitted that maybe, just maybe, Dorotea wasn't so bad, but I still had to contend with Craney. Alda made believe she was Craney, slithering her hand across my butt and making a smooching sound. Yuck!

And that's exactly how I felt when I went to Craney's office at seven. It was already dark, and her office cold, dank, and dimly lit. She sat on a high-backed swivel chair behind a massive, mahogany desk, all of which seemed miles away from the heavy, paneled door I had just dared to open.

"Come, dearie," she said. "Here, sit next to me."

She guided me ever so gently to a hassock smack up against her. She patted my shoulder and just stared down at me. "Your birthday!" she said as if the word were oiled.

I started to panic. She really could read my thoughts. I stammered, "My birthday?"

"Yes. You didn't think you could keep it a secret. I have a pleasant surprise for you." She patted my hand and ran her tongue around her mouth.

I couldn't tell if she was getting ready to devour me. Was this sarcasm before the kill? Again, I had the feeling there was a sniper—*Craney*—and I was about to be executed.

"I am going to have you over for your birthday breakfast in my chambers. Isn't that divine? Eggs benedict, and oh, maybe a touch of champagne, non-alcoholic, of course."

Dead, I thought, dead. My birthday and my death day, one and the same. I was not willing to go to my death a virgin! I guess I would die in many ways. At least, that's what I was learning from English poetry. "Ah–to die–to swoon–to love." In other words, S-E-X. But, oh crud. I had to do quick-second thinking about what to say to Craney. She was almost drooling over me; I couldn't stall any longer.

"Oh! How wonderful and what an honor, Miss Craney. You really are spoiling me."

"Yes, dearie, I told you, *you* are a Crane person, very, very special. *My* fledgling."

"Oh, no." I sighed, complete with a heaving of my chest. "On Saturday, I have signed out to go see my family's oldest—" Quick, I had to think. "—friends, the Gallos. Oh, I am so disappointed. Could we—" I was almost on my knees, but that would have made a racket, I was trembling so hard in the midst of this melodrama. "Could we do it another time?" I just about fluttered my lashes, but I was afraid I'd gag.

"Oh, my. I wasn't expecting that," she said.

"Please," I grimaced. "I am so sorry."

"Aha! I know. I'll come get you at seven on Sunday morning. Yes! Off to chapel and then to breakfast in my quarters."

"Thank goodness. I wouldn't have wanted to miss out!" I plastered a smile on my face and quickly found an excuse, a report due the next morning, to leave before I got sick.

Back in the dorm, I grabbed Katie and Alda. They hugged me as I recounted all the disgusting details of Craney's oozing over me. Katie reminded me that we better phone Joe Gallo, her father's boyfriend, to cover for us in case Craney called to verify my story. He would certainly understand our desire for privacy.

We thanked Alda for her present. She told us she would get Dorotea out of there early, early on Saturday and not come back until early, early Monday morning. After a few jokes about the kind of lingerie Katie and I would buy in town on Saturday, Alda walked Katie back to her room to say good night to Dorotea, her new best friend.

Chapter Fourteen

B-Day

Sunlight twinkled on my eyelids, sneaking through the slats of the wooden blinds. I was about to roll over when I sat up straight: it was here, finally! Alda, who was fully clothed, tiptoed over to the bed from behind me and presented me with my first pair of black panties. "Happy sixteenth!" she said, dangling the lacy things before my eyes and playing peek-a-boo through the legs.

She bent over to kiss me on the forehead, saying she and Dorotea were about to leave. She threw me a trench coat, told me to roll up my pajamas, run a line up the back of my legs like seamed stockings, slip on loafers, grab Katie, and go sign out as if we were leaving campus. She rattled all that off in one breath.

She wished us much love. She urged us to be careful even though she had given us the schedule of our monitor's room checks. Finally, she winked at me and told me not to succumb to Craney. "Seriously," she said. "Be careful. She really does make my skin crawl."

Katie and I waited until Dorotea had disappeared with Alda. We walked, almost ran to the sign out desk, signed, and left through Marmot Gate. Within minutes, we had scraped through the sappy branches of the balsam trees and started to scale the fire escape to my room. We looked at each other and said, "Here we go," pushing each other back to belly up the iron stairs. Whatever was going to happen, we had to be finished and in separate rooms by seven the next morning for my rendezvous with Craney.

I joked that I should carry Katie over the threshold of the fire escape when we actually fell through the open window onto my bed. I landed on top of Katie, feeling more like a beached whale in my trench coat and bunched pajamas pinning my legs.

Her smile was slow and tentative as she looked up at me and said, "Do we want to try on our new underwear?" She smoothed my straggly hair back away from my face and my gaze. And all was still.

We clasped each other in a quiet, soft hold and helped each other out of our clothes, feeling our warm, bare arms sliding together between each item and then, our bellies and our breasts. We had never seen each other completely naked before. We moved quiet and slow, just sensing and inviting each other closer and deeper with each glance.

Finally, we eased ourselves, legs entwined, onto the bed, more like one than separate bodies. Our hands felt for the borders: where did I end; where did Katie begin? Her small, light hand reached the outline of my breasts, and our hands and breasts melted into one another.

Almost an afterthought, a kiss. I kissed Katie a long, hard kiss. She answered fully, open-mouthed, her tongue filling my mouth. Our bodies took over. I saw my body arch over Katie's; her hand found my bottom. I felt the warm, damp space between her thighs and then, higher and deeper. She pulled me in as I felt her in me.

It seems we lost time. How many hours, I didn't

know. I also didn't know whose throat made those sounds, over and over, or where Katie found this drive and strength. How many times did I feel her weight on me, pulsing and pushing, the breath squeezing out of my mouth, mingling with hers?

Sometime after dark, we stumbled off the bed and ravaged our snack supply. We showered together and floated back under the sheets, enfolded asleep in each other's arms.

In my dream, we were building a wooden house together in Sicily. I smelled the lemon groves, and the sweat dripping off our tanned, taut bodies released its garlic incense. Katie wiped her forehead on her thin, white cotton shirt flapping in the hot, dry Sicilian breeze. I continued to raise my hammer with great sighs, but Katie's blows were forceful, heavy, and loud. Their banging set off a vibration. The doorframe she was working on shook as did all the walls we had just raised. We joked that it must be Mount Etna erupting, so loud and overwhelming was the rumbling. Louder and louder, all around, from under and overhead, on all sides. Katie's hand shook me too.

"Get up! It's...it's her, at the door!"

"Shoot! Katie, quick, under the bed. Craney! Yes, coming," I croaked in a hoarse voice as I threw on a bathrobe and doused myself with water.

I cracked the door and apologized. "Running late. So sorry. Please give me five minutes."

Miss Craney would have given me a lifetime, just not where I imagined her—outside the door, outside the school, anywhere but here. She plowed into the room with wide-sweeping strides and projected herself onto my bed. She would wait.

Chapter Fifteen

My Date with The Fates

I had never dressed as quickly as on my sixteenth birthday. I stood behind the chintz curtain separating my sink and dressing area from the room. My body felt so alive and velvety after Katie's touch, and here I was under the focused gaze of Miss Craney on the other side of this thin curtain. Could she really be waiting there? I felt my skin crawl. Ready for battle, I smiled and said, "Okay."

She sat me down next to her on the bed and produced a discreet, dark green box. She patted my knee and told me to open it. I sat staring at a lush, suede-bound journal. Embossed on the first page were our two names, Mary Margaret Craney and Pina Mazzini, and "To record our dreams." Did she do this for all the girls?

This was getting creepier and creepier. The only thing that was keeping me from running away was Katie's presence under the bed. I couldn't risk having Craney catch her, and if Craney pulled anything, Katie could report her, couldn't she? I also had to make sure Katie hadn't died of shock or suffocation.

"Lovely," I said while I quickly lowered my eyes to check the time—late for chapel—to avoid her eyes. "Oh. We have to go, right?"

Miss Craney sighed and stood to leave. I thought

I heard another sigh from under the bed. I imagined that Katie had breathed her dying breath.

Our walk to chapel down the empty, hollow corridor was stiff and silent. I was so aware of her towering presence inches away from my side. I pulled my elbows into my sides and sank deeper into my head. Craney only broke this silence to ask if I had my hymnal.

Her long, bony arm opened the padded stained-glass door. The escaping incense enveloped me, carrying me off to another world. My legs and bottom found the pew indicated by Craney. I was off into the sweet sensations of my night with Katie.

The smokiness of the myrrh wafted up my arms and legs, coating them with the memory of Katie's warm, inebriating touch. I felt swaddled again in her embrace.

A mournful sound shattered my reverie. "Amazing Grace" had become a dirge pouring forth from Craney's mouth.

A new chill stiffened the air on our slow retreat to her quarters. Once inside, Craney pointed to a straight-back chair at the small circular table set for two. The formal china and sterling silver baroque place settings lay cold and rigid in their appointed places. I obediently sat in my assigned seat.

While Craney methodically brewed the tea, I stole glances around the room: heavy, dark drapes, a clutter of old, mahogany furniture, a fainting couch, and a low, channeled ceiling. My air was disappearing; this felt like my last meal.

"Ahem." Craney bowed her head to catch my eye. Still holding my gaze, she poured the tea, smoothed her pleated skirt under her bony posterior, and sat opposite me. She smiled as if pleased with her work.

"Please." She extended a basket of rolls and toast. Her hand grazed mine. My stomach did a flip.

"Thank you," I mumbled, nibbling a small corner of toast just to fill my mouth to stop the watering.

"Here. Here's how we do the eggs benedict." She stood and approached me from the side. She took my hands in hers and manipulated them to butter strips of toast to slip into the shimmying egg. A dot of butter splattered on my knuckle. She bent her head low over my hand, still holding the knife. I panicked. She flicked the butter from my knuckle into her mouth and slowly licked my finger and hers. I startled, flipping the knife in the air. She jerked back to her full height, erect, a foot away from me.

"I don't tolerate stains."

Her speech was staccato, my look petrified, I'm sure.

"My dear," she chortled, "I thought you'd appreciate this. I was wrong?"

I wanted to puke and bolt. Would she block the door? And if I stayed?

I almost gagged when I heard the words come out of my mouth. "Oh, I love eggs benedict." My face must have betrayed my utter disgust.

She now seemed business-like and sort of depressed. She picked at her eggs benedict, forgot the cider, and kept glancing at her watch.

Finally, she leveled a blank look at me from across the table. Two, three minutes passed in silence. I was confused. My mind was racing, trying to figure out on the one hand, if I had disappointed her and on the other, why I wasn't just relieved that she seemed so distant. I even wondered whether I should make a bigger effort to suck up. But that was crazy and dangerous.

Her voice broke through my dilemma. She regretted that she had forgotten an important phone call she had to make.

I thanked her; my legs found the floor. She reminded me to "apply yourself fully and play by the rules" as she placed a wispy kiss on my forehead.

Craney had dismissed me.

Nauseous, I walked stiff-legged down the hall from her quarters and out across the green to Smythe hall. By now, I was running, running back to the haven with Katie.

I knocked on her door, not even waiting for her to open, and fell into her arms. We kissed and kissed and every few seconds held each other's head a foot away to check that we were really okay. Laughing, sobbing, and assured we were both intact, we collapsed onto the floor.

"Really, are you okay?" Katie asked.

"It was awful. I, uh… "

"Come on, tell me."

"She licked me. Oh God, I want to puke."

Katie closed her eyes. I thought she would vomit at that very moment. "What do you mean?" She held her hand to her forehead and then her mouth.

"She used my hands to butter bread and actually gave a slimy lick to a spot on my hand."

"Gross. Can't we do something? I mean, like what did you do?"

"I froze," I said as the same chill and nausea crept up my insides at this retelling.

Katie winced and hesitated before whispering, "Did she touch you, more?"

"She kissed me good bye."

"On the lips?"

"God, no." I pulled Katie to me. "I don't want to think about her right now. It's too weird."

Katie interrupted, "And wrong. I mean, can we tell someone?"

"And what?" I imagined Craney's revenge and the accusations against me. I turned Katie's concerned face toward me. I flashed her a resigned smile. "Kates, I need chocolate, soft, wonderful chocolate. That will take away the ugly taste in my mouth."

Katie's smile burst out. She shot up from the floor, ran to her dresser, fumbled with some paper, and flew back to caress my face.

I felt warmth and gooeyness. She was massaging chocolate between her hands and smearing it all over my mouth and chin. I held up my face for more of this wonderful make-up. I took her hand away and kissed her, sharing some of this luscious lipstick with her lips.

"I love you," I gurgled through the molten treat.

She licked long, lavish slurps up one of my cheeks and then the other. I spread some on her nose and nibbled it off.

By now, we were coated, hands, faces, necks, shirts too. We both lit up with the idea, "shower?" Even in our chocolate ecstasy, we realized that would be hari-kari.

After sponging each other off, we found Katie's bed and began where we had left off in the middle of the night. Our repertoire changed a bit: some solos, many duets, and often with full orchestration. Our loving was musical, a Siren's call, but this time to safe harbors.

Again, we took a midnight snack and showered.

Again, I dreamt of Sicily and building a dream house. Now, I was sawing some boards while Katie used a chainsaw with a sixteen-inch blade. She proceeded to cut through trees and beams. The ground shook with the felling of massive chunks of wood. Boom, boom, boom!

I stood in awe of Katie's might and smiled up at her face, which filled the breadth of my vision. No, not Katie's face...yes with a Halloween-like screech. "Jesus! Dorotea!"

Chapter Sixteen

Divine Tragedy

I sat up clutching the covers. I was no longer dreaming. This time I couldn't tell Katie to hide under the bed.

Dorotea was no apparition; she was flesh and blood and standing three inches from my face, screaming at me in German, fully open-mouthed, "Hieraus! Hieraus! Out! Out!" I felt like I was in the play Macbeth and I was the "damned spot."

She took a broom to me. I took a sheet wrapped around myself, clutched at the neck. All I lacked was the candle.

I had no choice but to go to my room and dress. I had a zillion questions and twice as many fears. Thoughts and movements seemed like a time-lapse sequence from a scary movie. I could barely put one thought together with the next. Could I even be sure that that was Dorotea—that she really had come in on us, in the *act*, or post-act? What did she see? I no longer knew anything, except one thing: I had to save Katie.

I listened outside Katie's door. Dorotea was still spouting, in English now.

"You, you…" she was saying. "You are good, Katie, yes! But she, Pina, she must go. I will see to that, but enough. We finish the talk."

I heard Katie mumble, "I'm sorry" in a small

voice, so different from an hour ago. She asked what Dorotea was going to do. Dorotea continued to babble that Katie was good, but not me, and that I must be stopped. Then, all was quiet.

I had the harebrained idea of going in to explain. Before I could think, I was in the room. Dorotea came at me with a wild look in her eyes. She curled her lip and targeted me with a wicked smile. "You will see. Beware!" And with a bloodcurdling "ha!" tossed back over her shoulder, she marched away from me. Katie motioned at the door with her head.

Katie joined me back in my room almost immediately. She repeated Dorotea's veiled threats, but added that Dorotea seemed particularly weird, almost trembling with fear and not rage. Although Katie had learned some German from her mother's distant cousins, she wasn't sure what Dorotea muttered in German about going to Craney.

My stomach tightened. I just about made it to the bathroom down the hall from my room. My throat closed up; my head throbbed. When would the shoe drop?

I slithered back down the hall to Katie in my room. We had to think. We also had to find out why Dorotea was here. What had happened to Alda's plan to bring Dorotea back Monday morning, not in the middle of Sunday night?

To say I was scared was an understatement. Katie, well, maybe she was safe. Her father was on the Advisory Board, and besides, Dorotea had said Katie was good. Yes, she was. Katie was also trying to convince me that we were in this together, and we should wait and see what Alda had to say upon her return later this morning.

We would have wanted to curl up together for another hour with the door locked, but after our near-escapes with Craney and Dorotea—or were they?—we didn't dare. That would be suicide.

I looked at my love. We had just touched heaven and now? I wanted to expire. I couldn't imagine a before or an after. Maybe I was really dead.

And yet, I felt a new life in me. Katie looked different too. She held my face with her awe-filled look, and through tears of joy and fear, she said, "I just love you so much."

Nothing broke her stare. She kissed my eyes. "I just love these eyes, like they're calling me to hold you." As she played with my hair, she went on, "Your hair… God, it's like begging me to curl it around my finger."

I was swimming in her eyes.

"Pina, I've never felt this way, even in communion!" Katie blushed and smiled, a slow smile, her head tilted towards me.

I sighed. "You are my world. I can't lose you now." And in a small voice, I said, "I'm scared."

Our foreheads met. We shared the moment in silence, our own special communion.

Chapter Seventeen

Alda's Return

Sharp, metallic screeches sliced through our moment of silence. We separated like limbs being amputated. Alda's troubled look, as she burst through the door, was as effective as a surgeon's knife. Her feeble attempt at a smile didn't put our pieces together again. We were in a Humpty-Dumpty fairy tale, but there was no make-believe.

Alda shifted her glance from my face to Katie's to try to read our story. Her own face seemed to reflect confusion: should she smile or grimace?

Katie and I finally hugged Alda, and I immediately started to cry. Katie squeezed my shoulder. "We've got to talk," she said, as she pushed Alda into a chair.

"Dorotea? Oh God. She didn't?" asked Alda.

"She did," I said.

"Oh boy," said Alda as she closed her eyes, cupping her nose and chin with her hand.

All three of us blurted out, "What happened?" at the same time. Katie and I explained our story, as well as its gaping holes: What did Dorotea see? What was she going to do? And why did she act more petrified than angry?

Alda listened and gasped in all the right spots, but something was *off*. Her wide-eyed looks and the sounds coming out of her mouth didn't match her stiff body and hands, alternately clutching together and flicking cuticles. Her reaction to our story was like steam after a hot shower, rising off her surface.

I found myself snapping at her, "What the heck happened on your end?"

Alda's eyes were shifting again. She apologized for having let Dorotea leave. She said it was almost the middle of the night, and she was unable to stop her.

"But why?" Katie was practically shaking Alda's arm.

Alda's hesitation, sucking her lips and staring to the side, was troubling, so unlike the normal Alda, quick with an answer, a humorous one at that. She claimed she was ashamed to admit she and Dorotea had argued over something stupid. When Katie asked what, Alda froze. She finally answered it was so stupid, she had actually forgotten.

When we pushed Alda with our "Huh?" and "What?" she whimpered a bit.

"My father yelled and yelled. I'm still upset." Alda stopped crying as quickly as she had started. We had never seen her like this, kind of like the heroines on daytime TV. I noticed she was peeking at us out of the corner of her eyes.

"She-it," I said. "C'mon, Alda, why did Dorotea leave? I might get branded as a lesbo and banished, and you're worried about your father's yelling?"

"Oh, right." It was as if she had to shake herself to focus. "My father yelled. You got that. Well, he yelled really loud at us because we were making so much noise arguing, and then, he slammed a door. Dorotea freaked out."

"You couldn't convince her he wasn't going to kick her out or worse?" I had started to joke and wondered if people joked that way about a man associated with the Mafia.

Alda said Dorotea must have snuck out and gotten a cab to Idlewild Airport or Grand Central Station. She switched the focus along with her demeanor. "What are *we* going to do about Dorotea? I guess she was more upset about our little fight than I thought."

Alda's typical playful spirit returned, and she was full of reassurance concerning Dorotea's harmlessness. She suggested she make up with Dorotea, and we would see everything go back to normal. She was trying hard to convince us Dorotea had probably seen nothing going on between Katie and me.

Again, I fretted over my fears about what Dorotea might do, but Alda clapped me on the shoulder and clamped her hand over my mouth.

"Details," she shouted. "I want all the sexy, gory details! Remember, I made it happen." She was dancing around us. Her silliness was so contagious, Katie and I soon found ourselves revealing even the juiciest parts of our tryst, almost without blushing.

Chapter Eighteen

The Walls Have Eyes

Daylight came. Alda said she needed a few minutes and would join us at breakfast. Scared that everyone would know everything about our night of love and look at us with dagger eyes, Katie and I walked, almost slinked along the walls in the direction of the refectory. The crisp, early October fog was a helpful, if bracing camouflage. We slipped off the path to hang out unseen behind a massive yellow pine.

"Something's fishy," I whispered to Katie. Now I was sweating, despite the chill, thick dew. Scraping off the sap that had fallen on my arm and navy Villager shirt, I scrunched up my face. "I don't know, Katie. Alda was fudging."

"She sure was slow in coming up with easy answers, like why they fought. Had to be something else. And she seemed real nervous."

We both agreed to be careful and observe every little move and sound Dorotea and Alda made. Katie said she'd be pure delight around Dorotea. I promised to stay away from Dorotea, except that we had French class together today.

After checking that the path felt safe, we went to breakfast where Alda joined us, playing her normal self. Katie and I asked Alda to meet us for lunch, figuring safety in numbers. Until then, I had some breaks and decided to go take a nap alone in my room.

I hit the pillow and went to la la land an instant later. All was comfortable, like pasta and sun comfortable! That could only mean my grandmother was doing her magic in my dream.

I began tossing and turning and started to come to. I had ideas about "something foul in Denmark," but then I was in Rome where I heard, "Beware the Ides of March."

I awakened. I was at Albert in my room. Right. I had been dreaming about Hamlet and Julius Cesar.

Just as quickly, I faded off again to half-awaken to "walk softly and carry a big stick." There was my grandmother looking like Winston Churchill, fading back and forth.

I was fully awake now, sitting up. I expected to see a neon sign, flashing, "Beware, beware, beware."

Chapter Nineteen

Off to French Class

I got out of bed to go to class. Classes couldn't be as bad as my dreams.

Still sticky from my wrestling match with the covers, I wound my way through the humid corridors, almost sticking to the walls, to arrive at my French class.

I started to become unglued when I spotted Mademoiselle in the doorway with Head Mistress Craney hunched over her. It appeared as if Craney had been dictating orders to Mademoiselle before she cranked her head in my direction. I froze; even Craney's gushingly warm grin couldn't move me.

After Craney slithered off, I slipped into my seat and discovered I had motor mouth in French to cover my anxiety. I was personally engaging Mademoiselle in a French discussion about the weather and the benefits of an Indian summer!

I came to my senses when Mademoiselle raised her voice, saying, "*Arretez*! Stop." She drew everyone's attention to me and said far more important news than the weather caused her to interrupt my meteorological exposé. I had been chosen for the Intensive French Living Program and was to be relocated to the prestigious Albert Hall.

Mademoiselle called for a round of felicitations

and added that while the class was offering heartfelt appreciation, they might also acknowledge Dorotea Cabanus who would share the honor, as well as a little French *chambre* with me in the French-speaking wing of Albert Hall.

I smiled a limp-lipped smile and was grateful for the loud clapping, which hid my deep gasp. I couldn't recover quickly enough to lower my eyelids before Dorotea filled my field of vision.

Within two of her huge strides, she stood before me, hand extended, with a formal nod of her fleshy chin. "*Je suis tres reconnaissante de partager la gloire avec toi.* I am most grateful to share the glory with you." She pumped my hand to the rhythm of a chorus of "bravos."

I think I dissociated for the rest of the class. I had a vague recollection of a sexual fantasy, mixed with horror. As I tried to focus on the brass doorknob, Dorothea's head loomed up through the frosted glass panes, a vision from my dream. I suddenly felt waves of nausea as I realized it was the same version of Dorotea's head as it floated above me in a sexual embrace in my living nightmare.

I ran to the bathroom, and when I emerged, I spotted Katie and glued myself to her side on our way to lunch. So far, no one stared at us; no one rolled her eyes. Katie kept on whispering, "So far, so good." I was just about to say I couldn't wait to tell her and Alda my French news when I caught a glimpse of Alda and Dorotea.

In an alcove of the loggia off the refectory, Alda stood blocking Dorotea's path. A sneer painted her face as she pointed and jabbed her index finger at Dorotea. There appeared to be a flash as Dorotea's glass beads swung wildly up around her chin and dampened with freely falling tears, broke, and glistened their way down the hall. Dorotea's shriek of verdammte vater, damned father echoed down the hallway.

Katie and I hung back, trying to make sense of what we had just seen. I certainly wasn't ready to eat with Alda and talk about my new roommate to be. And yet, there was Alda, smack dab at our sides, swinging both our elbows, almost waltzing us down the hall.

Katie threw me a puzzled look before pulling Alda to a stop.

"What's up with you and Dorotea?" Katie asked.

"What, my dear, are you talking about?" Alda answered, rolling her eyes at Katie.

"Duh! The two of you looked like flyweights about to slug it out," I said.

"Oh, Pina, I think Craney and your grandmother are getting to you. I haven't seen Dorotea since early this morning," Alda said, twirling us by the arms before excusing herself to use the bathroom.

Katie's look said, "Shush. This is a biggie."

"Yes," I said out loud, "We'll go to the library later." I made the form of a tree with my hands to signal I really meant Katie and I would meet privately under our yellow pine hideout.

Katie nodded she understood.

We had to put our heads together to deal with the newest of our mysteries. There were now three: Dorotea, Craney, Alda.

Chapter Twenty

Library and Ancient History

Hidden under the yellow pine hugging the path from Smythe, I could make out Katie entering the library and coming back out almost immediately. Smart. She was covering her tracks in case someone checked up on her. I had told Alda, who was acting normal again, I was going for a walk.

"Psst! Over here, Katie."

Katie flopped down with a huge sigh. "Finally." She hugged me hard, yet pushed me away with the heel of her hand. "I hate this hiding." And in a quiet voice, she said, "Will you really have to move to Albert Hall? How will we see each other?" She jerked her head away and gnawed on her lip.

I touched her cheek to make her face me. "We will. I swear I'll find a way—if I'm not kicked out."

"I don't get it," Katie said. "One minute Dorotea threatens to rat you out with Craney. The next, Craney's courting you and squishing you together with Dorotea."

"Maybe Dorotea's her spy. I won't be able to breathe with Dorotea in the same room. You know, I've had nightmares about both of them seducing me. It was gross. Dorotea's head was almost dripping drool, looming huge and lecherous above me in a sex scene."

"I think I'm going to be sick. Can they force you?"

"Force me to what?"

"Well, you know, threaten to throw you out if you don't."

"Oh. But Dorotea is so scared of queers, I mean, of us," I said.

"Pin, Dorotea is petrified, but it might really be of Alda. Did you get a load of Alda, jabbing her finger into Dorotea's chest and the sneer on her face? That was the worst bullying I've ever seen. My own chest squeezed real tight."

"Yeah. I felt ice cubes instead of my backbone. So much was happening, I almost forgot. And afterwards, she acted as if we were seeing things. Even back in the room, Alda looked at me like I was crazy when I asked about Dorotea."

Katie disappeared in her head; I had to call her a few times before she brought her eyes into focus. Her look was softer now, and she placed a hand on my knee.

"Listen, you're not moving to Albert Hall right away, right?"

"Right. Couple of weeks."

"We have time to act nonchalant with Alda and Dorotea to find out more. And, sweetie, we do need Alda on our side if Dorotea squeals."

"Yeah. I know. But Katie, us?" I didn't dare go there in my head. My insides were knotted up. No Katie? It would feel like dragging myself up the scaffolding for my impending hanging.

Katie had dropped her head. Her chin, drenched in cascading tears, rested on her chest. She started several times to talk and finally let herself topple over onto my lap. I stroked her head and risked a soft kiss.

"I've got to say this." Katie sat up and closed her eyes a few long seconds. "I can't lose you. I told you this summer. You were the first person, the first thing I ever had that was all mine. Like we were one. When my mother disappeared this summer, you were it, all I had, besides my dad and Joe."

"I know," I whispered as I reached over to pull her closer.

"No," she said, placing her hand on mine to stop me. "No, you don't really know."

Katie's eyes glazed over. Her voice trailed, long and low; it had become a long, wisp of a cloud.

I grabbed onto Katie and held on for dear life. Our tears mingled, warm and salty. I lifted her head and dove deep into her eyes, swimming in those deep blue wells.

"Katie, sweet Katie, we'll find a way. No matter what, I am yours." I was sniveling hard. I never wanted Katie to lose another thing, ever, and certainly not me.

We kissed a light brushing of the lips. In my heart, I promised to be hers forever, promised not to get lost or stray.

Chapter Twenty-one

To Sleep…To Dream

Katie and I walked our separate dimly lit ways back to the dorm. I tiptoed into my room and waved goodnight to Alda, mumbling that I was already half-asleep. She started to joke and protest, but I just disappeared under the covers, saying, "Yeah, Al, tomorrow…"

My mind was racing in sixth gear; it seemed it would roar. Maybe Alda would reveal something about what really happened at her house if I caught her off guard. If I got Alda talking about her family, I could ask her why Albert admitted her, an Italian. I mean Katie's dad, the prestigious Doc McGuilvry had pull; that's what got me in.

My mind was on overload. It shut off; my dreams turned on. I was dreaming about Fifi Gallo, Joe's father, and cannoli and lasagna. Fifi, all decked out in a tux in a church, was giving rings to Doc, Katie's dad, and his soon-to-be husband, Joe. Drinking bubbly Italian wine, he gave an equally bubbly speech about being a good guy, no more wise guy. I woke up with a sense of deja vu or maybe a premonition.

Murders, mafia, and Fifi's good turns this past summer floated through my early morning stupor. The dream of the roasting Sicilian sun on the future trip he had promised us put me back to sleep. I awoke for real, calling "Fifi, Fifi."

It was actually Alda's soft touch shaking me awake. Her dark eyes questioned, "Fifi?"

I was out of the bed and dressed in a flash. I needed to talk to Alda before class.

Her movements in her swaying ruffled baby-doll pajamas were slow. She seemed open and unprotected. A bright, liquid sun poured in the windows whose Bates collegiate drapes she had already pulled open.

"Alda, come sit." I patted the bed. "You know it wouldn't take much for them to throw me out."

Alda yawned and, with half-closed eyes, said, "No, cara, dear, they won't. Don't worry about Dorotea. Besides," and she yawned again as she lay back on my bed. "I don't want to talk about her."

I protested. "Alda, she was just about having a panic attack."

Alda rolled her eyes in response.

"C'mon. No one gets that scared of someone's father yelling," I said.

"Boring." Alda yawned again and leaned over to tickle me.

"Dammit." I pulled away and pushed on. "You're the one who scared her. I saw you poking your finger in her chest. And I don't need to have my eyes or my head examined!"

Alda sat up, groaning, eyes rolling. "I didn't want to tell you this."

This better be good, I thought.

"I was just telling Dorotea to be nice to you. Pina, she doesn't know how tacky it is to be Italian and poor at Albert!" Alda sighed and continued, "How hard it is to be you." She brushed imaginary lint from her chenille robe.

Bull, I thought. And how dare she! I was not poor. And, I was not dumb. This was all bullcrap.

At this point, I was shouting, "*And you!* What's your family's story?" I could feel the heat rise up my throat and my eye sockets tighten.

Alda sat up stiff, mouth open, hand raised to tell me to stop or…to push me away? The bedspread pooled in a mound around her. She had armor on now. Her momentary look of fear was sheathed.

"I, I uh…didn't mean to insult you." Alda winced.

I screwed my glare deep into her, drilling away. "Who are you?"

"Uh, uh…I told you, didn't I, my father knows some bankers, big shots. That's why they let this *eye-talian* girl in to mix up their Wasp blood." Alda cracked a hint of a crooked smile.

Still seated on the bed, she started to strip off her socks, and the belt of her robe with grand gestures. When she went to reach under her robe for her pajama bottoms, I felt the blood rush to my cheeks and other parts. She was purposely trying to steer me away from the conversation. I quickly got up to gather my books from my desk across the room.

I wanted no part of this tease. Too late.

In a flash of ruffles from her low-cut pink and blue baby dolls, her robe was off, and the pajama top in quick succession. Alda jumped off my bed. I tried to stay focused on her head.

The contrast with her dark, Mediterranean skin almost startled me. What caught my eye was not the lushness of her smooth skin, nor the giddiness of the ruffles, nor the swelling of her breasts even with the nuance of her light pink nipple.

Why hadn't I seen this part of her neck before?

It stuck out, incongruent with the soft and exquisite perfection of her chest. It caught my eye immediately. My eyes froze on it. It struck terror in my chest, in me, studying her now in depth.

The scar, the jagged line of a scar, crossed from ear to ear midway down her neck, puffy pink on its outer edges, brownish-red up its center. It could have been a bad make-up job from some past Halloween or a tattoo. She wasn't African; her culture, my Sicilian culture didn't use scarification, even though girls could be symbolically marked as inferior or damaged goods.

No. I had never seen this scar, thanks to her constant cashmere turtlenecks and roll-necked robes modestly covering her otherwise flagrant form. The abruptness with which her hand flew to cover it told me she hadn't meant for me to see it. But then, why the elaborate striptease?

I risked touching her hand as lightly as I could. My heart went out to her. No sex, no tease, just a deep gasp of sadness between us. I whispered, "You were hurt." A tear oozed out despite her saying it had happened a long time ago.

"A bad accident." She bit her lip while studying me as if to ask, "Will that explanation work?"

I didn't want to pry, but I knew this was bad, and I had to find out more about whom I slept next to. "How?" I dared to stroke the scar. This was no normal accident.

Her hand clasped mine and lifted it away. "Bad."

"Alda!" I didn't know whether to yell at her or comfort her. A part of me wanted to get as far away from her as quickly as possible. I grasped her shoulder. Even the heat of her bare flesh didn't distract me from staring directly at her and demanding, "Who are you?"

I shocked myself, pushing with, "Who did this to you?"

"Bad. Bad people." She pulled away, shaking her head. "No. No. No." She gripped my hands and said, "I can't. I can't. I can't talk about this. Trust me."

Elvis singing "Blue suede shoes" on the radio jarred me back to our room and the constant echo in my head of the question, "Who was Alda?"

Chapter Twenty-two

Off to Class

My cheeks still ablaze, I bolted from my room at the same time as Katie left her room at the lower end of the hall. Dressed in her plaid pleated skirt and loafers, she sashayed in my direction, smiling and relaxed.

It was a relief to see her so calm, a real contrast with what I had just experienced. But, it wasn't safe to express myself with intimate gestures here in the hallway this morning. Not that it ever was, but this time I couldn't risk more danger. And I couldn't find the right words to tell Alda's story. Not yet. I needed to think.

Katie checked in all directions before telling me how friendly Dorotea had been. She was so friendly, Katie said, that she even talked about having a tea.

"Lovely!" I put on a pseudo British accent and pointed my pinky.

"No, listen. She made a big to-do about inviting both of us. Yes, don't roll your eyes at me. You, too!"

"Moi?" I was on a roller coaster, and I didn't trust the safety bar.

"And, in fact, she even talked about how lustig, fun, it would be when you two roomed together in your French Quarter. But, you're right. It is all too weird," and in a quiet voice, she added, "and sad."

"Fun, all right! I don't know who to trust." I swallowed hard. "Katie, I've got to tell you about Alda." I was burrowing deep into my thoughts to figure out where to start when I heard a stilted, distant voice as we approached the loggia.

"May I help you? You seem a bit lost."

Lord. All I needed. Craney stood in my path, grinning at me.

"Oh, uh, just trying to solve a trig problem in my head, Miss Craney."

"And Miss McGuilvry sets up these equations for you?"

Katie smiled. "No, Miss Craney. I just try to steer her clear of obstacles."

"Well, my dears, I'd hate to be an obstacle. Oh Pina, let's go to chapel again."

I could swear Craney's fangs came out. I smiled.

She continued, "Especially once you are settled together with Dorotea in Albert Hall. Maybe we could invite her. You'd like that, wouldn't you, *ma chere*? *Oui*, she, too, is a lover of all things Gallic."

Katie knuckled me in the back. My silence had lasted a few seconds too long. I saw my life pass in front of my eyes: trapped. I gushed, "Oh, what an honor, *bien sur*, of course!"

Who was this machine? Craney's tailored, navy blue gabardine suit bearing the semblance of a human being marched off. Her control settings were switched on, to gushing and ingratiating this time. I still hadn't forgotten when the switch was in the ogre position the night she told me to tread lightly.

"Quick," said Katie. "Say something, anything normal like not about her."

"I can't." I was at least able to push out those

words. After Craney was well out of sight, I told Katie I needed to talk in private. I really needed the comfort of her arms.

She had a break coming up, and I devised a plan to get out of French. I would be "indisposed." Albert was still sufficiently Puritan not to question girls' monthly "troubles."

Since Mademoiselle, my French instructor, was also my dorm monitor, our hall was relatively safe right now, and Alda was in class.

I almost collapsed onto Katie, who was waiting for me in my room. She smoothed my hair back and dried my tears with the tails of her button-down shirt.

I explained Alda's scar as scientifically as possible, trying not to spook myself again and playing to Katie's strong suit, science. Katie held me across her lap while she continued to stroke my head. Both of us puzzled over whether it was a knife, saw, or razor cut around Alda's throat.

"So you're not thinking she tried to commit suicide," I said.

"No. But who are '*bad*' people? Like the worst people you know?"

"Maybe you're right, Katie. Maybe Alda's family is the old mob. Shoot! If no one's supposed to know about Alda's family, will they come after me? Try to silence me?"

Katie started that nervous thing she does with her hair, twirling and untwirling. "Nah. I think her folks would want to protect you too."

"I can't let her think I'd give away her secret."

"We'll just have to lay low. Like everything is A.O.K., just peachy-keen, and you really need her to be on your side if Dorotea goes crazy."

"Right. Dorotea," I frowned. "When is this bloody tea?" Katie began to hum "Tea for two" while she fluffed my matted hair.

"It's tonight, sweetie. It'll be okay. Go back to class. And make nice-nice with Alda."

"Okay. I'll see you and Alda in science."

I felt like my wits were back together. The walk down the quiet hallway and through the rosemary-scented loggia finished off the soothing transition.

When I got to the lab later in the day, I had enough time to pull Alda aside. I smiled an apologetic smile. "Sorry I bolted when I saw your scar. I have a thing about blood."

Her eyes twinkled. One of the "real" Aldas was back. "Can you keep the secret?"

"Sure can," I answered, my stomach doing flips.

Which secret was I keeping, in fact? The scar? The people who put it there, whoever they were? Alda's identity? Secrets. Dangit! I felt like I never wanted to hear another secret or "shush" or "I've never told this to anyone…"

Chapter Twenty-three

Tea for Three

After dinner, Dorotea opened the door to her room and rang a small bell. "Tea time!" She told us to wait outside until she welcomed us in, singing, grüss gott, greetings.

She had transformed the room into a German tearoom, complete with scented candles and a Bavarian embroidered cloth. A bowl of whipped cream sat on the side of a small, dark chocolate torte. Cups were glass in metal holders, from her Russian grandmother.

As she poured black tea for me, her fingers brushed my hand and rested there a second. "How gute to be your roommate soon!"

I smiled after Katie kicked me. "Pina's been telling me about it," Katie said.

I forced myself to ask if Dorotea would teach me some more German. We both chuckled. I didn't trust this new Dorotea. No rage and threats against me?

Katie stiffened and threw me a look. I knew Katie; I knew she expected worms to shoot out of the proverbial can when she asked Dorotea if she and Alda were mad at each other.

Katie hedged, saying, "After all, Dor, you did come back early from Alda's house?"

"Oh nay, nay," said Dorotea, putting her hand to her heart. "I was just alone for Albert. I was sick, home—oh, yeah, homesick for campus and Albert girls."

Katie kept it up, craftier than I had ever seen her. "You missed me, your roomie, really?"

"I swear, yes, I miss you too much. Oh, but stimmt, Alda and I, we are good, bosom pals. That's how you say, no?"

"Right," said Katie. Her look said "bull."

Dorotea got a twinkle in her eye and gossiped, "Alda's home, you know, big house, *big shots*, many guns…" She froze, saying, "Oops, bad word, not guns, gulls, birds, yes? Yes, gulls, moven in German."

Katie and I exchanged a look. Dorotea switched immediately to light chatter, telling Katie she might like to borrow some of her American books that I could read to her.

At the mention of Katie's books, Katie and I both swiveled around to check that her "Homosexualities" book was locked up. Katie certainly wouldn't have left it out.

After many thanks in English, French, and German, I got up to leave. Dorotea cracked the door for me before turning to hug me, asking, "Friends, now?" I nodded and stiffened. I thought I heard the click of Craney's Cuban heels and imagined a blur in the speck of light coming from under the door to my room. It was ajar.

Chapter Twenty-four

Tooth Fairy

I flew back across the hall and threw open the door. I half-expected Alda to be doing some exotic dance. But nothing. No one.

I sat reading at my desk for a few minutes. Alda opened and closed the door, obviously coming from the library, judging from the stack of books in her arms. I smiled as I looked up at her and asked if she had forgotten to latch the door when she left.

"Hmm," she said. "Bad neighborhood?"

"No. Nothing." I didn't want to start some intrigue now at nine p.m.

We chatted, joking mostly about clothes in the latest *Seventeen*. We put on a fashion show to model our winter nightshirts. Late October brought a true New England chill.

She wore a blue and white neckerchief around her neck and a cowboy and Indian tan and red flannel nightshirt. Mine was striped, blue and white, with a Henley collar.

I welcomed this return to normal. Perhaps I would sleep better tonight.

My tan twill bedspread was tucked more tightly than usual, and I made a big show of turning it down with a wide-arched gesture. Before I could open my eyes, I heard Alda gasp. A black academic gown lay spread out in my bed. Trimmed in ermine, European university style, this could only belong to one person: Craney.

I went to rip it out from under my covers. This dead animal skin swallowed my hand. For an instant, it felt like my cat at home, but dead, here in my bed, in Craney's gown. I vomited on the spot.

Alda was at my side, tearing it out of my hands. She helped clean me up, as I stayed slumped on the floor.

Where the hell did this come from? Craney! It had to be. Was she going to accuse me of stealing it? Of foraging through things in her room? Oh yuck.

Why? What was her thing with me? Sick! She did put this thing in my bed, between my sheets. She actually touched my sheets. Barf!

Boy, was I dumb? It was friggin' sexual. It was as if she put herself in my bed. Jesus, how was I going to sleep there?

"Alda, please." I choked back a sob. "Can you get me clean sheets? I'll get off the floor in a minute." I saw all the clean-up Alda had done. "Thank you, really…"

I began to sob as she soothed, "Shush. Tomorrow, we'll figure it out tomorrow."

I gurgled yes, made the bed with Alda's help, and curled up, momentarily and platonically protected by Alda's arm around my shoulder. I hardly felt her leave my side.

My grandmother took her place in a dream where she, too, just cooed "domani," tomorrow in Italian. Grandma must have sprinkled Sicilian sleeping powder. How I was able to sleep, I don't know.

Chapter Twenty-five

Domani/Tomorrow

Morning came soon enough as I started to surface through the gossamer layers of my sleep. A curtain drew back from my dream, from the comfort of my grandmother's bosom onto the black academic gown, a rancid, moldy sickness on the floor.

I turned away from the gown, like a morning-after drunk faced with the gut-wrenching task of cleaning up her own vomit. This black drape repulsed me. With its ermine trim, it seemed the shroud of a young household pet. I needed a voodoo doll of Craney or a curse.

The acrid smell of Alda's facial astringent wafted over from her sink. Its incense put the finishing touches on this funereal scene. I crawled to the other side of my bed and left the mess for later.

I escaped from the room to shower down the hall. The hygienic whiteness of the old brick-like tiles helped to wash away the image of the gown's lurid blackness from my sheets, my sheepskin rug, and my mind. I craved light and lightness. The crystal splash on my face brought some order to my thoughts. I wouldn't do anything yet, except talk to Katie and maybe Alda. She had comforted me, but...

Clean and somewhat clear, I put Alda off in response to her "what to do" questions and snatched

Katie from Yodel-land before Brunhilde could fawn all over us. I didn't want anything pawing over me but Katie.

We snuck out to the back fence under the tall privet hedges. As crazy as it was, especially now, we made out for a good five minutes. I allowed myself to luxuriate in this stolen moment.

Katie pushed me back by both shoulders, narrowing her eyes to a "What the heck?" I guess the extended kiss felt like a desperate gesture, as if I thought I'd never be kissed again.

She softened her eyes and her touch. If Katie never spoke another word to me, that look, those eyes…I could live a lifetime in her gaze. Her deep blue eyes always took me in as I was, all I was. One blink and I could hear her eyes whisper, "It's okay. Everything is just fine."

"I think it must be Craney. Who else could it be?" I said.

"Let's rule out Dorotea. We were with her all evening," Katie said.

"Alda was at the library."

Katie stopped short. "Was she?"

"Well…but why would she? And steal the gown?" I shook my head. "Besides, she was as grossed out as I was."

"So you think Craney is coming on to you? That's so sick, Pin. I mean, in your bed, her hands, her stuff… Oops, I'm sorry, sweetie."

"Yeah. What else could it mean? It's not just to show she's the boss; it's that and sex." I shuddered at the thought.

"Well, she probably won't say anything. She can't tip her hat. But, she could have an all-room search, and say you stole it."

"Man! You're right. I've got to get rid of it. But…"

Katie turned that look on me again. I melted, in love, as she stroked my head. "Pin, I think you need to slow down and rest. We'll figure out what to do. But for now…"

"Yeah, maybe the wisest thing is to do nothing, to act like nothing has happened. In public, anyway." I yawned

Neither of us mentioned Craney again for a while. If I got into Craney's head—this had to be Craney— her academic dress was the perfect projectile between my sheets, a skin-tingling symbol for her penetration into my head, into me. My stomach prepared itself for projectile vomit.

❧❧❧

Calm. I would just have to be cool and collected. Get through the day. Just the day. I would eventually have time to figure out the big questions: why me and could she molest me? I already had enough to straighten out in my head, like what did it mean to love Katie, and would I always be different.

I just wanted some peace and to fit in. Nothing was fitting here. Did I have to put up with all this craziness? God, I just wanted quiet, just a lot of quiet.

❧❧❧

I managed the day. No Craney encounter; no merry-go-round with Dorotea; no true-confessions with Alda.

Alda actually suggested that she hide the gown in

her closet. Although only covered with a chintz curtain, Alda's closet contained a hive of rolled sweaters and balled scarves with occasional gaping holes between them. She busied herself creating the perfect niche. She was back in the role of queen bee, depositing the gown's liquid folds into a socket in the hive.

The curtain fell; my eyelids closed. I blocked everything and attempted sleep.

Veils, curtains, and gowns waved through my dreams. Some had kittens for trim, others ermine. Memories of my summers with Katie in Maine wafted in the aroma of blueberries and heady balsam needles drying in the sun. Another pungent scent almost startled my olfactory nerve awake. Garlic?

I sank back to another episode in dreamland. Now Grandma Francesca was holding out a large clove of garlic. I heard chortling coming from the hole where a mouth should have been in a black-cloaked figure. Grandma, standing opposite this shadow in flowing white robes and long, pointed downy wings, was singing an aria in Italian. "Garlic is good. *Mangia aglio.*" Eat garlic. And then "The wicked witch is dead!"

I sat bolt upright and scrambled for the light. Just across the nightstand, Alda opened one eye and snarled at me. No matter who she might be, she still wasn't the wicked witch, and she certainly wasn't dead.

"A dream," I mumbled, "a weird dream. Sorry I woke you."

Alda got up, drank a glass of water, and offered me some.

"Pina, face it. You've got a real vivid imagination. No, don't protest, sweetie." With that, she ran to her desk and grabbed her Keene calendar of pointy-eyed girls and their pointy-eyed kittens.

She was jabbing her finger at the bottom of the page and did the same with my left index finger. "What do you see?" she asked, laughing an eerie laugh.

Oh God. I was staring at October 31.

"Honey, go back to sleep. It's pre-Halloween jitters. We're going to cure you. Tomorrow night—a grand slam of Ouija Board." She gave me a playful shove, and put out the light.

Chapter Twenty-six

Go ask Ouija

When I woke up to a cold, milk-white day, I pulled the Hudson Bay blanket up to my chin. Alda snored with a cowboy and Indian clad arm draped over her face. Even though I had dreamt about more witches and curses, I yawned and felt my muscles expand and melt into the padding of the mattress.

Alda was right. Halloween was coming. We would dress up. Bob for apples. Maybe even go out with Katie's dad, Doc, and his boyfriend, Joe, who were coming on Friday for my belated birthday, followed by my parents on Saturday.

Mmm! Kissing Katie under the cool water. No. That's not how bobbing worked. Oh, and Ouija tonight. Now that would be fun. I could ask Ouija if Katie and I would get married like in my crazy dream. I would also ask if there would be a pot of gold at the end of the rainbow!

Oh. Parents. I had better ask the Ouija if my parents would sense something different about me. Shoot. Dorotea, would she meet my parents?

I yawned again, almost dreaming the tingling effect of the bobbing water or cider around my lips. Finally, I rubbed my eyes. "Ouch!" I yelled. My eyes were burning.

I jumped out of bed to go splash water on my

eyes. My hands stank of garlic. I heard the dry rustling of garlic skins and started to skid on something. What the heck? A clove of garlic on the floor?

Alda was at my side in a flash. I couldn't open my eyes again and groped for her hand—her hand holding several cloves of garlic.

I rinsed my eyes in my small porcelain sink as Alda stood watching me. She looked back and forth from the garlic in her hand to me.

My face in the mirror asked the same questions: where had the garlic come from? Special delivery from Grandma and the Sicilian stregas, witches? From Alda? From Craney?

I held up my hand like a traffic cop. "Stop! I don't know. I don't want to know right now."

I blanched all emotion from my face. I thrust my chin towards Alda and said, "We'll ask the Ouija tonight."

I pushed past her, hid in my closet to dress, and departed with a dramatic whoosh of the door. I don't know if I was convincing; I was constricting every muscle, every nerve to dam up all emotion. One hairline fissure, and I would have cracked completely.

Classes came and went. I felt sheathed in a sarcophagus. I unwrapped my bandages enough to peek through to Katie. Under the gaze of Villager-clad ritzy girls outside the library, I pretended to question Katie about something in my science book. I rolled my eyes towards the library doors.

We met in side-by-side carrels. I spoke just above a whisper. "Look, I know I've been kinda weird."

"Yeah...?" Katie looked as if she was holding her breath.

"No!" I almost dared to reach for her hand. "No,

I'm not breaking up with you." I mouthed, "I love you; I really need you."

Her face relaxed. She was smiling with her watery blue eyes. She looked around and held her hand to her heart.

"I'm trying not to crack." I closed my eyes and puffed out air.

Her eyes said, "I know."

"Maybe…" she faltered, "Maybe this weekend… maybe my father…"

I flashed her a look that screamed, "No!" The stark "no" hovered in the air, and finally softened to a "maybe."

"Look." Katie wore her stern face. I had to pay attention. She had that effect on me.

"Sweetie," she continued. "I know you get really uptight about money and my father paying your tuition. That's not a big deal for him. I know it is for you. Taking anything is a big deal for you."

"Stop, Katie."

"No." She pronounced it with almost two syllables. "You're so afraid it's going to make you look weak or needy. Dammit, Pina, we all have things we need. Like hugging and love, and listening."

Her eyes seemed to go from my shoulders to my ears to my heart. She knew all the parts of me that needed tending. She was so right, of course.

I spoke softly. "I don't mean to hide from you. It's so hard for me to believe you care and that you want to give all of you to me…like, like I'm worth it."

"But…you…you really are, sweetie. I know that even when *you* don't or when you forget just how special you are."

"It's like you can really see me." I jerked my hand

to my eye. A big tear was about to drop four feet from my pronounced cheekbone.

Katie giggled. "You're such a tomboy. And I love it."

"I'll think about your dad and what to say. I promise."

With that, I was on my feet. I leaned over close to her ear. "Ouija, tonight. Just play along with me."

❧ ❧ ❧ ❧

In the refectory, Katie and I purposely avoided eating dinner with Dorotea and Alda. Too complicated. I actually ate with my head buried in *Catcher in the Rye*, only nibbling at my turkey and peas. Savoring the pumpkin chiffon pie for a minute or two, I made a loud scraping sound with my chair to alert Katie that it was time for Ouija.

I made my way out of the refectory by myself. For some reason, the loggia leading back to the dorm was dark, raising the sparse hairs on my arms. By the time I reached my room down the long, ill-lit corridor, I was in the right frame of mind to play Ouija.

Alda had set up the board on a low table with our two chairs and the turned-over waste paper can. Katie arrived immediately after me. The three of us looked more like three preppies in the formal parlor, waiting for dates to arrive, and not three troubled teens about to delve into the world of the occult.

Alda made some eerie sounds from the new television program The Twilight Zone and summoned us all to begin. We joined hands on the mover and called upon Ouija.

Of course the mover showed "Yes" when we

asked if Ouija was present. Alda started by asking, "Who are the lovebirds in this room?"

The mover indicated P and K. Alda continued to question, "Did they do it?" Katie blushed. The mover sped to a quick, scientific "Yes!"

I asked, "Is Alda jealous?" The mover seemed to be jerking to "No," but finally slid into "Yes."

Katie asked if we would marry. We were puzzled when the mover bypassed yes and no, and started "i" and then "n" and "s." We assumed all of us were pulling or pushing, but after "i-n-s-i-c-i" and then "l-i-a," we realized the board had spelled out "in Sicily" in Italian.

I looked at Katie. Katie didn't know Italian, and I don't think Alda knew we would be going to Sicily next summer. Could it be the board knew something?

I decided I had to get down to the business of the gown. I asked, "Did Alda put the gown in my bed?" Alda shot me a filthy look. Katie seemed to be pushing the mover towards "Yes" and Alda towards "No." The mover stopped at "?" and then zoomed to "H."

We didn't know any H's. I was about to leave the table. Katie started to reach up to touch my face. I caught my foot on the leg of the chair and plopped back down. Then with only two of our fingertips remaining on the mover, it sped to "M." Again, we shrugged. We didn't know any Ms.

Katie shrieked, "H.M., H.M. Head Mistress." Then, in quick succession, the mover spelled out "Beware."

By now, we could barely touch the mover. It sucked and puckered like dry ice, gluing our fingers to this charged, plastic magnifier. Its final message read, "Curse c" and the board upset itself with the jerky thrust of the mover. It lay crashed on the floor.

Chapter Twenty-seven

Return to Normal—Normal Parents' Visits

After the board's crash, I jumped up, cursing, "This is all bullcrap! I'm going to bed."

Katie started to "yeah-but" me and finally asked, "What about my folks?"

I answered that tomorrow was soon enough to worry about that. I grumbled, "good night" and pulled the blanket over my head, leaving Katie and Alda to clean up.

⁂

Katie and I met in the hallway in the morning. When she asked what we would tell her father and Joe, I said I wasn't sure. I would play it by ear.

Doc and Joe were cool. Katie had long before forgiven her father for the roommate situation. There wasn't a trace of resentment. They were especially generous with me. They gave me a small leather travel case for my birthday, wishing me dreams of great journeys. We did bob for apples and Doc and Joe did kiss, but not under water as they did in my dream. Katie and I also enjoyed a kiss or two.

As part of my birthday present, I asked for a few minutes alone with Katie in their hotel room. I explained it was so hard to get any privacy at Albert.

We had just about closed the door to their room. We stood against the wall and merely held each other.

"Katie," I broke the silence. "God, Katie, this is the first time I've felt safe."

"Yeah, I know. Really, we've got to tell my dad about Craney."

I pulled away from Katie. I didn't want to hear about Craney and whether or not she was trying to groom me. Maybe I still believed homosexuals were lechers and wound up as child abusers. I knew in my mind that that wasn't true, but somehow asking Doc for help, well…the whole thing might be my fault. Maybe there was something sexually weird about me. Maybe this slimy world of Craney's was really mine. Besides, I couldn't prove a darn thing.

"Hey! Come back here. Pin—c'mon. I won't force you to talk to my dad. Don't be mad." Katie held out her hands and softly pulled me closer. "I love you," she said.

A tear started to swell and run the length of her cheek. I kissed the spot and felt the wet warmth on my lip. I wrapped my arms around her as we pressed into each other. We stood still like that for what seemed forever. She whispered, "I just want to keep you safe."

We really didn't make out. Katie and I just held each other and vowed we'd get through this, faithful to ourselves and to each other.

I confessed I didn't know if I believed Alda. Maybe it was Craney, maybe Alda, maybe even Dorotea who was baiting me.

We also agreed we'd find a way to see each other when Dorotea and I were moved to Albert Hall. Katie said they'd probably switch Alda into her room. She knew she'd have to be on her guard even with Alda.

We only stayed about fifteen minutes before

rejoining Doc and Joe. Everything and everyone was so relaxed. It was pure fun! I felt like a kid again.

I really didn't want to talk about Craney. Then I overheard Katie telling Joe, as an investigative journalist, to check out the story about the former instructor Craney had allegedly fired.

"You know." Doc lifted his head from the paper he was reading and spoke to anyone who wanted to listen. "There have been rumors. I never believed them. Besides, if Miss Craney had a lady friend, well, that was her business, right?" He sucked on the stem of his pipe.

I definitely wanted to hear about this. "Well, Doc, what kind of rumors?"

"They called them 'particular friendships', but it was never totally clear whether they were with adults and consensual or…well, people couldn't very well imagine Miss Mary Margaret Craney capable of *that*."

"You mean abusing kids?" I said.

"Yes." Doc coughed as he lit his pipe for real. "I figured that was some bigot's attempt to smear the name of an Ivy Leaguer."

"But Dad," Katie broke in, pulling away from the chat with Joe. "Maybe Craney is doing that to Pina."

"C'mon, Katie. Don't." I frowned at her.

Doc raised his eyebrows and ran his hand through his thick, white hair. He exchanged a look with Joe. "That's a serious allegation, Katie."

I protested there was nothing to be concerned about.

Doc exhaled and held the pipe out, seeming to weigh his words. "If she ever gets out of line with you, you'll let us know, won't you, Pina?" He was studying both Katie and myself.

"Yes, of course," I mumbled.

I knew I couldn't prove anything, and Joe reminded me that there had been hazings of other minority students. He meant Italian and not wealthy, but I was also thinking about my other minority issue. That would be more than a simple hazing.

Doc looked from Katie to me, asking if we were being discreet. We just nodded. I realized that maybe the biggest help to me now would have to be my grandmother, or at least my dreams.

He was still watching me as I travelled deeper and deeper into my head, into my grandmother's world. He placed his sturdy grip on my shoulder, reassuring me he would believe anything I said.

When they left us, Joe embraced me, smoothing back the straggly ends of my ponytail. He gave me his private phone number and reminded us we weren't alone.

We cried as we watched them drive off. My parents' visit the next day would be totally different. Filled up with the safety of this day and Katie's folks, we returned to our separate rooms, ready to sleep. And sleep soundly we did.

❧ ❧ ❧ ❧

Halloween was still a day away. My parents wouldn't stay over, arriving early the next morning. I felt myself growing tense. They really had no clue about Katie and me, but would I seem different now? Now that Katie and I were intimate, could it show?

Well, they liked Katie; they had decided she and her dad were good for me. That would do for now. I would just have to be careful.

I managed to fall asleep despite my concerns.

Better still, I managed not to dream. I was up and dressed when Katie knocked. She admired my somewhat feminine white pleated-front shirt and flared wool skirt. I knew my mother would appreciate my outfit.

We met my folks in the formal parlor, the main one with Persian rugs, an old baby grand piano, and the Van Hals in the corner, a version of his clown-like character.

Out of their element, my parents were a bit stiff. They presented me with a soft, lamb's wool sweater in heather mustard, my favorite. I could tell it was a good brand on sale because of the cut label.

Kind of lost in the fingering of this luxurious sweater, I started to appreciate just how normal and wholesome this was. I heard my mother say, "Honey, don't you like it?"

"What? Oh sorry, Mommy, I love it. I was just picturing it with my brown tweed skirt."

Katie piped in, "Wow! Mrs. Mazzini, that's gorgeous." She winked at both of us, saying, "It might just disappear."

"Oh Katie, dear, if you like it, I know a shop."

"Mrs. Mazzini, you're swell." Katie planted a sweet kiss on my mother's cheek.

My father fingered leather-bound books on the shelf, pulling a volume of Coleridge. He called over to me, holding the Coleridge. "You know, I read a good deal of Coleridge and Poe in college. Still have that leather-bound volume of Poe at home."

"I love that one, Daddy," I answered. I looked up to see him smiling at me. I could only describe the look as pride.

My mother was eyeing a plate of shortbread cookies greedily. I couldn't help but say, "Mommy, wait till we go to eat. Those are kind of stale. I know."

"Just one, honey. They look so good." She finished by eating two.

She started to stroke a Belgian lace runner. We spoke of more food and Mothers' weekend in a few months, and more food. I chatted about things I didn't care about. Would the snooty girls see my parents? Hmph. Would the snooty girls see me?

My father invited Katie to join us for a lunch at the Olde Andover Inn. There were tourists of all sorts here; they'd fit in. I heard myself let out a big sigh, and realized I had worked up a ravenous appetite, what with all my worries. Our early afternoon turned homey with warm barley soup, pones, and baked apples with cream for dessert.

My mom cried a bit when she spoke of the empty house back home. Her tears brought me relief. Both Katie and I were reverting back to younger kids in a simpler world. I hardly thought of Craney, Alda, or Dorotea. My parents wouldn't have known what to do with any of them.

As they drove away, Katie and I reminded each other that tomorrow would be Halloween. I told Katie I was going to return Craney's gown, just folding it and leaving it on the cane chair outside her office door. She nodded in agreement and asked if she should come with me.

The parent's visits brought me a sharp clarity. Getting rid of Craney's gown would be clean. I would go by myself to her office at a time when she would be busy with chapel service. I would leave the gown, with no note, no explanation, leave unseen *immediately*.

Clear as the crisp, star-studded sky, promising frolics for the eve of all Hallows! I felt the brief kiss of

Katie's fingertips against mine as we separated for the evening.

Chapter Twenty-eight

Halloween

Heavy early morning rain pelted the windows, announcing a soggy All Hallows Eve. Even the black crepe paper streamers Alda had hung while I was with my folks sagged with a crippling fatigue. Alda was up early, already seated at her desk. She looked equally depressed.

I whistled and said, "good morning." She answered a slow "yeah" and turned to face me.

"You don't trust me, do you?" she said.

My mind was scrambling. I functioned on slow in the morning. "Why?" was all I could muster while rubbing the sleep from my eyes.

"You've hardly said a word to me the last two days. I don't even know what you're going to do about the gown."

"Well, our parents—"

"No. Listen. I get it. I've pulled some weird stuff, and I mean, the scar...give me a chance."

"Stop," I said. I really didn't want to get into the scar business now. I didn't trust her, but I did have to tell her about the academic gown since it was in her closet. "No, I don't think you put the gown in my bed. And I, I am finally going to put it back. Let's get it out of your closet."

I filled Alda in on the details of my plan to

deposit it outside Craney's office as soon as possible. She handed me the gown and continued to pull out other bundles.

"Costumes for later. I mean, if you and I are okay." Her eyes softened.

"Costumes? Sure." I scratched my head. All I could think about was getting rid of this black shroud. I could juggle costumes, masks, and conflicting friendships later. Katie would know what to do about Alda and Dorotea.

I bagged the academic gown and exited the room after a thorough hall check.

The hall was quiet: religious girls were already at chapel, others still sleeping or eating pancakes in town. I slipped out the security door to the outside and clung to the edge of the privet hedge. I peeked in the backdoor to Damper Hall. Not a sound.

I only had to make it one-third of the way down the darkened hallway. The long Persian runners padded my footsteps and the high walls with their large canvases cushioned any stray rustling of the paper bag.

There was the chair. In my relief at seeing it, I accidentally scraped its back leg onto the exposed marble floor. A sound of shattering glass and nail on chalkboard resounded back at me. My mind envisioned the dead rising up from graves and the gown floating out of the bag. I gathered my wits, left the bag, and sprinted off.

One last ten-foot section of carpet to go. I had counted them once, the last time I was here with Craney: fifty feet between Craney's office and the door, five sections of ten-foot Persian runners. Then, home free.

I could already see a single ray of light stealing

in from behind the last panels of brocade drapes lining the hall. I reached for the sculpted brass doorknob with my right hand. I could already taste freedom in the crisp October air.

A bony hand, Craney's bony hand, grasped my shoulder. She spun me around away from the door. She ushered me into the heavily draped alcove, the one I missed when I counted off steps and niches.

"Come." She pulled me deeper into the alcove and seemed to collapse back against the massive oak doors hidden by the drapes. "You will come to my chambers tonight at eight."

In the dim light, I saw her jerk her head away with a snort. An ether-like odor began to permeate the enclosed space. I was struggling to hold my breath when Craney's long arm thrust me back out through the velvet drape.

My legs could hardly carry me. I flung open the leaden door and ran to my room as best I could. I made it to the trashcan. I held the rolled metal edge and vomited bile. Resting my chin against the cold metal, I welcomed the cool washcloth Alda offered.

With a gentle tap on my shoulder, she whispered she'd get Katie. Katie came running in, followed by Alda, who hung back and allowed Katie to take over. She wiped my forehead and smoothed my hair. She even got Alda's astringent towelettes to freshen me up. I let myself go in her maternal care while the Platters' Twilight Time played on the radio.

The chamomile tea and a few Social Tea cookies made up for my lack of breakfast and fortified me. I actually heard myself say I could deal with this when Alda and Katie gaped at me. Yeah, we all wondered what *this* was. What would Craney do that evening?

Katie volunteered to come, but we all thought that it would be too risky for Craney to see us together again. Alda was quiet for a good five minutes, scratching her forehead and pulling on her thick, black hair.

"You've got to trust me. I'll go," said Alda.

For some reason, that seemed to make sense. Besides, the two of them, Alda and Craney, couldn't gang up on me. I looked quickly at both Alda and Katie. I wasn't sure if I had said that out loud. I imagined the theme music from the Twilight Zone.

"Menthol!" I shouted

Now, both of them looked at me as if I was truly crazy, not just paranoid, but hallucinating. Katie patted my shoulder and merely raised her eyebrows.

"Craney smelled of menthol. Like, what's that vapor rub called?"

Each of them had ideas about getting help. Each spoke of her dad, Alda choosing her words about her father with extreme care. I pooh-poohed their ideas. Craney hadn't done anything, really.

I joked maybe we needed a Sicilian curse. Alda opened her eyes wide. I had to repeat several times that I was joking.

"But," Katie interrupted. "Your grandmother dream, remember. She said 'the wicked witch is dead.'"

We all laughed as much as we could. It was better than crying. When the radio played "I Put a Spell on You," we really roared.

Alda said, "You guys, know, maybe it's not a bad idea."

We did homework while the radio played its usual blend of music. We giggled occasionally when the lyrics of a song were particularly fitting. "It's Just a Matter of Time" by Brook Benton was the final straw.

I raced to switch off the radio.

It was seven forty-five. Katie held me and told me she'd wait for us there. Alda and I walked in step down the hall, Alda telling jokes on a Halloween theme.

The fifty-foot walk to Craney's office felt interminable. In our silence, the dimensions of the hallway seemed to grow longer and higher. The walk had become a never-ending plank.

Outside Craney's office, Alda sat on the cane chair. I needed to continue walking off the tightness in my every joint and muscle. I had paced back and forth the extent of the fifty feet at least three more times when I heard the creak of Craney's door. Alda shuffled to her feet only to have Craney push her back down in the chair.

"It's time. Pina. Come." Craney had spoken.

I sat only after Craney had repeated her command for the third time. I kept my trench coat on. She motioned to the chair, mumbling, "Please do" in a voice that was neither pleasing nor welcoming.

She thanked me for the return of her academic gown. Someone had stolen it, she said. Between sniffles, she explained the tailoring of her gown, holding it up for me to admire. As she stretched out the gown's arm for me, my eyes started to water. Garlic.

Craney was on her feet now. Great. She was dismissing me. No. She was holding the gown out to me, throwing a knife-like stare at me over her frameless half-glasses.

"Unique, isn't it? Here." She reached for one of my hands. "Feel the ermine."

With that, she thrust the gown into my hands and commanded, "Dress me."

I couldn't protest; her closeness paralyzed me. I

obeyed, draping the gown over her suit. I stepped back as if to get a better look. The reek of rotting garlic hit my face head-on.

She sniffled again. "No damage. See." She changed her tone. Her eyes twinkled.

"You didn't take it, did you?" She turned the side of my chin towards her with the   prod of her arthritic index finger.

"No. No." I had cotton candy for saliva. I had to keep it brief. "Ah, no. I, uh, found it." I had to rob my face of the conviction she had snuck into my room to put it there herself.

She patted my shoulder. "Good."

It was then I realized she was sniveling when a drop fell on the sleeve of my London Fog.

She coughed and braced herself with one wrinkled arm on the desk. She took off her glasses and looked up at me from under her lids. "Well, good night to you, my dear. It is Halloween. Oh. And do you know the lament by Byron, 'We'll go no more a roving so late into the night?' A good one for Halloween."

I couldn't answer. She clasped me to her, then thrust me towards the door. She stood erect, reciting the poem.

"Damn!" was all I said to Alda once outside.

"What?" Alda's eyes seemed to check me all over for visible or invisible wounds.

"Just creepy. Weird and creepy."

"But…did she…uh touch you?"

"Yeah, but not like you're thinking."

She threw her head back and mumbled, "*Grazie, Dio.*" Thank God.

Chapter Twenty-nine

Halloween Continued

Alda was doing her best to zoom us back to the room through the moaning wind and torrential downpour. How could I have thought Alda would hurt me?

Dropping our shoes and sodden trench coats on the mats at the dorm doors, we caught our breath and continued down the hall, arms around each other's shoulders. There was no longer any come-on, sexual or otherwise. She felt solid; I felt safe.

Alda reached for the doorknob and nudged the door as she yawned. I leaned my weight into it. Glowing in the dark was a black, silver, and white skeleton creeping towards us. Alda and I both tumbled forward in a screaming fit and in frantic attempts to escape through the now closed door.

Katie, our misguided skeleton, was on the floor with us, attempting to scrape us up. She pleaded, cried, and begged for forgiveness. She had started to worry that we were gone so long. As a distraction, she dressed herself for her worst fears—that I was dead meat.

"Dangit, Katie. You were like a repeat of Craney in her gown just now. Get that frigging thing off."

"I didn't expect...I started to lose track of time." Katie threw off the costume and stroked me over and over. Her eyes were moist. She grimaced. "I'm sorry."

I recounted the short version of my visit with Craney, filling in more details about my emotional state. "I just knew she would touch me. I was afraid I'd pass out right there."

I admitted that my mind had also been fantasizing weird things. Like the smell of garlic and menthol. I flashed on death camps. I panicked that Craney was gassing me.

Alda was on her feet. She offered to make me some chamomile tea. Katie petted and fussed over me, but then she asked what Alda and I had been talking about when we were at the door.

"You were saying something like, 'We'll go no more a roving.' You and Alda?"

"Oh right. No, sweetie. We've got to look up this poem Craney recited to me. Gross, something about love."

Alda handed me my tea, and the two of them searched in our English Lit text for Lord Byron. They read it out loud, gagging especially over the line "Though the heart be still as loving..." and the beginning of the next one "Though the night was made for loving..."

Katie shrieked, "Yuck. It's like this old decrepit person is lusting over you."

"Let me see." I grabbed the book and let the words sink in. "Gross. It sounds like she's got to have me."

"*Putana!*" Katie and I turned to stare at Alda. She had used a really strong Italian curse both Katie and I recognized.

"Let me think," she said. "What did you say about Sicilian curses and spells, Pina? Do you really know any?'

"C'mon, Alda. It was a dream."

Alda had definitely gone some place in her head. Her eyes were travelling back and forth while she wrung her hands. Her eyes became slits; her lips pursed. "I'm going to call my father tomorrow. You do know he could help."

"Uh," was the only response from Katie and me. I realized there was something important in Alda's statement, but I was too numb to pick up on it.

Katie nudged me awake, saying, "I'm out of it too. Do you guys think I could sleep here tonight? Just sleep?"

Alda and I both agreed. Under other circumstances, I would have been whooping and hollering, "Yeah!" We wondered about room check, but Katie said Mademoiselle had already been by. Katie had told her she was borrowing a book while Alda and I were with Craney. Dorotea was away visiting her aunt.

If Halloween had anything left in store for us, we would all protect one another. We threw the mattresses and covers on the floor and felt like we were having a fourth grade sleepover.

❦ ❦ ❦ ❦

Before crawling onto the mattresses, the three of us built an arsenal of potato chips and brownies just off to the side. Memories of earlier birthday parties and sleepovers floated in my mind's eye. Our twistings and turnings over one another to reach for goodies created a true bed of crumbs. With each shift, we created dry crunchings and laughed, spewing still more crumbs under ourselves and down our nightshirts. All we needed was grape soda running out our noses to complete our return to childhood.

"Really." Katie crunched "We've gotta sleep."

I sputtered, "Yuck! You spat on me."

"Ladies, ladies." Alda was choking and giggling. "We've got to clean off the sheet."

We tumbled off the mattresses and flapped the sheet several times to balloon over us and hover and finally settle. After threatening to lick the last crumbs off each other's faces, we nestled into comfy sleeping positions.

Sandwiched between Katie and Alda, I closed my eyes and started to drool. My last semi-lucid memory was Mademoiselle's usual nighttime wish, *"dormez bien,"* sleep well, and the French figure of speech, "fall into the arms of Morpheus," meaning to dream.

There were pumpkins, apples, and Morpheus, the god, in my early dreams. And morphine, of course an association with Morpheus.

The next episode involved sleeping pills, menthol, and garlic. There was my grandmother, not Morpheus, with garlic again. She was mumbling that her father, the Doctor Daidone, could lift curses and spells that *"stregas,"* witches, had cast.

In this dream, my grandmother said she had heard me distinctly ask for help. She was muttering, *"I put a spell on you."* I couldn't see the victim of her curse.

"From your mouth to God's ear," she chortled. *"Be on the lookout for garlic."*

In the last episode, odors swirled around my nose. I was being asphyxiated.

I awoke with my nose in Katie's armpit. Her normal orangey scent had turned a bit musky under the many layers of covers and the stress of Halloween. Still somewhat lost in dreams, I ripped off the covers and sat up, tearing at my nightshirt.

Alda jumped out of bed to click on the light. "What?"

Katie, clutching the covers to her chin, grumbled, "Jeez. A dream?"

"Man," I said. "You gotta listen. It was a Nonna dream."

They got me water and listened to me rant. "My grandmother was making potions, I think. Giving people drugs, bad drugs, morphine and sleeping pills."

"Pina," Katie moaned. "I told you I thought Dorotea took a sleeping pill. Remember?"

"But she, I mean my grandmother was going to get back at someone. And I think that someone was after me. They were trying to asphyxiate me with some smelly stuff." I was babbling.

"Hey, cara you had your nose up in Katie's armpit. That's being smothered with Katie's smell. And come on. What does Mademoiselle say to us every night after 'dormez bien?' 'Tombez dans les bras de Morphée!'"

"Your mind just got to the root of the word Morpheus and popped out morphine." Katie added with a weary frown, "Pina, you've got to get to sleep."

Almost line by line, they made sense of my dream, tying each element to something real that had happened recently to trigger it: Katie's armpit, Mademoiselle's expressions.

I countered with "the garlic?" and "a spell?"

Katie, by now really cranky and in need of sleep, sighed. "Pina, listen, the song—on the radio—when we were doing homework? 'I Put a Spell on You,' by Screamin' Jay Hawkins!"

I thought I saw steam rising from Katie.

Alda patted my head, saying, "Hey, remember

you said Craney stank of menthol and garlic? She was probably using Vicks and garlic for a cold. You even said she snotted on you."

All three of us went "Yuck!' and Alda put out the light.

Alda giggled. "Besides, *'ciccia,'*" she whispered, using an Italian term of endearment with a twinkle in her eye. "Your grandmother did say she'd help."

Chapter Thirty

I Put a Spell on You

After the dream interpretations, we fell back to sleep, awakening to the early morning sounds of cardinals and nuthatches. The air was chill, and we expected to see the cardinals framed in snow. Not yet, but definitely too chilly to hang around on mattresses on the floor.

And too late. We knew we had to get the beds put back in case of a morning check. Katie also had to get herself out and into her room before Dorotea arrived back from her aunt's.

"Take care" was our new motto, and we meant every word of it. Besides, the room changes were coming up when Dorotea and I would be moved over to the French Quarter Program in Albert Hall. Katie and I would need to be extra cunning to get time together before we were severed, cut apart from one another. We were a bit dramatic.

Alda told us she would also be working on strategies to give us another birthday gift, just like the last one. I just stared at her since now was certainly not the time for that kind of fun and games! She merely answered that she had to call her father. Oh yeah! Her father again.

Huddled together wearing pea coats and stadium jackets, we walked to breakfast. We met other girls equally bundled up and risked some smiles. They smiled back.

We relaxed a bit and started to joke and bump our way along to the refectory. Rounding the corner to the long loggia, Alda started impersonating a Renaissance figure, pretending we were in Medici Florence. She struck a pose, combing her long beard with her fingers. She outlined our figures as if we were modeling clay.

"Jeez. Who are you now?" said Katie.

"Don't move," said Alda with a heavy Italian accent. "I will position you."

"Alda, stop it," I said. "You're bending my arm."

"Si. All the better to hold the slingshot," she said.

Katie laughed. "Oh God, Pin, you're supposed to be the David. Meet Michelangelo."

Alda doubled over with laughter. "You want to be a Pieta?"

"Who's the mother?" Katie giggled. Mid-laugh, she almost choked.

At the end of the loggia, dressed in a black shirtwaist underneath, Craney stood shrouded in a long, black shawl. Her face was ashen. She seemed to be quivering. I prepared to greet her as coldly as I could.

Katie held me by the elbow, hiding it with her scarf. Alda closed ranks on my other side. I stood protected, at least for the moment.

I shot my head up, chin tucked in, stomach tightened, rock hard. I caught a mere glimpse of Craney coughing and grabbing her chest and knifing her way through the adjacent alcove. She vanished, leaving a vapor trail of Vicks and echoes of snorts in the empty loggia.

I looked at Katie and Alda. We stared at each other in silence. Had Craney purposely avoided me?

This was even creepier. Why did she do that? I mean, I was glad she was gone, but it almost seemed like I made her go away. Yikes, I was losing my mind. Why would I let her get into my head this way? Jesus, I just wanted to be able to sleep in my upcoming French class.

We ate just enough and in silence, isolated in the farthest corner of the hall. We had nothing to say. What could we? Just one word, "Lunch."

Mademoiselle greeted me *en francais*, in French class. With much *joie*, she informed me she was being transferred from Smythe to Albert Hall to oversee our French wing along with Maitresse Craney.

I liked Mademoiselle, but the news that Craney would also be in our dorm chilled me. While I stood shivering at the thought, Dorotea strode in straight from her return from her aunt's. What now? I needed a break.

Dorotea gawked at me with a big-toothed grin. She nodded her head and pumped my hand in her newfound love or tolerance of me. On autopilot, I smiled a mirror response. I nodded and pumped back.

I was ready to shift into second gear and blank out when Mademoiselle's voice reached a new high note in French class. "Attention. *Immédiatement! Nous devons prier*. We must pray," she started.

I was awake now. Albert did not mix real prayer with the politics of schooling. Chapel existed, but it was more a national, Puritan moral obligation, rather than a religious meditation.

Mademoiselle was French, after all, and Catholic to the core. She intoned, "*Marie, Mère de Dieu, Jésus et la communauté de Saints, nous vous prions de protéger notre Maitresse Craney*. Look down upon *la Maitresse*, we pray!"

What? I was all ears. Mademoiselle was beginning

to say Miss Craney had just taken to her bed with a strange infection. "Let us pray!"

"*Une maladie mystérieuse*," Mademoiselle added, making the sign of the cross.

At the mention of sudden and inexplicable onset, I found my hand pinned to my chest and my mouth gaping open. It felt like my eyes were rolling in my head. None of these actions brought any clarity to my thoughts.

Did I do this? What was I thinking about power this morning? I couldn't have caused this, or…and my dreams? Shoot! I needed Katie to talk sense to me.

I claimed illness and stood to excuse myself from class. Just as I was exiting, I heard Dorotea inexplicably covering for me, explaining that I cared greatly for Miss Craney and must be overcome with concern for her.

I was overcome, all right—with the need to find Alda and Katie in study hall. Outside their classroom in Memorial Hall, I motioned to Katie, who excused herself for a break. I urged her and Alda to cut, just do what they had to do to join me as soon as possible in my room.

❧❧❧❧

By the time Katie and Alda could get away, I had fallen asleep. They had snatched some food from dinner and woven a good story to cover my absence.

"What the heck's up?" I heard over and over as they shook me. I might have been dead meat, but I wasn't dead yet. I hoped Craney wasn't either.

"You guys. I did it. I cursed Craney."

"What?" They rolled their eyes and extended their arms and hands palms up.

Katie sat down on the bed close to me. She spoke in sweet, soft tones, music to my ears. "Pin, you've got to calm down."

I melted into her; I swam in her eyes. "Katie, I think I'm the one who made Craney sick."

Mistress of sarcasm, Alda sniped, "She's got a cold, poor thing. She deserves it."

"No. She's really sick. Mademoiselle made us pray for her. Some rare infection."

"And?" Alda lifted her hands as if to add, "Who cares?"

"You said you smelled menthol. So she's got a cold. Sorry," Katie chimed in.

"No. Really. When I was creeping back here, I heard an ambulance."

"Oh?" said Alda.

"Wait." Katie smoothed the hair off my forehead and actually made me blow my nose in her hankie. "You're thinking it was your grandmother's curse?"

"Hah!" interrupted Alda. "Maybe it's my father. I told him about Craney."

Now it was our turn to look at Alda, eyes bugging, mouths gaping. "Yeah?"

"Nothing. I mean, like we didn't do anything." Alda was on her feet, whistling *Whistle While You Work.* She was heating some hot water for broth on a camp stove. She always got real busy when I questioned her about her dad.

Katie spoke up. She turned from me to Alda. "Alda, listen. Pina's dreams are real. Sometimes, they're really real."

"Hey, this one feels one-hundred percent real," I said. "It's like Craney's crawled under my skin and taken over. I've got to stop her at all costs. My grandmother, I think she's tapping into that."

Alda turned around and with one eyebrow peaking, she smirked. "At all costs?"

I sighed, and threw my slipper at her. "You know what I mean."

"Hmm," was her only response.

Alda checked the hall and made Katie run to the shower during room check. After Katie's return, Alda made a dramatic dance to her closet and emerged, saying, "Abracadabra," and produced her small bottle of Vin Santo and a tin of biscotti.

She made me drink two big gulps of the sweet wine, which relaxed me. I think I started to slur and feel very light, and giddy, and warm, and *marvelous*!

Katie and Alda jumped on my bed and we started to recite "Winken, blinken, and nod." We finished the bottle. It was really small.

Katie caught the last word of shoe and sang, "Shoo, shoo, shoofly." She sat up and poked Alda. "Tell us about your Pops. What's so special bout him?"

Alda rolled her eyes, which she could hardly keep open. She giggled. "'Wolfie'—ya know, like my last name—'Lupo' means wolf. He's fat. Ha. He's bald. He calls my Mama Jezebella."

"Oh yeah? Thought he was scary," I said. "Doesn't sound scary to me."

"But to our darling Dorotea…" said Katie.

"Oh pooh." Alda's eyes were almost crossed. "So my father has lots dnd lots of guns."

I was still able to make some sense out of our sloppy, gurgling chat. I glanced over to Katie, who looked wide-awake now.

"Guns?" we said.

When we shook her, Alda didn't move. We

learned the meaning of dead drunk. We did the only thing that seemed logical at that point. We left her in my bed and crawled into hers.

"Love you," I whispered to Katie. "You're so good when I get my crazies."

"Oh, sweetie," Katie said, brushing her lips across my forehead. "Just want to keep you safe and whole and sleeping!"

As much as I loved sleeping by Katie's side, my throbbing headache and some other heavy vibration caused me to shift my weight and push Katie onto the floor. None too soon either.

Dorotea stood before us, yelling at Katie. Katie was usually good at thinking on her feet, but she was on her bottom and the Vin Santo had dulled her senses.

"You, you, Katie, of all people, you turn your back on me too? What? There is a 'no-admit Dorotea' fan club?"

Katie struggled to open her eyes. "I uh…fell asleep. I'm so sorry."

I thought I had half a chance at saving the day, rather the night. "Oh, Dorotea, you know how upset I am about Miss Craney. Katie was only trying to comfort me. Please don't be angry."

I hoped Dorotea's constant sinus problems prevented her from smelling the alcohol. I also hoped her tender heart, for Miss Craney, might persuade her to believe me.

"Come," she said, bending down and offering Katie a firm hand. "Here, come, up. We finish talk in our room. *Schnell*, quick."

Katie mumbled agreement to Dorotea and "science" to me. We would put our heads together in science lab.

Chapter Thirty-one

Alda Comes Clean

Katie seemed ever so small as she stumbled off in front of Dorotea. The door slammed behind them. I was truly awake now. And Alda, could she really be sleeping through all this?

I could hear myself think in this alcohol-induced silence. Was I really responsible for Craney's illness? That's how the whole evening started; I wanted my friends to tell me—my fault or my grandmother's? Jeez! If I even thought I could, would I really try to make Craney sick? Did I hate her that much? Was I that scared and disgusted by her? Scared enough to hurt her?

I reviewed in my mind how frantic I had been the last few weeks. Breakfast with Craney, the journal, the black academic gown, images flashing by in my head since my birthday. Ah! And the all-encompassing thought of Katie, my birthday with Katie.

A new world had opened for me, a world of splendid titillation, but not without the side effects of craziness, abject fear, and all sorts of identity crises. Who the hell was I? Never mind Alda or her father. And did I have a backbone? I would need it.

I turned over the events of the evening in my mind. I looked over at Alda. She had drunk the lion's share. Maybe she really was sleeping and maybe she really did say her father had lots and lots of guns.

Jeez! Who was her father anyway?

I found myself shaking Alda awake. I heard myself saying in my sternest, middle-of-the-night voice, "I have to know!"

I rocked her back and forth with whatever energy and anger I could muster. "Dangit. Wake up."

A very puffy face emerged from the covers, eyes flickering. "Pina."

"Get up!" I had no mercy.

"*Minchia*! Okay, okay. Just don't yell. My head."

"Alda, enough! Spill the beans. *Who* is your father?"

"You really want to do this? Okay. He's...a... man..." She spoke one word at a time.

I finished her sentence, "Yeah, with lots of guns. More!"

"He's got a lot of power."

"Alda!" I slammed my fist down on the bedside table and stood, all five feet of me, hovering over Alda's head.

"He's in the family."

"You mean, the Mafia?"

Alda burped and excused herself. I thought she was going to vomit.

"Yeah," she continued. "I can't let anyone know."

"And Dorotea?" I asked.

"I think she saw some stuff she shouldn't have. My father told me to shut her up, but he didn't explain. Pina, believe me. I don't think my father's really bad, but I think some of his friends are."

"I guess it depends on your definition of bad." I looked away from her.

She reached up ever so gently and turned my head

around. "Please don't. You and Katie are the closest things I've had to friends. I don't want to do this again. Move and cover our tracks. Anything but that."

I felt my shoulders sag. Ice cubes formed all the way down my spine. But I was not a drill sergeant, not after a night of booze and no sleep. I locked my eyes on Alda. "Just tell me. Did your father hurt Dorotea?"

"No. I swear. Just…just that, Dorotea might have seen or heard something. My father thinks she might not be who she says she is."

"Jesus." I blew out a whole room of air. "Alda, I just need to think. Just too much tonight. Too many creaking doors for one night. Stop."

"Sure." She sighed and caught my hand as I started to walk away. "Please don't be angry with me. Maybe I exaggerated a little, you know how I am…I uh…got some things wrong, I think." Her voice was shaky. She looked at me, but seemed to be viewing a different movie in her head. "Oh, and you can't tell anybody," she mumbled, her head shaking with an involuntary tic.

I patted her and nodded. "No. Just sleep."

Chapter Thirty-two

Science Lab

I had awakened early. I bundled myself in my camel toggle coat and tiptoed down the hall barefoot. Once outside, I put on my Weejuns and slipped my earmuffs on to block the wind. I needed to walk.

I followed the line of the privet hedge and slid through the narrow space in the back fence. Free on the village green, I kept my head down against the wind and gazed back at Albert's frozen buildings. I wondered how many secrets those buildings held.

As dawn approached, I snuck back, catching a few sparse flakes on my nose. I felt cleansed. I didn't have to do anything about Alda's father, I would inquire as to Craney's health, and I would hear Katie's story about Dorotea in science lab. I'd manage to switch lab partners so we could chat between centrifuges and Bunsen burners.

I skipped breakfast, which suited my headache just fine. French class brought me the news of Craney's changing diagnosis: severe exhaustion and a mild case of pleurisy. We all signed a respectful get well card. I used a cursive P. Mazzini in the lower right-hand corner, wedged in among old Anglo Saxon family names.

Science lab was pretty quiet as our instructor, Dr. Hermione Eisenberg, allowed us great leeway. Unless flames or explosions alerted her, she was content to scribble equations and formulas, head down at her massive oak desk on the raised platform.

Katie shrugged her shoulders at me. She didn't know if things were bad between her and Dorotea. She had fed Dorotea some story about the upcoming room change, saying she would need to get to know Alda better if she were going to room with her. Dorotea had agreed, but then just shook her head at Katie and kept repeating, "Bad."

As Katie poured some water into the beaker, she lowered her head to read the level and whispered, "Dreams, Dorotea has bad dreams." She looked around at the instructor and continued, "Dorotea has dreams about Alda's father's guns. She wakes up screaming, 'Don't shoot!'"

I shut the burner off and took away the beaker. I leaned down to pull out the centrifuge and rack of test tubes. I caught Katie's eye and whispered, "Ma-fi-a." We both looked over to where Alda was working across the aisle.

Katie told me to meet her in the bathroom where we continued to whisper. "Alda's father" and "Mafia."

"Men threatening with guns," she said.

"Dorotea?" I questioned.

"Don't know, but she saw something," Katie answered.

We finished our lab, having produced some wonderful esters and some confusing glimpses into more emerging secrets. The aroma of mystery shrouded in banana, mint, and orange trailed after us.

Surrounded by other students, we couldn't do much more than sign language. I flapped my ears at Katie to signify "Listen up to Dorotea." Katie flashed a brown paper book cover on which she had written "Town—tomorrow."

I would find a way to get some time alone with Katie tomorrow. While Alda shopped for makeup, we would figure out more of what had happened to Dorotea at Alda's house or just let it be. We could just dream, not even grandmother dreams, just dreams of our past summer in Maine—the lake, the wanderings, the love.

Chapter Thirty-three

Shopping

Gray. My eyes encountered a cold New England gray. I awoke early after turning in very early. The emotional events of the previous day with its early dusk made eight p.m. seem late.

My future—with Alda, daughter of who knew what hoodlum, with Katie, love of my life; with Dorotea, handmaid of Craney or so I thought; with Craney, scourge of love and decency. All aspects of my future seemed gray and bleak.

For the immediate future, I had to get out of bed, dress, and go shopping with Katie and Alda. I had to fill Katie in on the details of Alda's father. Again, no shades of rose here.

As I dressed, I heard Alda humming Great Balls of Fire. I wasn't up for a striptease or charades today, just some calm. I longed for my tranquil, vagabond days in Maine this past summer.

Alda took one look out the window and one look at my face. "You need a break, don't you?"

I nodded.

"Sorry I added to your pile of crap with my family history."

"Shush." I sighed. "Let's just grab Katie and walk to town."

"We okay?" she said as an apologetic smile crept

across her face.

I patted her on the shoulder and ushered her through the door. She stumbled and barked, *"Merda."*

Oh lord, here we go again. I just wanted some peace.

Alda crawled back to the door. She braced herself against the wall and pushed herself halfway up. Mumbling *"Minchia,"* one of her colorful ways of saying the f-word, she grabbed a package from the floor, which she attempted to hurl.

I caught her hand. I deciphered part of my name on the brown paper bag wrapping. From the shape and feel of it, it was a slim book.

"Crap!" I spat out as I helped Alda the rest of the way up.

Katie was tiptoeing down the hall to meet us when Alda grabbed my arm, dumping the book into her satchel and commanded, "Let's get out of here."

We sped down the hall, our eyes a lighthouse beam sweeping to the left and right. I told Katie with a sidelong glance I would explain as soon as we were in the clear.

Once past the main gate, we disappeared behind the bandstand on the green. I took the book from the satchel and studied the label, typed. I held it up and shook it. "Another Craney gift?"

"She over her disease?" asked Alda.

"Unless it's a present from the grave," said Katie.

"From the netherworld," added Alda.

"Stop it. Enough! I'm sick of this crap." I pounded the grass.

"Sweetie," soothed Katie. "Aren't you going to open it?"

I ripped the thin grocery bag as if I were flaying

Craney's flesh. *The Children's Hour.*

"Huh?" was the consensus.

"Well, it's not pornography or a love story," said Katie.

I flipped through its seventy-five pages: no name, no inscription, brand new. The playwright—we discovered it was a play—was Lillian Hellman.

"Hey!" Alda snatched the book. "We're going to the bookstore."

Katie was trying to caress me with her soft gaze. Alda was on a mission. I was beat.

Setting a swift pace, Alda grabbed both of us by the arm and told us not to worry. She would look after Katie and find ways for all of us to rendezvous when I switched rooms in a few days. Her eyes twinkled as she divulged news of her secret plan to give me yet another birthday present, a sequel to the first. "Remember," she said, "woman doesn't live by bread alone." She planted a friendly kiss on each of our cheeks and had us skipping along to the Andover Bookshop.

Alda's birthday gift, another romantic tryst for Katie and me, sounded enticing, but not without complications. I was dragging, and I didn't have to think very far in the past to remember how all my problems began, but also all my blissful yearnings for Katie. We would have to be truly crazy or desperate to risk that again.

The bookshop was famous and familiar. Its wood-burning fire welcomed us into its comfy two floors lined with mahogany stained bookshelves and beamed ceilings. Alda disappeared into the section on drama.

Katie steered me into a tight niche, more like a warren sunken below the normal floor level—the section on murder mysteries. "I've got to tell you about Dorotea's nightmare," she whispered. "And maybe, just maybe, ravish you a sec."

"Shush. First things first," I said.

Katie started to pull a face when Alda returned, eyes darting. She crawled into the mini-cave and closed the hatch door a fraction.

Alda bit her finger. Her eyes apologized to me before she could even tell me she knew I wanted peace. "It's bad. It's a play about lesbians, well, supposed lesbians."

"Man, *enough!*" I bared my teeth. Katie slumped and breathed heavily. I expected to see fire bursting forth from her nostrils.

"Listen. I know you don't want to hear this. Maybe we could contact Lillian Hellman. I mean she must know something about lesbians." Katie had put on her lecturing voice.

"Duh?" was all I said.

"Well," Alda said. "Maybe my father..." She turned her palm outwards as if to ask why that wasn't a reasonable and rational option.

Katie and I exchanged a killer look.

"Yeah, right," said Katie.

I poked her with my elbow since Alda had sworn me to secrecy.

Katie recovered quickly, coughed, and stood, head-bowed to avoid the low eave.

"Look," Katie said. "We've got to figure out whether it's Craney or Dorotea or both. Let's get out of here and go to that crummy luncheonette no kid would be caught dead in. Even the drunks won't be there now."

We slithered out of our pit and crept over to Eunice's Cafe. Slopping waves of hot chocolate from our somewhat stained mugs, we made our way to the dimly lit stall with the formica table in the back. We sank onto and into the cracked phony leather cushion, which had given up the ghost a long time before. Molded into our individual forms, we each prepared a case for the demon of our choice: Craney, Dorotea, or both.

While Dorotea was a current thorn in my side, and come next week, she would be my personal prison guard of a roommate, I didn't think she knew recent American playwrights. Katie was also leaning toward Craney, but...

"Listen." Katie had blanched. She touched Alda's hand across the still-wet table. "Dorotea might think we're all having a thing, and she's picking on Pina because she's the most vulnerable. You and me, Alda, we're, well, you know, privileged, uh, protected."

"Picking on me?" I jumped up.

"Shush. Go on, Katie," said Alda. "You said 'protected.' You know something else, something about me."

"Okay, Alda. Dorotea has bad nightmares. She was screaming last night that Al Capone was at your house. She was wailing and ranting about kneeling down to say her prayers, convinced she would be executed with a bullet to the base of her skull. I heard her get up and rattle some pills. Then I fell asleep. Alda, she's petrified of your father. There, I've said it."

"Hmm," said Alda. "Al Capone? Couldn't have been. He's dead." Alda chuckled.

"Dammit!" whispered Katie and me at the same time.

"Well, maybe my father could fix all of them."

"What? Well, maybe just Craney." I laughed.

Katie gaped at me. "Are you crazy? Is it an Italian thing? Pina!" She looked around to see if the local hoods leaning into a nearby booth of big-haired girls had heard her.

"Hold on. I'm so tired of this crap. I'm joking. Alda, c'mon."

Alda sighed. "Katie, you've got to believe me. My father didn't do anything to Dorotea. There was a tough guy talking to my father, but—"

I butted in, "Wait. Alda, you said—"

"I was a bit drunk," protested Alda. "But, Katie, can you convince her—"

"Who?" said Katie, rather peeved.

"Dorotea. That she's confusing her Wild West stories. She can't, do you understand, she can't talk about that man. It would be suicide."

"Aw, jeez, Alda." Katie put her head down on the table. "Let me think. But, are we in danger?"

"Damn," I interjected. "Craney and Dorotea aren't danger enough?"

"Look. Silence is…" Alda began, playing with the greasy knobs on the miniature jukebox on the table.

"Yeah. Golden." I wore my best sneering face. "Dammit, get Pat Boone off that thing."

"Shut up! We make like nothing has happened, about the book I mean. My father swore no permanent damage was done. I've gotta split—need some lipstick." Alda popped out an old slanted tube, applied some, and blotted her lips dramatically on her slightly soiled napkin. Red and brown lips remained on the crumpled paper.

She waved, "Ta-ta" after we agreed to meet in an hour by the clock tower.

The door took forever to shut. Blanche, the

waitress with the grimy, short apron who had been draping her cleavage over the counter, finally noticed us. She tore herself away from the intense eye lock she had been sharing with the DA-hairdo endowed townie. We ordered melted Velveeta cheese sandwiches and Cokes. We were alone again.

I stared at Katie's raised arm supporting her forehead. She sighed, closed her eyes, and shook her head. "I'm freaked out about the book. It's creepy."

"But..."

"And I like Alda, I do." Katie was stalling. She played with the plastic Dutch boy and girl salt-and-pepper shakers. The girl slipped from Katie's hand, it was so greasy.

"But...?"

"Dorotea was petrified. I don't know if the pills were sleeping pills or...You know, she's been saying weird stuff. She accidentally stubbed her toe and said, '*verdammte fuss.*'"

"I know, damned foot. So?" I rolled and twirled the straw wrapper. I was so tired.

"Well, then she said in English, 'Off, off, gone. I could be gone. Good and gone!'"

"Katie, I'm exhausted. What the heck are you saying?"

"You think she might do something crazy?" Katie frowned.

"Like rooming with me? Or planting a book? Or stooging for Craney?" The smells of burnt coffee and bad beer were getting to me. I motioned to Blanche to turn on the exhaust fan. It was as if thunder struck and sucked out whatever life was left in this New England version of the OK Corral.

"C'mon, Pin," Katie said over the roar of the

fans. "I'm scared she might hurt herself. You don't want that."

"Course not." I looked into Katie's eyes. I, too, held my head up with my hand smashed against my forehead. I couldn't finish my cheese sandwich, which was now dripping down my other hand.

"I think Alda is scared too. I have a feeling her family has been relocated."

"Oh God," winced Katie. "Wow. Her father must really be ticked off and scared—what with Alda's big-mouth ways and Dorotea."

Katie had said it all. I think both of us were wondering who was in the most trouble, who was causing it, and what to do about it.

"Lay low," Katie said, suddenly looking super smart. Then, a bit less solid, she added, "You were joking about her father fixing stuff, weren't you?"

Chapter Thirty-four

The Doldrums

I lay sprawled across my bed, lost in the fog on the other side of my window. Fog in my brain too.

From the appointed meeting time with Alda at the clock tower a few days ago until the scheduled break-up of our threesome three days later—because of my room change—a certain calm reigned. Well, maybe boredom, maybe depression. Even Alda's new lipsticks seemed dull on her now droopy lips.

Katie walked around with her head in a book, her beloved science of course, or with sneak glances in my direction. She also reported on Dorotea's increasingly bizarre behavior, throwing or giving away her once-treasured German keepsakes, as well as more vivid gangster nightmares.

Alda's interest in her clothes waned, as did her curiosity about *The Children's Hour*. She went through the motions of friendship with Dorotea, actually inviting her to eat with us. Dorotea obliged, but her gestures during that meal were so strained that she dropped several pieces of food.

I read *The Children's Hour* without commenting on it to Katie and Alda. No one mentioned it, not them, not Dorotea, nor Craney. But I was becoming more and more depressed by the destructive power of gossip of any sort. I was now petrified of being called a lesbian—of being exposed.

How much of my current laying low was just being practical, and how much was hiding, maybe even hiding from myself?

What would happen if Dorotea or Craney uncovered the truth? Yeah. Goodbye Albert. Big deal. Well, it was. And Katie? Would my parents allow me to see her? Ha! After they died of embarrassment? Besides, I'd be a vegetable. They'd send me for shock treatments. I wouldn't even know my own name.

Shoot. I couldn't let that happen. I could try to date an Exeter boy. Yuck!

Oh. F-R-I-G! What am I thinking? Craney? What if she forced me? Holy crap! Why didn't she die of that stupid pleurisy? Man. I can't believe I'm thinking this way. Maybe I'm dead either way.

The knock on the door told me I was not dead, not yet. I checked to see that *The Children's Hour* was under my mattress and yelled, "Come in."

Alda and Katie came in, throwing sidelong glances at me. I'm sure they were trying to read my mood.

Katie approached me at my desk, lightly running her hand along my arm. I looked up and managed a feeble smile.

"Hi, sweetie," Katie said. With something approaching enthusiasm, she continued, "Hey, we figured out a way to leave messages. I mean, if we don't manage to see each other during the day. You know, once you move out."

"Oh?" I said. "Carrier pigeon?"

"C'mon," said Alda. "They poop."

"You know the weird lava rock by the library?

It's real easy to lift. Presto: messenger service, note underneath." Katie tried to catch my eye to create a twinkle.

"Look, you guys, that's really sweet. Albert Hall isn't that far from the library."

"But?" said Katie.

"I'm just…I don't know what I am," I said. "This can't end well."

"Hey. Who said anything about it ending?" said Alda as she pulled out a calendar. "I, for one, am arranging another birthday for you two. Here, in this room, unattended, unspied on. With Dorotea gone—who, by the way, will receive an invitation to her aunt's, sent by me, of course, in one week. My father will summon Craney to discuss acceptance of a certain sum to the Albert Foundation. How's that for no end?"

"Crazy," said Katie.

"Your father, he's all over the place," I said.

"No 'thank you'? You ingrates," Alda said. "I told you my father could take care of the situation."

"I wish he could," I said, imagining a 1930s Thompson machine gun.

Katie shot me a look, mouth hanging open.

"Look, you guys," I said. "I'm just friggin' depressed."

"Just say the word, and I'll make magic. Abracadabra!" Alda attempted a fancy move with her hands. She looked like an eighty-year-old woman doing wrist exercises.

Katie gave me a sweet kiss on the forehead and patted my head. "Hey, love, we have a way to pass notes now. C'mon. We'll help you move tomorrow. We're not going to leave you stranded across campus all alone with Dorotea."

"Yeah! And right next door to Craney's sub-office."

Alda said she was leaving to take a shower. I think she really wanted to give us a few moments together.

I just stared at Katie and clasped her hand in silence. She smoothed my hair with her other hand.

I heard myself say, "You know. I don't have to do this. French can wait."

Her eyes smiled back at me. "No, you do have to do this. It's your chance."

"But Katie, us?"

"We'll survive the three blocks of separation. And you, you can tolerate Dorotea."

"And Craney?" I was begging her to let me off the hook. Would she see my cowardice?

"I'm so sorry you have to deal with her. She really has been laying low. And I did tell my dad and Joe." Katie lowered her head but continued, "I couldn't stand it if you didn't grab every opportunity like this French immersion program because of me. You've got to go for it. We'll manage."

I let out a huge sigh. "I couldn't live with myself if you thought I was a coward—if I thought I was a coward."

Katie kissed each eyelid, whispering, "I don't."

The door swung open; Alda rushed in, also in tears. "I don't either."

I didn't know how much Alda had heard. I did know both Alda and Katie seemed like life jackets floating on either side of me.

Chapter Thirty-five

Dead Girl Walking

On the morning of the move, I awoke to a blackened room. It was too early and too stormy. I heard the thunder, as well as Alda's soft snoring. At least, that brought a smile to my face.

Looking around this room in the dark, I still managed to see some of Alda's treasures. I would especially miss her glow-in-the-dark, stone encrusted Our Lady of Pompeii, sitting next to the Venetian glass framed picture of Alda, Katie, and me taken at the Woolworth's photo booth in town.

These were my last hours of relative freedom before the move to Albert Hall. I snuck over to Alda's desk and munched on some of her biscotti. The long necked Vin Santo bottle was empty. I read the holy picture of San Sebastiano, martyr. Somehow, I felt like I, too, was going to be pierced through with spears, sacrificed in just a few hours.

I must have fallen back to sleep in Alda's puffy chair. The thunder was really monumental, or was it the end of my dream? My executioner was sounding the drum.

I sat up; my blood ran cold. I didn't know if I was awake, asleep, dead, or alive. Craney stood before me, cloaked in her black, flowing academic gown.

The ceiling light flickered on. "Your move is off."

She spoke each monosyllabic word with deliberate vocalization. "There's been a reprieve." Or did she say, after recess, winter recess?

The jangling of her keys preceded her. She disappeared in a swirl of black. The dry clack of the door confirmed her retreat.

I sat stunned. Across the room, Alda seemed plastered against her bedstead, arms spread out, hair seemingly electrified.

Light burst through the door as Katie flew in, tennis racket in hand. "Are you all right?" she gasped. "I saw her."

I covered my eyes. I didn't know whether to laugh or to cry. A laughing/crying jag took hold of all of us.

I roared laughing when I told them I thought Craney said "reprieve." I thought of crime movies and governors commuting death sentences at the last moment. Then I started wailing for real. The rollercoaster ride was fraying every one of my nerves.

Both Katie and Alda decided the winter break would give us all time to involve our families if necessary. I just wanted to sleep.

I was someplace in my head on a beach in Cefalu, Sicily. The froth of the warm ocean enveloped me while mermaids drizzled apricot nectar on my lips. Alda and Katie competing for the lifesaver of the year award broke my reverie; each one argued how to save me from the maelstrom.

"Stop!" I broke the spell. "Maybe Craney has definitely backed off. Let's just cool it," I pleaded when the door swung open.

Dorotea stood in the doorway apologizing. "I am so blue. My dream to be in the French dorm, chosen to be among the elite, *le cadre francais*. It is gone. Craney lied to me."

Craney had gotten to her too. Katie went to Dorotea and put an arm around her shoulders. "Shush," she said. "Come back to our room, I'll explain."

Chapter Thirty-six

A (Normal) Day in the Life…

Life had returned to its fall crispness and perkiness. We were drinking lots of orange juice and swallowing Vitamin C to make up for the lack of sunshine.

Our spirits had risen along with our hopes of normalcy. It had only been four days since Craney's change of plans. For us, it constituted a new normal.

Craney made no more appearances. We didn't question this reprieve or recess or retreat. We were on time for all of our classes and played by the rules, homework and lights out and all.

Alda and I spent some quiet evenings with Katie doing homework and board games in my room. Occasionally we invited Dorotea, whose mood continued to slump after Craney's change of heart.

Katie was worried about Dorotea. Her nightmares had become more vivid. My dreams had, in fact, turned dreamier.

Katie said Dorotea spoke to Craney in her sleep, asking Craney if she, Dorotea, had been a good girl. One night, according to Katie, Dorotea had awakened screaming she'd do anything Craney wanted. When Katie tried to comfort her, Dorotea kept on repeating that she, Dorotea, was not a good person.

Katie and I actually tried to be kind to Dorotea

since it was clear she was troubled. I even spent an evening with Dorotea, reading aloud in French, but it was too weird. Dorotea just stared at me. She gave me the creeps. I imagined her eyes were goats' eyes. Alda insisted Dorotea was not troubled, just trouble, evil trouble that had to be stopped.

Alda couldn't stop talking about the belated birthday present she had prepared for Katie and me. Everything was set to go off smashingly in a few days. Alda went around humming Eddie Fisher's Oh My Papa. She reassured us he always took care of everyone.

Katie and I weren't sure this was a great idea, but we were looking forward to some R&R. Besides, we had learned in our Classics class that you didn't look a gift horse in the face.

Chapter Thirty-seven

Belated Birthday

Coronets could have announced the day. Alda had set the stage for my belated birthday celebration. Dorotea had left early, thrilled to receive her aunt's invitation, Alda's fiendishly skilled forgery. Before her own departure, Alda phoned Craney's office. She let me hear Craney's secretary say Craney would be out of the office attending an Albert Foundation meeting. The bedrooms belonged to Katie and me for an entire luscious day and night.

Katie appeared in the doorway. She stood for a few seconds, still and lovely. Both of us held the moment as we held our breath.

We seemed a bit shy. It had only been a month since our first encounter, but we were no longer impulsive, horny kids. It felt as if we were a seasoned couple on one hand and newly disrobed nuns on the other.

I approached Katie and lifted off her trench coat to reveal a beautiful cotton cut-lace gown. I was almost trembling.

She clasped me to her and softly stroked my throat and my neck. She unbuttoned my flannel nightshirt. She kissed each button as she undid them.

"I'm wondering how to do this. I love you so much," she said.

I took her hand and pressed it to my lips. "I

know," I whispered. "This time is different."

We lay on the bed and cuddled and stroked each other. I sighed. I was so free, so transported. I felt as if we had already touched each other deeply and become one.

Katie's face had never seemed so open. I felt layered inside of her; she was my second flesh. She saw through my eyes; I breathed through her pores.

We must have been there, that way for hours. Or maybe a lifetime. Our arms, hands, and fingers found each other, open and magnetic. It was impossible to say where she began and I ended. Her legs were my legs, my breasts, hers.

I cried out with her in me, her breath, her moan echoed back on me. We fell back, full of each other.

We dozed off, spooning in each other's arms. I never wanted this to end.

I awoke in the early morning to Katie's honeyed smile, her head a few inches away.

"You're lovely," she crooned.

"You're lovelier," I whispered.

"I'm thirsty." She coughed a silly, make-believe cough.

"I'll get something." I slipped on a robe and got money for the collective soda supply down the hall.

"Don't disappear now." I smiled as I grabbed the doorknob to exit. I twisted it back and forth a few seconds. Locked. Ooh, that sinking feeling. I tried to recover, laughing out of nervousness. "Ha! We're trapped *forever*! Together!"

We giggled a bunch. Katie thought it was a joke. She got up to try the door and collapsed back in bed in a burst of "ha-has." We jumped back in bed. I just shrugged, sighing, "Oh well," when a ray of light darted across the wall.

Katie started to hum the theme from *The Twilight Zone*. I grabbed her arm and scrunched up my face.

"What is that?" I said, pointing to a black spot, a large black beetle on the wall above Alda's dresser. "A bug, a hole?"

When Katie got up to investigate, the black spot had turned back to the normal off-white of the walls. I ran to her side, dragging a chair. She went to touch the once-black spot when her finger disappeared into a hole.

"Aw crap, a peep hole. Quick. We've got to get out of here." I pointed to the door.

"How?" she whispered. "It really is stuck."

We put on a minimum of street clothes, with no idea where to go, except out. We'd use the fire escape. It led to the rear of Smythe Hall with only the privet hedges as backdrop.

I couldn't see anything through the fog outside the window. I raised the window and stepped out, guiding Katie onto the metal cage. I thought I knew how to unlock and secure the fire escape hinges as I had snuck out with Alda one night. Panic set in this time.

We hardly let go of our handholds as we crept down to the hinge release point. After a few attempts at unlatching the last set of stairs, I was able to work the mechanism. We moved onto the first steps when I felt the stairs give way under us and start to swing back and forth. Someone had tampered with the swinging stairs.

Katie held onto me as we careened, a living pendulum, ten feet above the ground. We were truly unhinged.

As the dangling stair reached its low point, I pulled Katie away from the grille work and let go. We were sore but temporarily safe after our four-foot fall onto cement. We hid out under the privet hedge. I fought back the urge to faint. Katie had turned on her side to vomit. I cleaned her mouth with an old, compressed tissue I found deep in my pocket.

"Where do we go?" I asked through my gasps. "Craney saw it all through the peep hole. She's going to get us."

"Do we have money?" Katie had started to dig in her pockets. "We've got to get away."

"Let's think. Alda or your father?" I said, producing some crumpled dollars and two quarters and a dime. "I can't think straight," I was beginning to ramble. "Where the hell is Alda, anyway? It's ten A.M. She's supposed to be back."

"Right. She'd look out the window, no?" Katie said.

It seemed like an eternity had gone by as we continued to gape at each other and the occasional ant also seeking refuge. It took a while to bring Alda's face into focus. It was the only thing with some color and definition piercing through the fog coating the side of the building. She must have been waving at us for several minutes before we realized she was signaling she'd be right down.

She snuck into the privet hideout beside us.

"*Minchia!*" Alda cursed as she wiped the smeared blood from the scratches on our faces. "I didn't screw up this time. I swear. But what? What the heck happened?"

Katie and I shrugged. "Locked door," said Katie as if that said it all.

I shook my head and sighed. "Yeah, don't forget about the peephole. Oh and the broken security hinge on the fire escape."

The laughs that escaped from our mouths were anything but funny. Alda shook me, and held me by the shoulders as she raised her voice. "*What*?"

"Dorotea?" I asked.

"She's not back yet. I checked," Alda said. "What do you mean a locked door? I had no problem."

Katie was able to roll her eyes at Alda. "Dammit, Alda. That friggin' door was locked from the outside. Craney's work." Katie spit the last few words.

"Uh," Alda seemed to be counting hours and schedules in her head. "She was supposed to meet with my father in New York yesterday and be back around noon today."

"But did they meet?" I asked.

"But the peephole…" Katie frowned. "When did that happen? And, Alda, where the heck were you?"

"Yeah, Alda, where were you?" I yelled.

"Geez. Now you don't trust me?" Alda stammered, "I have a…well, an arrangement with an Exeter guy."

Silence and the near freezing air stilled the scene for a good five minutes when our combined sighs brought us back to pertinent questions. "What was on the other side of the wall containing the peephole?" was the latest inquiry. Theoretically, a broom closet. We had never investigated. And none of us had noticed the peephole before this morning.

"Hold on, everyone." I stopped our musings. "What do we do now? I'm losing it. Enough of this cloak and dagger crap. I'm going to be exposed as a flaming lesbian. I'm a goner."

I was seriously sick with fear, vomiting and

weeping. I panicked as I pictured the life I had known wiped out. I didn't see individual things and people erased; I just froze in the icy sensation of death. Tears and saliva coated me. I needed help.

"Okay," Alda spoke up with an air of authority. "Katie, you're safe because of your father. You go back to your room."

Alda's hands were around my waist. She was pulling me up. "C'mon," she said. "I've got another plan for you. Katie, you go first. C'mon now, hurry. Back to your room, Katie. I've got Pina." Alda was clearly in command.

Back up in the room and cleaned up, I remained almost comatose in extreme fear, delirious in the same bed where hours before I had been love-struck. Alda reported I had tossed and turned and ranted, "Dorotea, Craney. Craney, Dorotea."

In my hallucinations, Dorotea appeared to be evil personified, fuming at Craney for cancelling our French program, suspicious that I may have caused it. Craney, too, made an appearance, issuing me a reprieve, maybe just until this torturous episode.

According to Alda, I screamed out, "Just kill her. She's evil." She told me that I had been whistling The Wicked Witch is Dead and called for my grandmother.

I woke up soaked in sweat. Alda told me I had wanted to kill both Dorotea and Craney. Thinking more clearly now, I laughed at this death wish. I hurried to admit to Alda that yeah, in a way, I wanted them gone, but of course, I wouldn't kill them.

Alda rubbed her hands and said it would all work out. Her father would be pleased too. Had I really been thinking clearly?

After what had seemed like eons, I asked Alda

what had been going on. "I didn't kill Craney or Dorotea, did I?" At the time, I really wasn't sure if I had been delirious or…could Alda have slipped me a pill?

"Nah. Don't worry," she answered.

"I think you kept saying your father would take care of business. You were joking, right?"

Alda produced a great big grin. "Sure!"

I was fighting hard to stay lucid now. I needed to make sense to Alda. I needed her to understand who I was. "I can never get 'even' with people. I can't. It makes my skin crawl. When I make a mistake, I want forgiveness, you know?"

"Uh huh," she said. "Pin, you worry too much. But you are right. They will throw you out." She looked as if she were picturing this on a movie screen. "Your parents will be furious—or they will pity you and send you to that hospital, Bellevue. But after a little bit of shock therapy, you won't mind."

What was Alda's problem? "Stop! Crap, Alda, you know that's what I'm scared of, not just losing Albert. I'll be excommunicated, officially, and from the pulpit. I guess I could live with that. But people will look at me like I'm dirty, like I'm wrong, all wrong. I'll never see Katie again. How could I go on living?"

"You will. You just won't know who she is after the shock therapy. But don't worry, I keep telling you there's always my father."

"Alda. Drop dead!" I said, rubbing my eyes and wringing my hands. I was still kind of out of it. I shook my head to try to break through to the real truth. "I can't. I can't. I'm just not that kind of person. I don't think."

"What kind?" laughed Alda.

I don't know how long I slept, if I slept, if I dreamt. I had a feeling something really weird had gone on with Alda, but what was going on now was definitely not weird and not illusion.

I felt something, warm and wholesome—it just had that safe feeling—by my face. I just wanted to hold on forever. Katie was whispering, "It's okay, Pina. I'm okay too. But, sweetie, listen, I think you have an official note."

Chapter Thirty-eight

The Official Note

A butter-cream light poured through my window. Katie was fully clothed, sitting next to me on the bed; Alda was nowhere to be seen.

I blinked a few times and tried to figure out the day and the circumstances. I was thinking more or less straight.

Katie repeated that she was okay. Why wouldn't she be?

"Kat, I uh…What day is it?"

"It's Monday. You've got to get up," said Katie as she tapped an ivory colored envelope against her hand. "Sweetie, you have to read this. It's on Craney's stationery."

"Oh Jesus. It's all coming back to me." I scratched my head. "Where's Alda?"

"No clue. Listen, Pin, the note. You've got to—"

"Kat, Alda was really weird, really scary. Do you really trust her?"

Katie got up and came back with a washcloth. She wiped my face and held my head between her hands. She looked straight into my eyes and said, "Open it!"

Finally putting all the pieces together, I understood how this letter could change everything. I reached out for Katie's hand and ripped the flap with my other hand. The note said, "Report to my office at once on a matter of extreme urgency." Signed Mary Margaret Craney, Headmistress and dated that morning.

All I could think to say to Katie was, "What time is it?"

Katie was chewing her lower lip. "Seven. Why?"

"Why didn't she summon me last night?"

"Pin, is that important now? Are you following this? Don't you get it?"

"What's to get? I'm going to be thrown out," I grunted.

"Is that the only thing you're worried about?" Katie caught my eye. She had raised her voice and was pursing her lips. "Pin, dangit, I've already called my father. He's totally upset but can't do anything until he knows what's what, what she accuses you of."

"Katie…" I threw my head back. "We can't prove anything except that we're in love. But you know, like in that book *The Children's Hour*, all the relationships wound up ruined after the whole ordeal." I stared off into space.

Katie threw back my covers and pulled me from the bed. "Pina, you've got to get dressed. You've got to find out what she's going to say."

"And Alda and Dorotea?" I said.

"She-it, Pina! Why the heck are you worried about them now? I haven't seen either of them."

"Alda's up to something. I think. But it was like I was drugged. She was cruel to me. Like she was laughing at me, I think." I was struggling to remember.

"Get dressed now! We'll talk about Alda later," Katie ordered. "I'll walk with you up to the entrance to Damper. I'll wait for you, I promise. Just remember everything Craney says. And don't argue."

"What? And take her garbage in silence?"

"You've just got to get her to spell it out, to do something we can nab her on."

My mind wandered. Just how much would I have to let Craney do to me?

I got dressed in my most serious clothes, all navy and white. It was hard to concentrate. Everything distracted me from the task at hand: to walk the gangplank to my perdition. I even looked for the peephole and thought for a second this was all a dream I had imagined.

"Katie, it's gone," I said, pointing to the approximate spot where I believed the peephole had been.

"What?"

"The hole, the peephole. Holy smokes!"

"Oh my God," Katie shrieked. "It couldn't have just disappeared."

I jumped on a chair and ran my finger over the flat surface of the wall. When could it have been repaired? I tried to punch a hole with my finger. Nothing, just a faint whiff of cold, fresh off-white paint.

"How soon could your father get here?" I snapped, jumping down from the chair. "Now I'm really awake. What if I didn't go to Craney's?"

"You've got to go," Katie said. "We'll call him right after you talk to her."

We walked the three blocks to Damper as if they were thirty. The wind blew against us; my feet felt leaden and frozen. I would never get to Craney's office it seemed, and that was fine with me.

What would she say? I could stand the words. I expected them. What would she do? Hit me? Call my parents? Oh my God. I forgot about that part of it.

Katie tried to get me to talk. She reminisced about Maine earlier this summer and swore her father would fix everything.

"You sound like Alda," I said.

"Huh? Thanks."

"I think Alda was hinting her father would make Craney and Dorotea disappear."

"C'mon, Pina. You were so out of it last night."

"That's just it. I can't be sure of anything."

"Just listen up now. Nod, apologize, whatever you have to do to get the heck out of Craney's office as quickly as you can. We'll get my father involved."

"And my folks?" I was imagining my mother's face, her gray-blue eyes swimming, her cheeks flushed. She would hold her heart and hyperventilate. My father would be ultra-polite and apologetic to Craney, but pulled back with a stiff face.

"We're almost here. Your folks love you. And my father will talk to them. They like him. But listen. I love you. I'm right here. I'm going to stay right here and wait for you."

Katie had stopped and pulled me behind the huge yellow pine. She placed her hands on my shoulders, looked into my eyes, and said, "I want you to carry my love with you." She reached into her pocket and put something into mine. "You can hold onto it."

I reached deep into my pocket as she pushed me out from under the tree in the direction of Damper's entrance. I turned the object over and over, a small velveteen heart. I would carry Katie's heart with me.

Chapter Thirty-nine

The Office of the Head Mistress Mary Margaret Craney

I was there. At the door, I read the inscription on the brass sign, Office of Head Mistress Mary Margaret Craney, as if it were an oracle. I wouldn't have any answers until I knew the questions. And I certainly couldn't ask my questions, like why me? Or what did she want with me? And most crucial, did she really mean to seduce me?

I knocked. My stomach knotted, my throat closed. I wondered if I should have gone one last time to the bathroom. No answer.

I knocked again, hoping this would all go away. I heard voices, but there was only one sharp voice, Craney's, instructing me to enter. Craney was alone in the room.

She sat behind her massive desk, just like the last time I was there. I walked ever so slowly the length of the interminable Persian runner just like the last time. I stopped three feet from her desk and shuddered just like the last time.

"Approach, Miss Mazzini," she said.

I advanced one more foot.

"Where is Dorotea?" she boomed.

I started to shake. "I don't know, uh, Miss Craney."

What the heck? Aw, man! Katie said she hadn't

seen her. Alda…the invitation to Dorotea's aunt's. No. Alda, what the hell did she do? Could her father…? Oh man, I've got to concentrate on Craney. Just drain myself of all my thoughts.

She was standing now and sliding open her middle drawer. She extracted an envelope, which she waved at me. "Where?"

I dug my nails into my skin to give me courage. "I really don't know, Head Mistress."

"Do you know what this is?" She poked her head forward, thrusting the envelope a foot away from my face.

"No, Head Mistress." I tried to squint to see if there was anything written on it—a name, an address, something. I tilted my head as if to think. I couldn't even get a glimpse from that angle.

"It's an envelope, yes? Containing a message, yes?" She prompted.

"Yes, Miss Craney."

"Do you have any ideas about the message?" Her lips had become chisel-like. I thought of monster voles.

"No, Miss Craney."

"Well, I'll tell you, Miss Mazzini."

By now, Craney had picked up an ivory letter-opener with the head of a shrew carved into it. Pewter accented the carved ivory head. The pewter eyes reflected the yellowish light in the room.

I fingered the heart in my pocket. The nappe of the velvet calmed me as I anticipated the slice of the letter opener. Craney continued to emphasize her words with the point and alternately the head of the letter opener.

"Miss Cabanus' aunt just called to inform me that Dorotea seems to have gone missing. I have reason to believe you might be involved. You were, shall we say, not friends."

"No. I mean yes. We had become friends. We were going to room together, as you know. She just invited me to tea four days ago."

"You did not say you were not involved." Craney jabbed the point into her blotter.

"I uh, don't know anything about her uh, disappearance. I thought she was going to her aunt's," I stammered, not knowing whether to admit that.

"Well, that may be so or it may not. This letter." Miss Craney made an abrupt pause to get water. She looked at me over the rim of her half-glasses as she slowly extended her hand to grasp the Waterford tumbler.

She continued while tapping the letter. "This letter. I found this letter, which Dorotea had dated and deposited in my box apparently the day she left. It's marked 'Ask Pina, in case of emergency.' We know what's inside, don't we, Miss Mazzini?"

I was wet under my arms, and my underpants stuck to me. I attempted to shift my weight; I was still standing. Craney had reseated herself and pulled her chair in close to the desk.

"Honestly, Miss Craney, I don't."

"I might have just an inkling," she said, flipping the envelope over and over.

I tried to see the words "ask Pina," but I couldn't make out anything. Was Craney bluffing?

"Aren't you curious? The slightest bit?" she asked.

Had she really read the letter and what did it say? She was trying to trick me into giving her info that wasn't even in the letter: that I was a, uh, lesbian. God. I had to freeze my face and my thoughts.

I forced myself to say, "With all due respect, Miss Craney, I'm concerned. I had grown quite fond of Dorotea and had looked forward to rooming with her to improve my French and German. How can I help?"

The heart was almost throbbing in my pocket. I peeked at my hand, which I slid out flat by my side. My fingertips were blood red from the dyed velveteen.

"Clever girl. I knew I could count on you. Let me see how. Hmm."

Miss Craney had sat back in her chair and removed her glasses. Stroking her chin, she smiled. She opened her eyes wide and grinned at me.

"Yes," she said. "You will help."

As her smile broadened, her tone became liquid gold and honey. All authoritarian notes disappeared. She stood, came around the desk, and slithered behind me. She placed her hand on my neck and said, "Yes. You will help."

A shiver ran down my back. I didn't dare slump since I could feel the heat radiating from Craney's body, her breath on my neck. Her posture mirrored mine, her chest a mere inch or two away from my back. I tried to think. My body convulsed, trembling.

"There, there," she said, grasping my shoulder. "I know it's a thrilling thought to help find a misplaced person. And we would be working ever so closely." She slid her fingers down my cheek.

Leading me by the waist with her bony hand, she scrunched me down in a chair next to hers. She sat down again, tapped the envelope two times against her desk, and said, "We'll put this envelope away for now as long as we're putting our heads together, no?"

I had no other choice for the moment. "Yes. I uh…will do what I can." I desperately needed to go to the bathroom.

"You'll do more than that. I will show you the way. You're such a clever follower. Are we clear, Pina dear?"

"I really need to use the restroom." I needed to pee, but I also had to think. How was I going to get Craney to spell out what she wanted? Could I play dumb a little longer?

"Are we clear, Pina?"

"I'm not sure what you mean, exactly. Can we finish this after...?" I realized I didn't know where the bathroom was.

I looked quickly all along the draped walls but couldn't locate any door. Before I knew it, Craney had grasped my wrist and was escorting me. She pulled me behind velveteen drapes. I felt them slither along my face and sides. There was a paneled door. Craney flung it open and commanded, "Go!"

I have never peed within earshot of someone about to punish—no, not punish me, torture me. I had to pee so badly I couldn't hold it in any longer. After a torrential downpour, I felt Craney could see every inch of me, inside and out. It seemed as if she had taken possession of me.

I delayed as long as I could. My body felt so taut, a solid block of wood. I wished I could disconnect my nerves from whatever sensate experience awaited me on the other side of the door.

As I crept out, Craney took hold of my arm to usher me into an adjoining room. I was midway between fainting and going someplace far, far away in my head. My powers of observation were shutting down so that the only thing I registered was a monstrous ebony canopy bed with a polar bear skin dead center.

I believe I fainted. I came to my senses, seated in an uncomfortable wingback chair. I smelled vomit, my vomit, and saw Craney flicking particles off her bony hand. She towered over me, speaking.

"No need to service me when you're not well."

"Thank you," I mumbled. "I have a history of fainting. Anemia, they say."

"Don't thank me for this reprieve."

Oh lord, I thought. That's that word again.

Craney continued, "We have a working contract. You do understand?"

I needed to get out of there immediately. I also needed her to spell out her threat.

"I don't really understand." I winced.

By now, Craney was bending over, her eyes almost level with mine.

"You have until Mothers' Weekend to decide just how much service you could be to me. Think about it. I would hate to have the authorities blame you for Dorotea's disappearance. Why, I would have to divulge the contents of this letter, my dear—rambling and damning accusations. Though, maybe just the sloppy sentimentality of the jealous, young thing Dorotea was."

Craney paused and stood up. She patted my head and moved behind my chair. I didn't dare breathe. I believed Craney had just commuted my sentence.

"Ahem," Craney began to whisper in my ear. "I would have to have a long chat with your mother, uh, Giuseppina Mazzini." She spoke my mother's name as if the vowels scorched her tongue.

"Yes. Your mother would become privy to all I have learned about you. I am sure she would be most interested and determined to get you the best help available. On the other hand, how proud she would be to know you were to be my right-hand girl. Don't you think, dear Pina?"

I managed to say, "Yes."

"As I was saying." Craney was beginning to tie up her speech. "You have a week. I have had my eye on you. It's not often one disappoints me. You'll learn to appreciate, I'm sure. Now run along, and do be careful with yourself."

Craney exited, disappearing in some recess without looking at me again. I fumbled my way through the drapes and back through her office. The rug seemed to run on forever, but finally I pulled open the door and fell out onto the threshold.

The air was sweet. I stayed crouched on the floor several minutes before I ran the fifty feet to the exit doors. The yellow pine hiding Katie opened its branches, clasping me in its safe embrace. I toppled into Katie's arms and wept.

Chapter Forty

The Debriefing

Katie's arms seemed like the only safe place left in the world. They transported me back to my security blankets from the past.

All was good now; warm and soft, Katie's scent of lilies and lavender slowly enveloped me in multi-layered folds of tranquility. Katie let me cry for what seemed like forever, cooing occasionally that she was right there and would take care of me.

As I started to slow my weeping, Katie turned my head with great care and tenderness.

"Pin, look at me. We can't stay here."

She peeked out through the branches, adding, "Too many Albert people. We've got to get to town."

"I don't care. I can't move," I said.

"Yes, you can. You have to." Katie grabbed me by the waist, saying, "The coast is clear. Come."

We made it to the fence where I paused.

"C'mon," Katie said. "Eunice's is the only place they won't report us for cutting and won't eavesdrop on our conversation."

I grunted, "Okay" as we wove our way through the fence and onto town lanes.

I managed to squeeze myself into the farthest corner of the last booth in the back room of the restaurant. Katie held my hand hidden by the display of salt, pepper, ketchup, and menus. We could always pretend to be picking out songs and pushing the greasy buttons on the miniature jukebox behind the menus.

"Slowly," Katie urged.

"I don't know where to begin. I still feel like I'm in shock. My body's one mass of crawling bugs." I shuddered as I sank back into the tufted, faded plastic cushion.

"Did she…I mean…did she touch you?"

"Yeah. But no. It was creepy, and she touched my neck, but…God, I wanted to vomit, and I actually did—even a few drops on her ugly hand. Probably the only thing that stopped her from doing more."

"Pin!" Katie lowered her voice. "Did she touch you *in that way*?"

"No, but I know she wants to. She hovered behind me, almost pressing on my back. I felt her breath on my neck."

"Oh God."

By the look on her face, Katie was probably figuring out what we could tell her dad.

"Katie!" I squeezed her hand. "Just listen. I need you just to listen now. It almost felt worse than if she had molested me. Her words were like snakes slithering over me in every direction. Her looks undressed me. She even made me pee less than a foot away from her."

"What? Jesus! I'm sorry. I want to touch you, but you've been saying it's like your skin is crawling."

"Yeah, it is. But your voice and your eyes…" I wanted to reach across the table to Katie with my other hand, but…I sighed. "She didn't molest me. Yet. She gave me until Mothers' Weekend to think it over."

"Did she really say that?"

I shook my head. "Katie, she was really slippery.

  Dolores Maggiore

She didn't spell anything out except to say I would have to cater to her and service her."

"Puuke! And if you don't?"

"She's going to tell my mother."

"Huh?" said Katie. "Tell her what exactly? I'm really confused."

"Aw shoot, Katie. About me, about us, and stupid Dorotea has disappeared!"

"You're not making sense. I thought Alda sent her a phony invitation to her aunt's."

"That's just it. Phony. But you're missing the point, Katie," I said, trying to sort out the important points about how scared I was about us.

Katie interrupted. "Did she go to her aunt's?" She scrunched up her face as The Great Pretender came on the jukebox.

I lowered the volume and whispered, "Alda." I had allowed myself to get caught up in that part of the story.

"I don't get it." Katie was frowning, especially at the line in the song "You seem to be what you're not." She snapped off the sound and wiped her fingers on her sleeve.

I tried to continue the story in proper order. "Well, I don't know where Dorotea is. It's weird because her aunt phoned her in missing, according to Craney."

"So, Craney is lying, or Alda, or both!"

"Who knows," I said. "I think Alda knows something. But I also think Dorotea suspected that someone phonied up the invitation."

"Nah. She was so excited to go to her rich aunt's. Don't you remember?"

"Hold on, Katie. Let me put my thoughts together.

Craney has a letter supposedly from Dorotea. She claimed the envelope reads 'Ask Pina, in case of emergency.' She hinted at its contents but wanted me to tell her what I imagined it said, so I would spill the beans on myself!"

"Sly witch!"

"Craney? Bitch is more like it," I said. "I couldn't see anything written on the envelope. She threatened that if I didn't comply with her wishes, she would tell the cops that I had something to do with Dorotea's disappearance and then reveal the contents of the letter."

"You think it's a bluff?'

"Maybe, but…but…I mean what if Dorotea didn't go away? What if she made the peephole?" I felt my chest tighten and beads of sweat gather on my forehead. The more possibilities I imagined, the more anxious I felt.

I must have turned white because Katie leaned across the table to shake me, saying, "You need to eat something. Let's stop for a minute."

I welcomed the pause. The chili, which appeared on our table almost immediately after we ordered, tasted so comforting. The soft, understanding smile of our favorite waitress, Blanche, exuded compassion.

I took a deep breath. I needed to tell Katie the most important stuff. I managed a smile in Blanche's direction. She wiped her hands on her apron and patted our shoulders as she backed away, leaving us to continue our story along with our soupy chili.

"Craney threatened to tell my mother about me. That was her final blow: the authorities and my mother. Or, if I comply, she would rave about me to my mother."

"Tell your mother what?"

"C'mon, Katie. This is the real killer…about us. Craney's words were, 'All that I have learned about you.'"

There were a few moments of silence. Dishes banged in the background. Guffaws came from the dartboard area up front. I flipped through some of the real old songs and the country songs on the jukebox. I could be a local yokel here, didn't have to be Ivy League. I could just hang out here in Andover.

Katie continued to try to make better sense of my story. "Craney said you would have to cater to her."

"It was all sexual, and when I said I didn't understand, she said she knew I did. This whole thing makes me sick."

Katie made several attempts to speak, scrunching up her face each time worse than the time before. "Pin…what about the peeing?"

"She stood right outside the door while I peed. Please don't make me explain more." My head was almost on the table.

"Sorry. I'm just trying to figure out if she'd really do it. Seduce you, I mean."

"You've gotta be kidding. Of course she would." I had lifted my head and shot a hurt and befuddled look at Katie. "Don't you get it?"

"Yeah, yeah. Sorry. It's just too much. And your mom? How crazy would she get?"

I closed my eyes and covered them with my hand. I started to choke on the words. "I think, I really do, she'd have a heart attack. I couldn't live with that. And I'd be dead meat. Don't know where they'd send me…a hospital…shock treatment."

"Well, you couldn't live with Craney pawing all

over you, could you?"

"I just want to die," I whispered.

Katie turned to see if anybody was around. The room was empty: too late for breakfast, too early for lunch. She reached for both of my hands.

"Sweetie," she said. "Let's call my father."

"Yeah. But wait. The other thing…"

"More?" Katie shrieked.

"Alda. Alda asked me if I wanted her father to take care of Dorotea. Do you remember?"

"You mean the time you were joking about killing…was it Dorotea or Craney?"

"Yikes! I remember saying something like, 'Yeah, if your dad only could…'"

"C'mon, Pina. You don't think Alda took you seriously? Then why hasn't her father taken care of Craney? Oops. I'm joking."

"Quit it. I know it sounds crazy, but Alda was always saying her father would take care of everyone. And the scar on her neck, and, and…the witness protection program…"

"You don't know that for sure. Her father wouldn't really…"

"What about Dorotea's dreams and the talk of guns and bad men?" I was working up a good sweat again. "I've got to talk to Alda."

"And say what? 'Oh, by the way, did your dad knock off Dorotea?' But come to think of it, Dorotea was real shaky and sad the last few days. Do you think…?"

"What? I'm tired of thinking."

"You know, she was giving stuff away. You know what the signs are."

"Suicide? Aw, damn! Craney did say 'in case of

emergency.' Nah, Katie, Dorotea was really charged up about her aunt's."

Katie gasped. "Maybe she had everything figured out, how to stop being Dorotea, the girl with no friends, no class, no courage. Maybe she found a way to get rid of that girl."

"Maybe I should just run away." I began to fantasize about Maine, hiding out in one of the dilapidated cabins of the old boys' camp. Then I remembered: winter, no stoves, the lake frozen, no Katie...

"Where'd you go just now? Look at me," Katie said. "You can't just run away. C'mon, let's do what we should have done from the start: ask my father and Joe for help."

"I won't ask him for anything else." There it was again, my stupid pride. Katie was always telling me I was afraid I'd look weak if I accepted help. Hah! And now?

"Are you crazy? After all you went through to help clear his name in that murder investigation in Maine last summer?" Katie's blue eyes flashed red.

"Yeah. I guess. What are you going to say?" I mumbled.

"Well, Craney has been on your case from the start. But then, there's that book where she had your two names embossed."

"Big deal."

"The academic gown in your bed and the book about lesbians, and the peephole and the fire escape."

"Can't prove it."

"And finally, she's holding you hostage, claiming you're responsible for Dorotea's disappearance and threatening to tell your mother about us if you don't comply with her wishes."

"And her wishes? They could simply be 'Play by the rules.'"

"Well, I'm going to say all that to my father and remind him of the rumor about Craney and the young instructor she seduced and then fired."

"And?"

"Dammit, Pina, I'm trying to help. We've got to do something. Besides, maybe Joe, as a journalist, could track Dorotea down."

"Maybe. And then Dorotea, in person, in the flesh, could accuse me of being a lesbian. Dead ends, all dead ends."

"C'mon. We're going." Katie had strong-armed me and was leading my semi-limp body through the back and front rooms and out the door.

The cold air was like a snort of smelling salts. I was alert. Everything was clear now. I had to act. I wanted Katie, and I wanted my parents to be okay. The rest was, well, just the rest.

Chapter Forty-one

Doc and Joe

Katie literally dragged me the three icy blocks to the phone booth. We welcomed the shelter from the wind and the opportunity to stay close to each other without looking conspicuous.

Katie asked me if I wanted to speak to her dad. I was willing to answer questions via Katie, but I was sick of talking.

Up until then, Katie had acted like a whole cheering squad contained in one diminutive body. Although she was only six inches taller than I was, she usually appeared much more slender. At times, it seemed a breeze could run away with her delicate body. Today, she had been my rock.

Her father's private number was ringing. His deep, mellow voice said a resonant "Hello." Katie managed to form the word, "Daddy" before she started to falter. I could hear her father shouting, "Katie, Katie, are you all right?"

I yelled, "We're okay," and wrapped my arms around Katie's shoulders.

"Pina, what's wrong?" Of course he recognized my voice.

I pinched Katie and shook my head. "You've got to do the talking."

Katie took the last few sighs before starting the

saga. "We're okay, Dad, but we do need your help."

"It's Headmistress Craney."

"No. Absolutely not. We've been discreet."

"No, Katie, don't." I whispered.

"Well. Sort of. Two times, but no one was there. It was safe. We think."

Oh, God, she did.

"It's Pina. Miss Craney has been on her case from the beginning—said she was watching her like a hawk or something."

I was embarrassed, but Katie was going to bat for me. It felt different coming from her mouth. I missed a few exchanges but really tuned in when I heard Katie say, "Daddy, I think she's trying to molest Pina. She's like a real lech."

Katie stomped her foot.

"No, really, Dad. She's done things."

Her dad's "What?" was so loud I could tell what he was thinking.

Katie continued, "She's hidden stuff in Pina's bed and books about lesbians in her room, but we can't prove anything. Dad, there's a lot more—Oh, did Joe ever research that rumor?"

"Yeah, the one about the young instructor."

Katie held the receiver away from her ear and just stared at it.

"Dad. No, listen. I'm not exaggerating." Katie had started to cry. She tried to get me to take the phone, but I refused.

"I'm scared, Dad. She's threatening Pina and Pina, uh…Pina's talking about running away. Daddy, she can't."

I attempted to mouth the words "I won't; I promise." I hadn't realized how upset Katie was.

"I can't go on here if Miss Craney kicks her out. And I can't bear to see her hurt Pina. She's threatened to tell Pina's mother."

"That she's uh…well, you know. Well, with me—like you and Joe. Dangit, Dad, a lesbian!"

"Can she do that? But Pina just cares about her mother. She thinks her mom will have a heart attack. You know her mom, Dad. She's so emotional."

I rolled my eyes at Katie and pointed to my watch.

"Is it true they do shock treatment on lesbians?" Katie continued to grill her father.

I fired an imaginary gun at my temple.

"No. That can't happen. I'll run away with her. No. She'll be…she'll be ruined, dad."

By now, Katie was staring at me and trying to get me to hold the phone, while attempting to smooth my hair at the same time. I was tearing up. The booth was dripping too with our breath and condensation and fogged on the other side. I kissed Katie on the forehead.

Katie finally answered her dad. "No. I promise we won't do anything stupid. Miss Craney may be backing off right now. She actually gave Pina a week to decide."

"What? *Decide what, dammit*?" Doc's voice came through loud and clear.

Katie was doing as good a job as I had putting things in sequential order.

I finally grabbed the phone.

"Hello, Doc," I said.

"What in the name of the good lord is going on?"

"Okay, Doc. I have until Mothers' Weekend to decide to give in to her. She's put her friggin, excuse me, hands all over my neck and my waist, and she's looked at me like I'm naked. There, Doc, that's what's going on."

"Look, honey, I know you tell it like it is, you always have, but I need you to slow down. Tell me what she's done," said Doc.

He was calm and organized, but his deep baritone always made me feel his warmth and caring.

"That's just it. She's only put her hand on my neck and around my waist. But...but..."

"Pina, that's not right."

"I uh...know, but...I can't pull away from her. She raises her voice, stares in my eyes, and says stuff like 'You understand what I want.'"

Doc's moment of silence told me he had no immediate answers. I think he knew that too based on the way he mumbled, "You don't have to take it."

"Right. But...but she's going to tell my mother, who will die of shame, if not of her heart condition. And I'll die of a lobotomy."

"Stop! I am sorry, I am truly sorry, Pina. We'll find an answer."

"Oh. Katie didn't tell you. Her horrible roommate, Dorotea, has disappeared and Craney is threatening to tell the authorities I had something to do with it—which I didn't."

By now, my cheeks were burning hot. Katie grabbed the phone. She was under control now and told me to go take a walk in the fresh air.

I squeezed open the door and the moisture in my nose stung. The temperature must have dropped. I ran a few blocks to stay warm and to clear my head.

I came back to the booth in time to hear Katie telling Joe that Dorotea's aunt lived in Watertown, Massachusetts, meaning that Dorotea would have changed buses in Boston. Joe could check with the bus authority.

I motioned to Katie that I wanted to speak to Joe.

"Hi Joe, I miss you," I said.

"You too, ciccia. My dad sends his best."

"Oh, is he visiting from Maine?"

"He was, but now we just spoke with him on the phone."

"Good. I've been thinking about him too. Uh… Joe…I uh…"

"Say it, Pina. It's okay."

"Joe," I started, not sure of how to ask this. "Do you think your dad knows somebody named Baciadalupo?"

"Just anybody, Pina? C'mon, toots, out with it. Remember you're talking to Joe, Fifi Gallo's son."

"Yeah, but your dad's not like that, anymore. Well, anyway, I wonder if this Baciadalupo is a tuff guy. I mean a real bad tuff guy."

"Hm. Any more info?"

"Uh…maybe. Maybe they've been relocated."

"Oh. So you're asking me out of curiosity or asking me to put on my journalist's hat or…"

"Would your dad get in trouble with the cops?"

"Can you tell me why you want to know?"

"He's my roommate Alda's father, and he might have had something to do with Dorotea's disappearance. I think she may have seen something she shouldn't have when she visited the Baciadalupo home."

"Listen." Joe's tone was serious but warm. "You girls have to relax. We'll figure something out."

"Joe, I don't want your dad, Fifi—"

"Not to worry. Boy Scout's Honor."

I giggled. I couldn't picture small, handsome Joe as an Eagle Scout.

Doc got back on and yelled for both of us not to do anything crazy. He promised to get back to us really soon, maybe tonight.

First Katie, then I, we begged him not to contact Craney.

Katie grabbed the phone. "Dad, she's really creepy. She's not like the professional woman you had described to us. Please, promise."

Judging from Katie's repeating, "Promise," I'm not sure he promised. The click of the phone sounded too dry, too final.

Katie became serious. "We've got to be really good at being super cool. Model students. Squeaky clean. My father will come through."

Her pace was fast, business-like. As for me, I knew my business now was with Alda, at least for the moment. I had to find out what she had done.

Chapter Forty-two

Alda's Lamp: Just Rub it the Right way

Katie and I worked our way back to campus, walking at a snail's pace to avoid the ice and to delay our arrival.

We had just cut some classes, and Katie wanted an excuse for missing science. Our instructor, Dr. Hermione Eisenberg, found Katie gifted in the sciences and willingly accepted her claim of having to nurse a sick student. Right now, I was the sick student. Usually, I supplied Dr. Eisenberg with the correct chemical formula for her daily dose of humor; she got a kick out of me. Katie and I received no demerits for missing the double lab.

Cleared that hurdle. Then I was solo. On my way to find Alda in our room, I crossed paths with Mademoiselle. I immediately broke into my best French. I was desolée, crest-fallen, I said, to postpone my French immersion program with Dorotea. She was so taken by my effusiveness, that she didn't ask why I had cut class earlier that morning. I supplied the answer just the same; I had allegedly been searching for Dorotea. I actually beat my breast and intoned the French equivalent of *mea culpa, "ma faute, ma faute, ma très grande faute."*

After that encounter, it was clear sailing to my room. I couldn't wait to rip Alda's head off. How dare she hurt Dorotea?

Whoa! I had to breathe. Once again, I had no proof. But again, I had no control. I had voiced a disgruntled wish, not a real desire for Dorotea to disappear. I didn't mean it. Well, I did, but not like that.

Whatever had happened, whatever evil genie had granted this half-wish, I wanted to take it back. I didn't want to hurt anyone. Hmm. And here I wanted to decapitate Alda.

Damn. That thing that Katie said to me—that I didn't like accepting help. Was it really that it made me look weak? Maybe it was just this feeling of being out of control. If Alda had done something, she took all control out of my hands. I didn't have a clue what she had done to Dorotea.

Well, somebody did something, and that meant they did it to me too. Ha! And I was going to pay for it either way. Do it with Craney—I think I'd rather die. Kill my mother? And then, electrocute my brain in some hospital for the sexually ill.

By now, I had covered the length of the dorm hallway and I had my hand on the doorknob. How was I going to get Alda to confess, to tell the truth? Novel idea.

With that thought, the door opened. Alda reached out her arms and pulled me in, saying, "I'm so sorry, Pina. God, what are you going to do?"

"What the heck? What are you sorry about?"

What did she know, and how the hell did she know it?

"I, uh, I hid outside Craney's office. I overheard," Alda said.

"And how did you know I had a meeting with

her?" I shot back.

"Man. You're sounding paranoid!"

"Cool it. I'm not joking."

"I can see that. I was over at Damper Hall, and I saw you outside Craney's door. Will that answer do?"

"Yeah, maybe," I grunted.

"What's up? You're giving me the third degree."

"What's up, Alda? What's up? I'll tell you. What the hell did you do with Dorotea?"

"What?"

Alda walked to her desk on the other side of the room. She turned her back to me and started to talk two different times. She only managed to chew on her lip and swallow hard. I actually saw a tear that she smudged away.

"Yeah," I repeated. "Where's Dorotea?"

"I have no idea. Besides, what do you mean, 'What did I do with her?'"

"Bull, Alda. You're full of bull. You bragged about how your father could take care of everything for everybody. So, you're such a good friend, you wind up screwing things royally for me. Now I have to have sex with Craney or have her blow my cover to my folks and ruin my near and distant future! Tell me, which death should I pick? Go on!"

"Hold on. I don't know what you're accusing me of."

"Your father?"

Alda contorted every feature of her face as she asked, "What about him?"

I pushed on. "You basically told me he could make Dorotea or Craney disappear."

"Well, to tell the truth, he could."

"Did you stop and think I didn't want that?"

"Ha! You're so worried now. What about when you said you wanted to kill Dorotea?"

"For crap's sake, Alda, I didn't mean that."

"Oh, I can hear you saying, 'Ah, Alda, if only your father could…'"

"So," I braced myself for the plain truth, "you really had your father do something?"

Alda just shook her head. "Pin, you really are a jackass. You'd rather believe I'm just a mafiosa brat."

"Well, you just confessed you granted my wish."

Alda turned on me the worst sneer I'd ever seen. "I did nothing of the sort. You're just going to believe whatever you want. How could you?"

I stopped on a dime. I sat without ceremony and listened, really listened to her tone. It sounded like she was truly hurt. I was going to be excommunicated and electrocuted, but she was hurt.

A softened note brought me out of my head. Alda was facing me, holding out her hands open-palmed. Her look was one of disbelief, but she was saying, "I guess, I guess…I could understand how you might believe it was true. I mean with all my bragging…but you know I do talk bull."

Alda reached for my hand as she approached my bedside where I had dropped, exhausted.

"And now? Are you feeding me baloney now?" I asked.

"Why would I? I don't want to lose your friendship," she said.

"Alda, I'm done for. You'd have nothing to lose, nothing to gain. Sorry, I don't believe you. And because I'm going to be screwed both figuratively and literally, I'm not inclined to care."

"Pin, Pin, listen. I swear. I did nothing. But you're

right; my father could have done something. He didn't. But…Craney…"

I screwed up my face and snarled, "What? Now your father will fix Craney?"

"We could work it out, Pina. I mean my father could pull his support and money."

"Oh, and Craney would disappear?"

"Pina, what do you want me to do? You're accusing me of getting you into this, and you won't let me get you out of it."

"Man, Alda. Listen to you. And did you arrange for the peephole? Dang! Let me see; is it still there? Son of a gun! Right, it's been patched. Seriously, did you set things up so I'd be scared out of my gourd and willing to do anything to have you help?"

"Pina! You're crazy. You think I'd do that?"

Alda went over to her desk and started slamming books on the floor. She cursed in Italian. I heard *minchia and cazzo.* She opened the top drawer of her desk, letting the smell of lavender escape from the scented stationery inside. She took out her address book with her father's personal numbers.

She slammed the drawer, grabbed her stadium jacket, and said, "I need a break from this, from you. I've got to talk to my father."

I had this strange feeling I'd gone too far. Lordy, lordy. Here I stood to be punished beyond belief, and I was afraid I'd said too much. What was I imagining now? Her father was going to do me in?

"Alda," I mumbled. "I don't want to believe this. I uh…"

"Don't worry," she said cold like the Arctic, cold like death. "I'll come back, or maybe I'll just run away."

"No…I uh…" I didn't know what I wanted to

say. I really did like Alda, but…

"*Non ti preoccupare!* Don't worry, *cara,* dear." She seemed to spit out the "dear."

"We've got to talk," I said.

"We just did."

"But if you did, I mean, if you know…"

"Yeah, yeah," she said.

"Alda, I don't want your help, not like this, not the mob. I'd rather die," I screamed.

"You've made that clear. And maybe you will and ha! Maybe the mob will snatch me away." She turned and back over her shoulder, she threw me the Italian sign for *ciao,* and stepped out into the darkened hallway.

Chapter Forty-three

Katie's Comfort

After Alda left our room, I stretched out on my bed and stared at the ceiling. When no answers appeared there, I rubbed my eyes until I saw twinkling stars against the white orange peel dome of the ceiling. Still, they were no help.

Alda was definitely a live wire. I didn't know what spark or shock to expect. No answers, no control.

I had to face it. I was done for. I should pack. My mother would be there in three days. Just three days to live. This wasn't living, though. Wouldn't even be able to enjoy a last meal. How did folks about to be electrocuted do it?

I started to visualize an electric chair and a gas chamber. I couldn't decide on a preference. Maybe if they put a mask over my mother's face instead of mine. How could I face my mother?

I wasn't seeing anything too clearly. Some hours passed, and it was close to dusk. I squinted in the direction of the door and made out a slow blur. Katie tiptoed in.

I had no sooner whispered, "I'm here," when I felt her hand slip into mine. She sat on the edge of the bed and buried her face in my hair.

I heard her muffled, "What are we going to do?" but we continued to just rock back and forth in silence.

Finally, she helped prop me up.

"Listen," she said. "My dad called."

"Oh?" My voice ached with desperation.

"Well, no, nothing great, but it's calmed me down." Katie's voice trailed off.

"Your father will be able to fix it for you." I sighed.

"No, Pin. I've decided if you go, I'll leave Albert. I can't stay."

"Yeah. Thanks. But your father won't have you lobotomized or excommunicated or worse."

"Right. He did say he would come up and talk to Craney and your mom, but he can't make it until Monday."

Katie tried to make me look at her, brushing the hair away from my eyes.

I let myself look into her eyes. I managed a weak smile. "That's great, Kat, but I'll be dead by Sunday."

"Don't say that. I'll tell your mother it was my fault. I'll tell her Craney's making up stories. Yeah, that's it. It's just a rumor started by Dorotea."

"And the peephole," I said. "Who knows if there are pictures?" I turned away from Katie.

"We'll do something. My father will figure something out. He will," Katie pleaded.

"Sorry, optimism just hurts my stomach right now. Besides, I have to tell you about Alda." I sighed. "Jeez. There's really nothing to tell except we blew up at each other. She swore she didn't do anything to Dorotea."

"Where is she?"

"Said she needed to get away from me. Think she was going to phone her father."

"What for?"

I gagged. "Probably to tell him to knock off Craney."

"You kidding? C'mon, Pina, it's too late for that."

"Joking or knocking off Craney?"

"Stop! What did she say?"

"Doesn't matter, really. Like I should believe that she didn't have her father do something. Even now she says her father could fix it with Craney, pull money or something."

"Hmph. But where is she now? It's late."

"Don't know. I wouldn't care if I never saw her again."

A silence settled over us, broken only by the rumblings of my stomach. Maybe I was wrong about last suppers, but I really couldn't imagine going to the cafeteria and facing a hundred collegiate girls yakking about dates and Salisbury steak.

I started to grumble. I grabbed Katie's hand.

"What do I tell my mother? 'Hey Mom, guess what? I'm a fag, a ho-mo-sex-ual, a lez be-en?' God, she'll walk out on me. She'll smack me." I wailed, "The worst will come later."

Katie hugged me hard, so hard I had no more breath, no more energy. She brushed her lips across my forehead and gently lowered my face to the pillow.

She said with some authority that I needed to eat. She was going to scout around and bring back food. First, she made me promise I wouldn't do anything crazy. I didn't have the energy and besides, my mother and Craney would do a good enough job in a few days.

I must have fallen asleep. I hadn't dreamed of gowns, ghouls, or Craney. In my dream, instead, there was a sumptuous meal that my mother and Katie were feeding me. I knew that was a dream since I had these ferocious hunger pangs and growls coming from my gut.

Almost on command, Katie entered, balancing a cafeteria tray in one hand, a Coke under one arm, a box of chocolate chip cookies and a bag of Wise potato chips in her other hand. She had managed to waltz out of the refectory with her untouched hamburger, as well as a second serving.

We ate in silence and rounded off the meal with an ice cream cup from the machine in the basement. A last meal it wasn't, and certainly not sumptuous. It didn't matter.

Katie had other news to feed me. She had caught a glimpse of the sign-out book. Alda had signed out early with the explanation "needed at home." Her anticipated return remained blank.

"She's scared," Katie said.

"Of me? Ha!" I shot back.

"You think she's trying to get her father to do something?" Katie said.

"You mean if he hasn't already. Remember, Dorotea is missing," I said.

"Hmm. Didn't you say Alda finally told you Dorotea had seen something she shouldn't have?"

"I don't know. That's not going to help now. But you said you had two pieces of news."

"Right. My father…He called again. He told me that Joe has been working on a newspaper article about that former Albert instructor. You know, the one Craney hit on and then fired. And hey, you'll love this, Joe's father, Fifi, is helping too. Craney may have pulled a lot of similar stunts. It's downright serious, he said, if Craney had her blackballed. That's what they're trying to find out—legally."

"Legally?" I picked my ears up at that. "And Fifi, legally, really?"

"Yeah. Joe told my father some judge owes Fifi a favor." Katie smiled, but it seemed pretty tentative. "It might take time," she added. "More time than you have."

"Face it, Katie. It's over."

Katie came and stood in front of me. "Look at me." She lifted my chin and kissed my eyes. She held my head to her chest. "I love you. Whatever happens, I will find you. I promise."

I managed to pull away enough to mumble, "In the hospital?"

"My father will help. I know he will."

"Your father will convince my parents that I'm normal—like your father who wears pink shirts and darn near hugs Joe in public, like he's normal?"

I pushed Katie away just far enough to pull her back immediately to apologize and tell her, "I love you so much. I do, but I can't see a way out. I don't think anybody, even your dad, could convince my parents that being a homo is okay."

"But your parents like my dad."

"Yeah, maybe. As long as they don't have to hear the word 'homo'."

Katie slumped onto the bed at my side. I leaned over and hugged her. "Let's just hold each other," I said.

That was the last thing I remember. We awoke several hours later. We started to panic that Mademoiselle had come in for room check. But at that point, it felt like the situation couldn't get any worse, and we closed our eyes to everything but the moment.

Chapter Forty-four

Katie's Comfort Continued

Katie and I slept, arms and legs entwined. The few times my eyes opened during the night, I closed them instinctively as if to lock in all the warmth and safety I felt inside me at that moment. With Katie's soft breath and the heat radiating from her flannel wrapped body, I imagined myself an infant coddled in a living cradle. I would stay here forever.

A thick milky grayness inched through the blinds. The morning of one of my last days had arrived unwelcome. As I attempted to focus, I sensed more than I saw Katie leaning over me. She seemed a night watchman holding back the dawn.

I put my finger to my lips. No words were needed. We stayed that way, eyes fixed in one unbroken flow. I poured my heart into Katie's ocean of love.

We rose in silence and padded about the room, looking for remnants of food. I found a half-full tin of biscotti in Alda's closet to go with the hot chocolate we made with her electric kettle.

Katie had opened the blinds before sitting at my desk to share our breakfast. The pines drooping in the morning sleet matched my mood.

Katie reached her hand across the desk and touched my wrist. "Do you want to talk about it?"

I closed my eyes and sighed. All I wanted was to

savor the chocolate bits in the biscotti. "I guess."

"We have all day," Katie said.

"Right." I snickered. "It's Preparation Day for Mothers' Weekend. How appropriate!" My frustration poured out in sarcasm.

"Oh, Pina." Katie swallowed some chocolate. She hesitated and then asked, "Have you decided, really?"

"Katie!"

"I mean I wouldn't hold it against you if you—"

"Stop! No way. I could never. That's sick." I could feel my cheeks burning. I clenched my fist. Katie grabbed it and pressed it to her lips.

Katie teared up, replacing my hand gently on the desk. She lifted her eyes to mine and said in a barely audible voice, "I don't know what to do."

"Me neither, but I know my answer to Craney."

"What are you going to tell her?"

"Don't know yet. Don't know what I'll say to my mother either." I let my eyes drift over to the dreary scene out the window.

"You've got to tell your mom before Craney does, right?"

"God, yes. She's coming tomorrow early afternoon."

"Does she have reservations at the Inn?" asked Katie.

"I can't worry about that. Besides, it's too expensive," I snapped.

"Okay. Listen. I'll get my father to book her at the Inn. This way, you can keep her off campus until you have to."

"Right. Sorry I snapped." I touched Katie's hand. "I don't know what I'll do without you."

"Stop. We're going to fix this. Look, your mom

likes me. I know she does. It's like she fusses over me and treats me like a daughter. Do you want me to talk to her? I could. I really could."

"No. I have to do this." I bit my lip.

"But she loves me."

"I know, and maybe I can tell her that way—like you're so lovable, I fell in love just the way I did. Like not with a girl or a boy, just you. I did, you know that."

A dry knock at the door interrupted our mutual avowals of love. I wiped my tears and told Katie to stay back. I opened the door to Mademoiselle, head lowered, hand to her chest.

"Pardon," she said in French. *"Puis-je-entrer?"*

"Yes, of course, please come in." In my surprise at seeing her, I had forgotten that Katie was there.

"Hello, Miss McGuilvry." Mademoiselle broke into a warm smile as she reached for Katie's hand.

I was thoroughly stumped. Mademoiselle was in my room at eight A.M. as was Katie, in her nightshirt, and Mademoiselle was not angry.

"Je suis desolée." Mademoiselle spoke to me, head lowered once again. She turned to Katie to translate, "I am saddened."

She continued in English. "I am to tell you, you must report to Miss Craney's office today at noon. I am so sorry."

She turned back to me and in rapid French explained that she was being called back inexplicably to her family in Montargis, France, that her father, Docteur Lesage, supposedly needed her. She added that she wished she could help me. She embraced me with the traditional double-cheeked kiss and pressed a calling card into my hand. *"Si besoin est…*if needs be."

Mademoiselle exited as she had appeared: an

unexpected messenger. Perhaps of bad and good news.

Katie and I just stared at each other. Both of us scrunched up our faces, speechless.

Finally, I muttered, "Well, someone knows something."

I turned the address card over in my hand. I would keep it safe.

I reassured Katie that the upcoming meeting with Craney didn't scare me too much. I now knew I could stall her.

Katie stood up, squared her shoulders, and tossed her pageboy back over her shoulder. She appeared years older, despite her Mickey Mouse nightshirt.

"I have to go with you." She thrust her chin in my direction.

In tears, I grabbed her. "Yes," I said. "You will. Just to her door."

Chapter Forty-five

The Eve of Mothers' Weekend

A new calm seemed to settle over me. I dressed in my favorite Fair Isle sweater and turquoise wool skirt. I rubbed my hand slowly over the still unpilled knit. I knew I could handle this ordeal calmly. I had lost enough control for a lifetime. I was determined to take it back!

Katie returned from making the phone call to her father. She too appeared at ease. She had taken care of what we could: her father had made the reservation at the Inn for my mother and called to surprise her.

I didn't have a plan yet about what to tell my mother. There was a lot to tell, but in stages. The most important thing was to spare my mother the humiliation of hearing mortifying news from an authority figure, Miss Craney. Let's see…that I was a queer, that maybe there were pictures proving that, that I had caused a girl, Dorotea, to go missing, and last but not least, that I would be ostracized, chased from this prestigious institution and every other one in the future.

But for now, I took Katie by the hand. I smiled and in a low, sweet tone said, "I love you. That's the most important thing. I'll be okay, Katie, and that's because of you."

Katie placed her hand on my cheek and said, "No, that's because you're you. We'll do this together.

I'm ready."

I helped Katie with her pea jacket and wrapped her scarf around her upturned collar. I started playing with her hat, pulling it down over her eyes, but she held my hand away. "No, I have to keep an eye on you."

We laughed as she adjusted my earmuffs and attached the frog toggles of my stadium coat.

The walk, side-by-side to Damper Hall and Craney's office, flew by, aided by the wind and my newfound determination and cockiness.

Katie mumbled, "You certainly ate your Wheaties this morning."

I stopped and said, "Uh huh. I'm ready for a tennis match right now! I'll do this from here."

We had arrived at Craney's door.

"Break a leg?" Katie whispered with a puzzled look on her face.

"I'm going to," I answered, raising my chin.

I had decided I wasn't going to wait for an invitation from Craney. I knocked and entered her office without ceremony nor permission.

Craney was pacing. She hadn't finished setting the stage or the control for this contest of wits. Her wide-eyed look and wringing of hands betrayed her unpreparedness.

She attempted to regain the upper hand. "Sit!" She tried a power serve, but her tone faltered as she missed her mark.

"I'll stand, thank you." I added "Head Mistress" for respect. I had returned the play.

She coughed and smiled, trying to get into the best position for her next move. She chose a soft lob.

"My dear, I just thought I'd give you a gentle reminder, tomorrow being Mothers' Weekend."

"Yes. I know. I do my best work the night before tests and trials." Right back at her.

She tried to get me with a short lob. "My dear, you have choices."

"I'll take that under consideration," I shot back.

I astounded myself with my cockiness. Where was it coming from? And then…

Craney fired a long shot, "Hmm. No news from Dorotea, and so sorry, dear Pina, your sweet friend Alda's not here to help you."

"Hmm. So strange." I had to keep up, run ahead of her. I was almost out of breath and in the backcourt.

Craney attempted a drop shot. "And dear Katie, a motherless child. Such a shame. Where's her father's help now?"

"That's quite all right, Miss Craney. My mother loves Katie like a daughter. We'll be together for Mothers' Weekend." I let that drop back on her.

"Oh." She came up short.

"Don't worry, Miss Craney. See you on Sunday." Game!

I exited, triumphant. I elbowed my way through the velvet drapes, grabbed Katie by the hand, and raced down the hallway to the exit doors.

"Huh?" asked Katie.

"Sweetie, my tennis lessons really paid off." I smirked. "I told her 'till Sunday'. Hot damn!"

"You sure about this?"

"Sure."

"Stop! You're speeding. What the heck happened?" Katie kept yanking on my arm to tell her the details.

Now, outside, I risked letting out a sis-boom-ba cheer. "Yay. Katie, I did it."

"What? Flipped your lid?"

"I stood up to her. Finally!" I said.

"Jeez, Pina…You did?" Katie softened her tone.

"Yeah. I had to."

"Oh no." Katie stopped short on the path to our dorm. "She'll kill you."

I grabbed Katie's arm and pulled her along, skipping and laughing.

"But, she didn't. Besides, I have nothing to lose except my self-respect if I don't speak up. Don't you see? I was so darn scared. I let her scare me. All she had to do was act like she knew I was a queer, and I froze. It was as if that look of hers, the one where she's almost undressing you with her eyes, that look could see everything and could tell the whole world. Like I was walking around with a big 'Q' for queer on my forehead."

Katie pulled me into our dorm, which was totally empty. Everyone else was off with early arriving moms. She wrapped her bulky blue wool-coated arms around me. She held me so tight, I thought the anchor from her pea coat button would leave its imprint on my cheeks.

"No, Pin. You have a 'W' up there. 'W' for wonderful!" She mussed my hair and murmured, "God, I love you."

"But, but…I was so ashamed…" I lowered my head. Katie pulled it up and looked me straight in the eye. "No. Not anymore!"

Filled with the notion of nothing to lose, we lay about on my bed for a good hour. Craney could do whatever she had to. The girls were gone from the dorm, as was Mademoiselle. We could just be.

We laughed at some of my posters on the wall of Don and Phil Everly and oohed and aaahed over the one of Mont Saint-Michel in France. We talked of going there someday together. We were just two sixteen-year olds doing what sixteen-year olds do: dreaming, being silly, liking our closeness.

Katie sat up without warning. "What do you mean about your tennis lessons?" she asked.

"Well, it's like I saw her words coming at me like tennis balls, hard shots I had to return, backhand, forehand, anyway possible."

"Just focused on the ball?" Katie said.

"Yup. Like Althea. You know, my favorite champion, Althea Gibson."

"Yeah, right, my little Althea!"

We talked a bit about tennis and whether Althea Gibson faced discrimination as a Negro (and as a lesbian, maybe) in 1955. What psychological games did she have to play?

Katie sat up again. She had stopped laughing. "Your mom?"

"I know," I said.

"Oh, sweetie…"

"Yeah. Craney's not finished with me by a long shot. It's not over—" I said.

"Please don't say 'till the fat lady sings.'"

I leaned over and ruffled Katie's hair. She apologized. I hadn't forgotten about my mother and how serious this was. I was just taking a long breather.

"I am scared," I whispered.

"Can I do anything?"

"Keep telling me how much my mother loves you—and your dad."

We decided to go to Eunice's for burgers and malts. No Albert girls would be caught dead there with their mothers. We told each other stories about our previous summer in Maine. We giggled about all the pranks we had pulled and how my mother had begged Katie to help me be more ladylike. We reminisced about Katie's father and Joe and how they had fallen in love, like us. All of these things had happened, Katie reminded me, under my mother's gaze. This time, though, my mother could not choose not to see. I would have to open her eyes the very next day.

Chapter Forty-six

Mothers' Weekend

A crisp, cold morning greeted me. I shivered with the November chill—and at the thought of my mother's visit later in the day.

Katie warmed up the day, bursting into the room, chirping, "Good morning, Sunshine!"

I rolled my eyes and smirked. "Come here, Miss Sunshine."

"Well, I didn't want to be all gloomy," she said.

"Yeah. That'll come soon enough." I let my voice trail off, matching my mood.

"Pina, I can walk you to the Greyhound Station to get your mom, then disappear. Okay?"

"Yeah, that'll help." I sighed.

Dressed and ready to deal with the day, we walked mostly in silence. Katie made me promise I would wake her up later that night to tell her what happened. I agreed, knowing I would need her later just as I really needed to run away with her now.

Too late to run. The flashing neon sign of the long, gray racing dog came into view. We had arrived at the station. The loud speaker crackling out the incoming bus from New York City told me it was way too late to run.

I felt Katie's fleeting touch on my cheek and watched her walk away. I could tell by her slow gait that a part of her wanted to stay here and fight this out with me. Only Katie wouldn't fight. She would melt my mother's heart with her soft, lingering look of love and admiration—or my mother and me alike. Maybe.

❧ ❧ ❧ ❧

The Greyhound slid into its bay. My mother descended the stairs elegantly and slipped into the role of the old-moneyed mother of a prep school girl. The only problem was my mother was neither old money nor new, and I was a student at the Albert Academy only thanks to the generosity and pull of Dr. McGuilvry. We both had roles to play out. The curtain had lifted.

The last thing I needed was my mother attempting to put on airs. Craney could pierce that bubble with a pinprick! I wasn't yet convinced that Craney had really found Katie and myself *en flagrant délit,* as Mademoiselle would say. I wasn't even sure when or what "in the act" would have looked like to Craney. Did she have actual proof? Didn't matter. Craney's accusation would be proof enough for my mother.

Getting kicked out of the Academy would definitely kill my Ivy League hopes. I didn't think Doc could salvage anything. Craney would blackball me from anything good in the future. And my parents, once I was yanked out of here? What? Send me to a convent? Watch me like a hawk? Make me date the ugly, bepimpled son of a distant Italian friend? Or, realistically, following the current cure for lezzies, send me for shock treatments?

The worst would be the shame. I'd never hear the end of my parents' asking, "How could you? You must be sick." Was I?

My mother's peck on my cheek and typical greeting, "Hi, honey!" brought me back to reality. I took her suitcase, a new classy one for the occasion, and admired her lush felt hat. We were off to an okay start—that is, until she picked at my cheek to see if "that" was a pimple.

We had dinner in the small restaurant next to the Inn where she was staying. That gave me the opportunity to get a head start on the Pina-Katie stories I knew she would be exposed to. Craney had the reputation for inviting parents to a luxury tea and then slowing her pouring to ask, "Oh, by the way, do you know your daughter's pregnant?" I didn't know how Craney would approach my mother, only that she would.

How to begin: with the tried and true version, "You know, Katie and I have been really good friends…" or "Gee Mom, I have something really important to tell you…" No. I couldn't do it.

"You're not eating," I heard her say. I immediately shoveled some peas into my mouth, serving the double purpose of satisfying her and keeping my mouth busy. Before I knew it, I found myself saying, "You know, Mom, I really like Katie."

"I'm so glad," she said. "You've finally found a good friend. And what about that nice Italian girl, Alda?"

Shit. Here we go. "She's good."

"Oh, I'm so glad I'll be able to chat with her mother. The father, no. I think he's involved." She trailed off. I knew she meant Mafioso.

"But Mom." I started to panic. I needed a running start, uninterrupted so I wouldn't chicken out. "Listen! Katie…"

"Yes," she said.

"Well, we're really close."

"Now, have you gone and had a fight with her? What is it with you? Why do you always have to start something?" She reached for more salt.

"Mother!"

"Well, you usually do."

"Mom, stop! We haven't had a fight. Nothing like that. Mom, Katie and I, well, it's like I love her."

"Mmm. Uh huh. Pass the sugar, please."

"You know, like l-o-v-e. We didn't mean for it to happen."

"That's natural, like sisters or twins."

"Mom, we're not sisters."

"I know, of course. But, close, that way."

Well," I stammered. Did she need a picture? "Well, that way, and not. Well, not platonic."

"How's that, honey?"

"What I'm saying is I like her like a boy, like I'm her boyfriend."

"Oh, honey, that can't be." She seemed to be doing a boy's fall shopping list in her mind: one pair of boy's socks, a pair of jockey shorts, boy's loafers; no, they won't work.

"Mom, *that* can be. It is."

"Pina!" Now she stared at me, as if checking to see if I had breasts and girl features. "Pina, what exactly do you mean?" She looked down at her lap to brush off imaginary crumbs.

"Mommy, just look at me. I think I've fallen in love with Katie. There, I've said it."

A far-away look crossed her face as she smoothed the peak of her custard with her spoon, back and forth. Finally, she looked up with tears in her eyes.

"Oh my," she said. "There are some girls like that, just too good to be true. And we stay bosom buddies the rest of our lives through children and husbands and grandchildren."

Shoot! I thought she was getting it.

"Yeah. Kind of like that, but..." I closed my eyes, shut them tight, and covered my face with my trembling hands.

"Wait. You don't mean..."

"Yes, I think I do."

"Not one of them?" she said. She held her breath, gulped some water, and started to fan herself with her hankie. I guess it seemed safer to both of us not to mention the "L" word, to keep it as far away as possible.

"Yes, Mom." I stopped short of saying, *I am, what? A lesbian? A queer?*

"We didn't raise you that way."

"And what way is that?"

"Don't get smart with me! You're not sick, like them."

"*They*? They are not sick. They're...I am...No! I'm not."

"Sick or not, what would people say? What would they think of your father and me?"

"You didn't do anything wrong."

"Then just wipe that thought out of your head. You tell Katie you made a mistake; you like boys, I know you do. Remember that handsome boy two summers ago?"

"Billy? God! Now you want me to sleep with boys?" Jeez. Why did I have to start getting sarcastic?

"Who said anything about sleeping with boys, miss? You're not a hussy."

"Uh..." God, I was tempted to—

"Oh...so you've gone and slept with her?"

"Slept?" Aw, man!

"You know what I mean."

"No, Mom, I don't. I love Katie. She is one of those girls, too good to be true. And so is her dad, not a girl, but a one-in-a-million."

"Yes. Dr. McGuilvry is. And what does he think of this?"

"He's fine with 'this,' and so is Joe. And they're fine together!"

"Oh. *Oh*? Oh, Jesus, Mary, and Joseph. What is this? A den of...of perverts, of...not normal. I should take you home right now."

"Mom. Remember, you just said 'too good to be true'. You agreed 'one-in-a-million.' Mommy, why are you crying?"

"Well, yes. I know there are people like that."

"Like me?"

"But you're supposed to get married."

"Says who, Mother?"

"Those, those other girls, they got married. They had children. Well, one did. And the other..."

"That one, your friend Rosa? She divorced almost immediately, and I think her husband was homosexual."

We sat in silence. My mother whimpered a bit in the emptied dining room. A sweet waitress quietly served more tea. I thought she looked homosexual with her strange, not-quite-pixie hairdo. Her eyes seemed to read my whole story and to blink approval. I guess I could understand my mother; she must have felt as if she had been dropped into a queer world.

I was glad to focus on her a minute. I played with my straw and realized my throat was tight, my shoulders were up around my ears, and all of me was rather slouched into the high-backed bench.

My mother's voice gently cut the air. "Why?"

"Why what?" I asked. "It happens to some people. They don't know why."

"No," she said. "Why tell me now?"

I blew out my breath and sank even further down onto the seat of the bench, if that was even possible. I hadn't planned this far ahead. Slow. I'd start with Dorotea.

"Mommy, I think Katie's roommate has a crush on her." I scrambled to latch onto a story, any story.

"Oh, so everyone loves Katie?" That came out of her mouth with a bit more hurt than I expected.

"Mom, you once admitted Katie would have been your ideal daughter. Yes. Dorotea is jealous and started rumors. She may have even told lies about other things to Head Mistress Craney."

"Ah. So, are you a thief or a cheat, or God knows what, as well as a pervert?"

I really didn't get the depth of my mother's hurt and anger. All I could whimper was, "What, Mom?"

"You know, I didn't like that Dorotea with her German ways."

"What?" A woman of surprises, my mother. I guess she was living proof of the proverb "Hell hath no fury…" I was trying to grasp the fact that she felt scorned because I was scorned. Maybe this was beginning to make sense.

"Mom, it's not because she's German. She's got problems; she's depressed and doesn't like it when other people look better than she does."

"So. She's the thief of other girls' reputations."

"Mommy, we've got good reputations. Everybody likes us, well, almost everybody, kids, teachers. Well, they liked us. Then something got weird with Dorotea and Alda's folks. And Miss Craney—she's really weird."

"And you and Katie? That's not weird?"

"We're not hurting anyone. I want you to go on liking Katie the way you always have." I sobbed softly before asking, "Can you still love me?"

"Oh, honey. I do love you. I'm stunned and confused." As she reached for my hand, she sighed. "You may be right about my friend Rosa and maybe even Daddy's sister Athena, but..."

"Aunt Athena? Really? But you like her...and she's my...my godmother."

I unfurled myself out of my snail position. And slid across the table to hug my mother. We both cried. It was a good time to end this for the evening—on a good note.

My mother asked me to tuck her in at the Inn next door. The walk to the Inn proved brief but blustery. We walked arm-in-arm, quietly in step with each other, closer to her than I had ever felt.

I hesitated at the door to her room, drained and afraid our chat would continue, but she leaned on my arm to help her in. Inside, I remained standing and watched as she modestly slipped into her flannel gown.

She needed to sleep on all this, she said, and would send me back to school in a taxi. She said we'd have a lot to talk about the next day. She hugged me tight, and her next-to-last words were, "Give my love to Katie." But my mother was always proper. Maybe her "love" meant nothing.

As she turned her now-haggard face to be comforted in the soft down of the pillow, she mumbled, "Tomorrow...time enough...to talk to Miss Craney... to decide what to do."

In the taxi back to my dorm, I tried to relax and let the darkness and slap-dap of the tires calm me. I realized I had told my mother the most important thing. That was some relief. Not a whole lot, but some.

Chapter Forty-seven

Back at the Dorm

You take care, Missy," the cabbie said. "Sure you're okay?"

We had arrived at the dorm. No, I wasn't sure I was okay. I dragged myself out of the cab.

As I walked up the front steps of the dorm, I told myself I would worry about all this tomorrow. That wasn't working. Different voices in my head quarreled: *Face it. You are sick; nah, it's just a phase.* Still another, *if you had just been more ladylike...*

I attempted to talk back, *I'm okay; it just happens this way, sometimes.* A stuffy authority explained, *arrested development, that's the Freudian view.* Finally, a gentler, seemingly kinder voice piped in, *we'll take good care of her at our facility.*

There were so many voices, I no longer knew if they were all in my head. I did hear myself say out loud, loud and clear, "But it's love..." My words echoed back at me down the long corridor to Katie's room. "It's love...it's love..." I had to see Katie, now.

I shook her gently. She pulled me close and held me for an eternity. The voices stopped.

"Go on, tell me," she said.

What to tell? I was still numb from the fistfight in my head. All those voices. I couldn't scare Katie like that. Ha! I couldn't scare myself again. Couldn't, wouldn't, fall apart.

"I don't know...I really don't. I think it went okay, like the way I expected my mother to be. 'How could you, blah, blah...' and that was after I kind of had to spell everything out."

"Everything?"

"Katie, I'm so tired; you know what I mean. Like I love you and all."

Katie cupped my cheeks, her soft gaze begging me to tell her everything was okay.

I was staring at the birthmark on her earlobe, getting lost in it. I needed to sleep, afraid the voices would come back. Finally, the voice that broke through my fog was Katie's.

"Pin, I love you. I have to talk to your mom, really. Let me..."

"She did say she loved me still. Even talked about a friend of hers, Rosa. Sounds like she was a queer. And my aunt..."

"That's great, no?" Katie was smiling. I didn't know why.

"Katie, I can't. I'm just petrified. Like tomorrow might be the end." I was hiccoughing and sopping wet with tears. It was happening even though I told myself No! I was falling apart. I just had to get it together.

I swallowed hard and mumbled, "We have to see Craney tomorrow. Tomorrow..."

"Shush. It's okay, Pina. We'll talk about it tomorrow."

Katie pulled the sheet up around me, taking care not to rustle too much. I felt a butterfly kiss on my forehead, and I knew I was warm and good and safe.

❧ ❧ ❧ ❧

I awoke to the tolling of bells. I couldn't understand why Katie was scrambling over me, mumbling "stupid alarm." I felt good and whole in every part of my body—and holy too. In my dream, we had entered a small Sicilian church from a movie, radiant in the shaft of sun piercing the crimson stained glass. I was murmuring, "Life is good."

"Wake up. The alarm just went off," Katie said as she tapped my shoulder.

"Mmm. Life is good." I could smell the incense.

"Life is good? Sweetie, you've got to wake up."

I opened my eyes: no crimson glass, no shaft of sun, no radiance. A wind-up alarm and a gray New England morning. Yet, the incense-filled church dream had left me warm and mellow. My church-going childhood sense of wholeness and holiness filled me.

Katie stood smiling at me by the side of her bed. She leaned over and brushed the hair out of my eyes. "Life is good, sweetie. We'll do this together."

I propped myself up on my elbow and just stared at Katie. God, she was great, but would my mother go crazy if Katie came? I reached for Katie's hand.

"What if my mother—"

"Goes nuts? I'll leave. I'll start by telling her she's been like a mother to me."

"C'mon, I can't talk about this anymore." I hurled myself out of the bed.

"Let's just go to the Inn; she won't explode there. I'll get ready right away."

We left the dorm bundled against the cold, me in a tightly stretched jacket over a Norwegian ski sweater, Katie sleeker in her goose down ski jacket.

"I feel like a dough boy," I said.

"You look like one." Katie laughed. "But at least you're protected."

"I kind of feel like that. Thanks for coming."

"But it is like she's my mom." Katie wiped her eyes with her mitten.

"Jeez, Katie. I forget sometimes it was just three months ago. You must miss your mom. I'd be…I mean you never say anything."

"I don't know what to say. She's gone, and I'm angry and sad."

I took Katie by the arm. We walked that way, arm-in-arm, in silence for two blocks. Katie sniffled occasionally. Then she stopped and turned towards me.

"Pina, I loved her, but she was never, never, never there. Now, at least, she's really gone." Katie coughed and adjusted her scarf. She took a deep breath before continuing, "You're here now. Your mom's here. We've got to do this."

Katie took my arm again. She giggled. "Come on, dough girl."

Chapter Forty-eight

Mother's Room at the Inn

Katie pushed ahead of me as we approached my mother's room.

"Let me, please. I'll leave if she's weird," Katie said.

I bit my lip and shrugged.

Katie knocked and softly spoke my mother's name. "Mrs. Mazzini, it's me, Katie."

The door opened immediately. My mother clasped Katie to her.

"Oh, Katie, dear," my mother said. "How are you?"

Katie burst into tears. I had never before seen her cry like this. My mother had her arms around Katie and silently motioned to me to close the door. She led Katie to a chair and offered her a hankie.

Katie managed, "I'm sorry" in between sobs.

"No, dear, I am so sorry about your mom. She was good to me. I know I've told you this before. I've been wondering how you're doing."

"I'm okay," Katie said. "But I needed to see you, to explain."

"Shush, now. First things first."

"Yeah, good morning, Mommy." I didn't mean to be so relaxed, but…

"Oh, Pina, come here. Let me fix your hair." My mother pushed my straggly hair behind my ears and kissed me on the cheek. "You didn't say you were bringing Katie." She was all sugar and cream.

"Uh, is it okay?" I said.

"Of course. Should we eat here at the Inn?" my mother asked the two of us.

"Mom," I hesitated, not wanting to break this charming spell Katie had put on her. "We've got to talk about Miss Craney."

Katie made a face at me. "Pin, we've got plenty of time. Your mom's hungry."

"You tell her, Katie," said my mother.

She had us out the door and down the stairs before we knew it.

Unbelievable. She was acting like yesterday never happened. Katie was her ideal child, and I was a dutiful daughter whose hair and tomboyish mannerisms just needed a mild taming.

Hmm. Always discreet. When would she explode? I knew Craney's attempts to humiliate her would be pure torture. She would shrink into her little Italian girl self and fade into shame. It didn't take much to mortify my mother, nor me. I knew it by heart; I was her daughter.

"Pina, pancakes or eggs? Pina, pay attention." My mother had been speaking to me.

"Uh…A piece of crumbcake."

"You've got to eat something more." She turned to Katie to ask, "Has she been eating right?"

Between gulps of coffee, Katie managed, "Oh yes."

"Now," my mother said. "Have you been discreet?"

I was nibbling on a parker roll, lulled into a familiar numbness by my mother's banter. She finally dropped the bomb. I looked around to see how many Albert girls were here. Not many, probably preferring the Exeter Inn down the road. Still, my mother wouldn't make a stink.

Katie kicked me under the table. Her smile could have killed. She blinked and lightly touched my mother's hand across the table.

"You would be proud of us. Pina's a model Albert girl."

I almost gagged. I started to say, "Katie, she means," when Katie pinched me.

"Yes," she said, "Your mom wants to know if we've embarrassed her."

"Well, ahem, yes. I hope people aren't talking."

I think my mouth hung open for several minutes. My mother was wiping her hands on her linen napkin and leaning over to kiss Katie.

"It almost feels like you're my mom too." Katie sniffled and stared up from under her long, wet lashes. Their looks mirrored each other.

My mother patted her eyes with her second flowered hankie and then shook it gently in Katie's direction, "Oh, Katie, you've always been a daughter to me."

Could this be? Was there going to be a real bomb? Was this just another level of the sand my mom hid her head in? Maybe that sand wasn't such a bad idea.

"Hey. What about me?" Oops! I really was glad my mother loved Katie. I wanted some of that for me too.

"Yeah," said Katie, shooting me that look. "It's Mothers' Weekend. Tell your mom how much you love her."

God. Katie's right. Why was it so hard for me to do that? "I love you, Mom, thanks for coming up," I said, almost a whisper. My mother squeezed my hand across the table.

We had made papier-mâché with twelve tear-soaked paper napkins. Two hankies lay drying over the edge of the table. When my mother pulled out her Harriet Rubinstein Old Rose lipstick, applying just a genteel amount, that was the sign it was time to leave.

As she stood up, my mother said, "That conversation, the one about Miss Craney, why don't we continue it upstairs?"

Katie excused herself and said she'd meet us there. I figured that was her way of leaving my mother and me some privacy. I didn't know if I wanted any, but Katie had a clever way of making me face my fears.

We were just about seated in my mother's room when I said, "Thanks, Mom." Too much silence was frightening. Who knew what my mother might ask.

"What's to thank?"

"I mean the way you are with Katie. It's great." I could do this, I thought, like really try to talk to my mother.

"Oh, that," she said.

Chicken!

"Yes, that! You treat her as if she walks on water."

"Well, she is special, isn't she?" she asked, standing up to fix one of the waves in her hair in the mirror. She pushed the loose curl up in place.

"Right, Mom. She's great. You're great. That's why I love…you…both." Jesus. I've said it. Shoot. She'll probably twist it all up.

"What's that, honey?" She squinted at me from the mirror above the mantle.

"I was saying you're both great, you and Katie, and…I uh…that's why I love you."

"Hmm." She sat back down and leaned over to flatten out my skirt. "Yes. I guess we're two in a million."

I didn't believe it. Yikes! Was it safe to let down my guard? I wished Katie would hurry.

"So…" said my mother. "Miss Craney. Were you…? What were you…?"

"Hi!" Katie burst in. "Oh, excuse me."

"My mother was just asking about Craney," I said. I hoped she wouldn't ask about sex in front of Katie. My mother had a real thing about sex. She couldn't even use the word when she told me my sixteen-year old cousin was pregnant.

"Katie, sit here," my mother said.

Katie sat at the edge of the wingback, studying our faces. I tightened up my jaw and squinted, hoping Katie would read "careful" in my look.

She chewed her lip and cast the most imploring look at my mother. "Mrs. Mazzini, Miss Craney is wicked. My father thinks she might even be a child molester. He's coming up tomorrow."

My mother blanched then fanned herself with her hankie as the wave of her flush crept up her neck. She opened her mouth but continued to stare ahead in silence.

I approached my mom and touched her arm. "No, she hasn't abused me that way."

"Yet!" said Katie.

"Pina! Please tell me now what's going on." My mother was holding onto the arms of the chair.

"Craney, uh…Miss Craney has been…"

"The word is grooming," said Katie.

"Mommy, she's threatened if I didn't—"

"Didn't what, dammit?" My mother's movements became staccato, her tone frigid.

"Service her," I mumbled.

"Mrs. Mazzini, she won't dare say 'have sex.'"

"Katie!" My glare was a gun with a silencer.

"Or what?" my mother asked.

"Well…I'll be kicked out…like I'm a les…well, a…well, you know. But she's also accused me of being involved in Dorotea's disappearance. I'm not."

I started sobbing. I knelt down next to my mother and held onto her knees. "I didn't do anything wrong. I swear. She's crazy."

"Except…" My mother seemed to be searching for the right words. "You and Katie…" My mother swallowed hard and continued, "Did Craney see something?"

"We don't know," Katie said. Katie got up and stood next to my mother and me. She placed her hand on my shoulder.

"Miss Craney has been after Pina from the start, but we had no proof she was really sick. Oh yeah, we have that journal where she wrote your name and hers."

"It all started on my birthday," I explained, seeing my mother's narrowing gaze.

Katie threw me a sidelong glance, acknowledging in silence that our intimacy had also been a birthday present. Then she frowned, saying, "Remember how she warned you from the start. What was it? Yeah, 'I'm watching you…' but then, she got all chummy and made our skin crawl."

"Mommy, she was almost petting me. It was gross."

"And you said nothing? You couldn't have told me?" My mother was puffing out her cheeks.

"But, I wasn't sure. And she invited me to her private room. I didn't know. Maybe she was just being nice? I had no idea how things worked at a swanky place like this. I was out of my league. But she's done far worse."

"Jesus, Mary, and Joseph. Pina, *what?*" She said, pulling out yet another hankie from her purse by her side. My mother was perspiring and fanning herself. Her chest heaved with massive sighs.

I was sobbing again. I couldn't do this. All I was doing was upsetting my mother, the last thing I wanted.

Katie pulled me into a chair. She patted my shoulder and stared out at the hills through the window. I wanted to go away, far away from my mother's gasping and Katie's pensiveness. I just wanted out.

Katie broke the silence. "Mrs. Mazzini, please. Miss Craney has been planting her things in Pina's room and sending her books about…uh…suggestive books, and she's like a lecherous, old man…only a woman."

"Enough!" My mother stood and turned to take her purse by the double handle. "We'll see about this. Pina, get my coat, please."

"What are you going to do?" I helped her with her coat. After she finished buttoning the collar, she reached out and clasped me to her. She called Katie over and held the two of us a few moments more.

"I'm going to do what should have been done a long time ago."

Katie and I hurried to put on our jackets. I had never seen my mother standing so tall. In her four-foot-something frame, she seemed to loom large as she walked solidly in her Cuban heels, bearing us along on either side. She informed us we would go directly to Miss Craney's office, adding she didn't give a whit about Mothers' Weekend.

Chapter Forty-nine

Mother's Visit with Miss Craney

As we approached Merrick Memorial Gate, this brave, new version of my mother started to disappear. She withdrew her arm from ours and slowed her pace. Physically, Mom seemed to shrink before our eyes, shielding herself with her purse clutched to her breast. I saw her raise and then lower her eyes to take in a group of mink-clad mothers and cashmere-coated daughters.

In a barely audible voice, she mumbled, "It's so… so big. Where do we go?"

Katie took hold of my mother's arm in a possessive, daughterly fashion. She held on with both hands and leaned into my mother to speak. "I'll show you the way."

Katie lifted her head. Her face took on a mask of determination: set and firm, and protective. I feared we had just lost my mother as advocate. At least she had been moving in that direction.

How could I let her do this? Craney would gobble her up.

We had arrived at the end of Craney's hallway. We walked down this now familiar Persian runner.

My mother knocked. I clung to her back, a gosling riding her tail feathers as much for my own safety as for hers. The door swung open. Craney's smile oozed honey.

"Dear Mrs. Mazzini, I've been expecting you." She ushered my mother in with a gracious sweep of her left hand. She thrust her open right hand to the center of my chest. "No," she uttered, baring her teeth.

The last thing I saw was my mother awaiting Miss Craney's orders, an assigned seat and her place. The door slammed shut.

I covered my mouth. Katie put her finger to hers. We tiptoed to the door, held our breath, and cupped our ears to capture any words the cold walls would give up.

My mother's voice was saying, "Honored."

Craney's said, "Occasionally…magnanimous… opportunity to the deserving, but…"

Jeez! The first part was so clear. Craney had lowered her voice for the "but."

"What a bum!" Katie mumbled.

I motioned for her to be quiet; my mother was crying. Katie placed her hand on my arm and shook her head. I must have looked like I wanted to kill. Katie mouthed, "You can't."

My mother asked, "A second chance?"

"Pardon?" was Craney's response.

I heard Craney push her teacup back across the glass penholder. A fingernail scratch on a blackboard. She was definitely zeroing in for the kill. She raised her voice. "Ahem. The accusations are many."

My mother retorted, "Yes. I'm sure" with a new sternness to her voice. "I certainly want to hear what my daughter has to say for herself!"

My mother's chair scraped the floor. I almost fell into the room as she opened the door.

"Come, this moment," she demanded.

It was over, all over. Craney had cowed my mother. Katie touched my fingers as I inched away, pulled by my mother into Craney's office.

"Sit," said my mother.

Craney was smirking at me. "Well, the disappearance of Dorotea, Miss Mazzini, how do you explain that? Or…do you have a different answer for me?" She inclined her head, closer to mine, holding my gaze.

I knew Craney was asking if I had decided to be her slave.

My mother nodded at me. "Go ahead."

"I think she was depressed, but she seemed happy to go to her aunt's," I said.

"Out with it, Miss Mazzini!" Craney glared at me. Her command hung suspended in the air.

A wave of confusion and doubt seemed to wash across my mother's face followed by a flash of anger.

"Ahem! If I may…" My mother raised her voice, "You've called the police, I hope."

"The family…they seem to be taking care of things," Craney muttered, fumbling with a pen on her desk.

"Let me understand then," my mother said. "So, Dorotea did in fact arrive at her aunt's; she's not missing from school."

"Well, yes—"

"I'm beginning to see. I certainly am!" My mother glared at Craney.

Craney struggled to stand, holding onto her desk. She leaned into me, her beady eyes inches from mine. "I asked you a question, Pina! Are you involved in Dorotea's disappearance?"

"No!" I said.

"Honesty is fostered here at Albert. I'm asking you again. I will not tolerate your 'no.'" Craney's nearby lip started to curl. She oozed seduction and power.

My mother pulled me closer to her. I read disgust and horror on her face. She got it, the whole picture, and she was determined not to let Craney get her or me.

"Pina, did you have anything to do with this?" My mother snapped.

"No."

My mother cleared her throat. "Miss Craney, sit down."

Craney drew in her breath as she regained her chair.

"Miss Craney, my daughter does not lie," my mother said.

"Be that as it may—"

"Allow me to finish, please!" My mother cut her off. "I occasionally check Pina's facts, but she is not a liar. Nor do I believe she is fabricating stories about your threats—"

"How dare you!" Craney blanched.

"Yes, I dare. Threats to expose her as a lesbian if…if she didn't…what? Comply? Pina is not your plaything!" Mother's voice ricocheted off the walls.

My mother sat back in her chair, scarlet and perspiring heavily. My insides were roiling; yet, I had to suppress a smile itching to cross my lips. My mother passed me a hankie in complicity.

Miss Craney drank a large draft of water. Her voice quavered. "Hmm. We have a history of dignity and discretion here at Albert. We eschew scandal at all costs, and your daughter's lewd, aberrant behavior—"

"Enough!" said my mother.

I felt a twitch. Craney digressed; she wasn't going to answer my mother. I guessed that maybe I wouldn't either. Sitting in the chair with steam almost rising off her, my mother seemed more like a raging bull than her petite, demur self.

Having regained her composure, my mother leaned over the edge of Miss Craney's desk to admire a bronze owl.

Miss Craney pointed to the owl. Her voice was flat. "Symbol of the Goddess of—"

"Wisdom," my mother said. "Athena. Yes, I do know. In our family we, too, honor wisdom and strong, educated women. I am neither strong nor educated. Athena, my sister-in-law—so, yes, we know all about goddesses and wisdom—she's one of *those* women: educated, independent. Paid her own way *and* can pay Pina's. *She* is Pina's godmother and a role model for Pina. She has not needed a husband."

My mother picked up the owl, dusted off the spot it had sat on, and replaced it. She looked up at Miss Craney, who sat hands braced on either side of her on the desk.

I blinked at my mother. I didn't dare breathe.

Miss Craney slowly shook herself alert. "There must be consequences for Pina's, ahem, behaviors."

"Yes," said my mother, encouraging me. I gave an assertive nod.

My mother smiled broadly. "Saying no to an authority figure does not come cheaply."

Miss Craney gasped. "I have to reflect upon Pina's expulsion. Morals, particular friendships…"

"Moral high ground?" My mother sighed as if bored with this whole meeting. "You and I both know this is not about Dorotea. Miss Craney, the truth is out.

I know who and what my daughter is; I can say the word 'lesbian.' Let's be honest. Dorotea is not a threat. You, Miss Craney are the threat!"

Miss Craney closed her eyes, twitching ever so slightly.

"Come. It's time for us to leave, Pina. Oh, and Miss Craney, you'll be seeing Dr. McGuilvry later tonight," my mother added.

"But, it's Mothers' Weekend," Miss Craney sputtered.

"Yes," said my mother. "I have claimed both daughters for today. And what a pleasure it will be to visit with her dad."

"You'll, uh…stay, Mrs. Mazzini?" Craney asked with an almost imperceptible tremor.

"Of course. To give you time to reflect," said my mother.

A smaller, frailer Miss Craney stood with difficulty from her great chair. She pointed to the door and startled when my mother said, "Do call for us later."

We heard a quiet, "Yes, of course," as we exited through the velvet drapes. The thick, lustrous fabric muffled my mother's words, "Right now, I'm taking my girls to lunch." The alcoves and companion drapes seemed to wave in approval.

Chapter Fifty

Flush

Katie and I hugged and petted my mother so much she blushed all the way out of Damper Hall. We helped her down the stairs to the loggia, whose only occupants today were its statues.

I stopped my mother and spun her around. I pondered her standing there for a moment while I dreamed up some harmless prank. My mother smiled back at me, as if to say, "Okay, what are you up to?" She was going along for the ride.

I gently positioned Mom against the stone wall to mimic the statues of Venus and Athena. Katie threw her scarf around my mother's shoulders.

"Hail Queen," Katie and I intoned.

"Girls, stop. You're being silly." My mother placed her hand on her reddened cheek.

I grabbed Katie's arm and nodded for the hymn to begin. We sang "Hail Holy Queen" from our Catholic School days. We enunciated the line "Oh Maria" doo-wop style – O-MA-RI-A and screeched, "Triumph all ye cherubim" in the worst falsetto possible.

I hugged my mother hard. "I love you so much, Mommy. You are one in a million."

"Oh...honey," my mother sobbed.

"I love you, too!" Katie said with a sheepish grin.

"Oh my girls..." My mother dabbed at her eyes

with her hankie. "You're so silly, my angels!" She used the same hankie to fan herself despite the November chill.

❧❧❧❧

In the Olde Anchor restaurant, my mother announced she was feeling flush and ordered a four-pound lobster for us. We wore silly bibs and held mock claw wars.

My mother coughed and checked around her with darting glances to see if the other staid, well-dressed diners were looking at Katie and me.

"Girls, really. Behave yourselves."

My mother composed herself and brushed imaginary crumbs from her burgundy silk dress. She cleared her throat. "You know, Pina, Miss Craney will probably expel you."

I sucked my lower lip a second and turned away. "Yeah. I know." I knew, but nothing had really sunk in. In a quiet voice, I added, "I am sorry, Mommy."

"No." She paused and sighed. "It will be all right. I don't think she'll publicize it."

"Why?" I scrunched up my face. It was hard to imagine Craney having mercy on me.

"I guess I took the wind out of her sails." My mother laughed. "No one was going to accuse you of being a liar."

"Yeah! Craney probably figured she'd disgrace Pina and shock you, Mrs. Mazzini. And the way you talked about Pina's godmother…Wow! Craney almost fell off her chair." Katie was grinning from ear to ear.

"Well, Katie, I think your father's visit might also be a serving of humble pie for her. She might fear litigation." My mother dabbed at the last bits of lobster tamale on her lips.

My mother's choice of words, her mannerisms, her carriage seemed altered. She applied her lipstick with aplomb and used her compact to spy on the loud woman seated at the table behind ours.

"But, Mom, what about Dorotea?"

"The police might question you, but I doubt it. Pina. Aunt Athena can afford any school you would choose. We'll talk to Daddy and see."

"Oh…Daddy. How's he going to take this?"

"Don't you worry. He knows about his sister."

"No. I mean about me. About…Katie, about—"

"Pina," Katie broke in, "remember my father. He'll help, big time. You might not get kicked out."

"Yeah, but I have to face my father. *You* might not get thrown out, Katie, but me?"

"But my father said he was working on something." Katie crossed her fingers.

"Pina, Daddy's a smart man. He loves Katie."

My mother took our hands, licked her lips, and spread out the embossed menus once again. "Ladies, ladies. It's time for crème brule, pumpkin soufflé, or apple crisp?"

❧ ❧ ❧ ❧

After lunch, I walked my mom back to the Inn for the nap she said she needed after the morning's events. Katie went to the bookshop.

Seated next to me on the loveseat, she patted my hand and turned away to block a tear.

"You know, this isn't what I would have wanted for you. I do love you. I want you to know that, honey."

I leaned over and threw my arms around her. "I love you. Especially now, Mommy. I know this is hard for you."

She smoothed my hair and dabbed my eyes with her hankie. "We'll work it out. Don't you worry about Daddy."

"Oh, and Mom, thanks for how you are with Katie."

"Pina, listen to me. Katie is in our lives. She's been one of the family and will continue to be. Now let me rest. I have to look sharp for Dr. McGuilvry later tonight."

Chapter Fifty-one

Bronte's

Mothers' Weekend at Albert had come and gone; my mother remained.

Katie, my mother, and I were enjoying the coziness of the blazing hearth at Bronte's restaurant while we waited for Dr. McGuilvry to arrive.

Somewhat later than expected, Doc entered the restaurant, where he often called Albert's Board of Directors to order, and left his overcoat at the coat check. Katie ran to greet him and all but tackled him with her powerful hug. She led him by the hand over to my mother.

"Giusy Mazzini, it's good to see you. You look well."

"Doctor McGuilvry," She extended her hand, but he had already bent over to kiss her on the cheek. "Thank you," she said.

I rushed over to be scooped up into his arms. Every time this giant of a man gave me one of his bear hugs, wafts of his Bay Rum and the nub of his Aryan Island tweed vest brought me back seven years to the first time I met him and Katie. He reached out and pulled Katie into this joint embrace. All was good.

"Well, ladies, I'm exhausted, but I wanted to see you all before turning in. I see you've all eaten; I'll just have some tea," said Doc. "Giusy, I want to thank you before anything else. I should have been the one to confront Miss Craney, but my conference in Rome prevented that." Doc stifled a yawn.

"Yes, but she accused Pina, not Katie," said my mother.

"Be that as it may, I'm sure these girls have been through enough. I regret that they didn't tell me all the details from the start." Doc took a sip of his tea. "You're a brave mother; of course you have a brave girl in Pina. I'm afraid that by sending her here, I gave her a monumental task: break into Miss Craney's 'system.' I knew she was rigid from working with her on the Board of Directors. Heard she was a bit bizarre, but..." Doc seemed to be weighing his next words.

"Doctor, Pina knew what to expect. She said she could handle it," said my mother.

"Please, call me Ron. Yes, the peer pressure, the academics, the money. But Miss Craney's, well, hovering over Pina, the unwanted attentiveness—should I say fawning over Pina?—her gifts, her spying...I hadn't expected that. Unfortunately, Pina and Katie say they have no proof, but we'll see about that.

"I imagine the biggest trial for Pina must have been figuring out what her role was in all of Miss Craney's warped machinations." Doc took another sip. "The other struggle, that's the toughest. I know; it's a hard awakening to realize who you love—and to accept it."

"Oh," said my mother. "You knew?"

"Yes and no. I was speaking for myself. I had to untangle the same questions, but late in my life. So much time wasted in the struggle. So much unnecessary shame. You really are quite a brave mother, Giusy. I wish my mother had been like you."

"I'm not sure I understand." My mother wrinkled her brow.

"You do know Joe, Joe Gallo, my companion. I was…scared. Scared of what people would say if they knew."

"Oh…oh, but Ron, you've always done the right thing."

"Yes, my wife thought so too."

"I am sorry." My mother lowered her eyes. I placed my hand on my mother's arm. She smiled at me and reached for Katie's hand. "Thank you, Ron," she said. "Thank you for telling me."

Katie and I kept looking at each other. How long would they talk like this? I was beginning to squirm. Did my mother really get what Doc was saying? Katie and I knew he and Joe were homosexual. Found that out last summer. And my parents met Joe, but…well, she'd figure it out. Doc was pretty honest. It had to come up in his meeting with Craney.

I couldn't contain myself anymore. "I'm not expelled, yet," I blurted out.

"Dad, you should have seen Mrs. Mazzini. She was great." Katie tugged on his sleeve.

"I called her bluff." My mother blushed.

"Mrs. M is being modest, Dad. Tell him about your sister-in-law, Mrs. M," said Katie

"Ron, my sister-in-law, Pina's godmother is… she's…"

"Homosexual?" Doc took a sip of his tea and gently replaced the cup in its saucer. "Like me and Joe?"

"Well, like Pina," she said.

"As I said, Giusy. You are a brave mother."

Doc turned to us and said, "Girls, I know I've left

you out of this conversation tonight. I don't want you to worry. I've been working on some things with Joe—some old stories about Albert and a certain instructor fired by Miss Craney, which I'll explain later.

"You know, it was a long flight from Rome. I am really tired now, and I have a nine A.M. meeting with Miss Craney tomorrow. I'll see if I can do as well as you, Giusy! What say we meet for lunch tomorrow?" Doc leaned over to hug us all before retrieving his coat from the check. He waved his hat. "Good night, ladies!"

Chapter Fifty-two

Doc and the Mistress

In the morning, a pale blue sky and hints of an intense yellow sun hung in the frame of my window. I had slept alone in my room to give my thoughts some space. I didn't recall any dreams. The almost-holy moment, that one instant of the perfect sunrise, *that* belonged to me alone this morning.

I just wanted to immerse myself in the maize waves undulating through my blinds, lulling me back to sleep.

Craney! I jolted myself from my stupor and jumped out of bed. Katie and I had agreed to eavesdrop on her father's conversation with Craney.

※ ※ ※ ※

Katie and I huddled in the hall outside Craney's office, hidden behind the velvet drapes covering the doorway. The scraping of the chairs and the voice of Craney's maid announcing the Earl Grey signaled the beginning of their session.

After the clinking of cups, we heard Craney clear her throat. Her voice seemed to lack its normal icy control or its alternate, phony dulcet tones.

"Dr. McGuilvry, it's always uh...a pleasure. What...well, to what...? You honor me with your presence after all these mothers on Mothers' Weekend. Oh, I am so sorry. I have grown somewhat forgetful… your wife…"

"Thank you for seeing me, Miss Craney. I am a few weeks early for our Board Meeting, and I do have some concerns about staffing and finances. Yet…"

There was a long pause. I looked over at Katie, who was crossing her fingers. I just wanted Doc to get on with it and cut through his doctorly blah blah.

"News, sometimes, travels slowly, even from here at Albert." Doc was taking his time—or setting up Craney.

"Well, yes," said Craney. "I, too, have news, some of which relates to funding and staffing. But, I am concerned, no, I am deeply, deeply troubled. Your protégée Pina Mazzini has caused us undue worry. She seems to have single-handedly precipitated our potential undoing."

"Our undoing?" asked Doc.

I could hear him shift his bulk in the leather wingback. He made a deep, cough-like chuckle.

"Miss Craney, I'm a pretty stout fellow. It takes a lot to 'undo' me. Please…"

"The daughters of two of our biggest donors have disappeared. And…"

"Oh my. You say Pina did this 'singlehandedly?' But do tell, whose daughters?"

"Wolfie Baciadalupo's and Adolph Cabanus's."

"Hmm. Of questionable funding, themselves, no? Miss Craney, help me understand. What do you believe Pina did? Does Pina have any connections with The Italian Brotherhood? That is what we call it up here at Albert, isn't it? Or maybe Pina has joined the Nationalist Socialist Party? I'm having difficulty understanding Pina's influence here."

I was flat out on the floor, laughing silently. Katie was a deeper shade of crimson.

"Dr. McGuilvry, you do have a sharp sense of humor."

"Tell me how Pina did this," said Doc.

"She wanted the rooms all to herself. You see, these girls, Alda Baciadalupo and Dorotea Cabanus, are the roommates of Pina and your sweet daughter Katie."

I snapped, "Liar!" Katie almost gagged me.

"Miss Craney, I thought we were being serious. Roommate troubles? Conspiracies? And you haven't said that Katie was involved," said Doc.

"Uh, I don't really think that's pertinent."

Craney was having a coughing fit. It sounded as if Doc had stood up to get her some water. She was gurgling, "but...but" through her gulps of water. "I have proof," she managed to spit out, "Dr. McGuilvry, here's the proof."

"Ahem," said Doc, unfolding paper. "This note from Dorotea Cabanus, marked 'in case something happens to me,' yes? But there's nothing else inside the envelope. This is the proof?"

"Well, it's there. There's more. 'Miss Mazzini is a lez-be-an'! On the flap. Can't you see? She has done something grievous to drive Dorotea away. She may have even corrupted your daughter."

I heard Doc clear his throat and in a low voice say, "I wonder who corrupted me?"

Craney kept on repeating, "Beg pardon?"

"Corrupted? My daughter?" Doc said clearly. "Why, they've been close summer friends for over seven years in Maine. Close friends...corruption is a strong word. And you don't think it's my daughter who's done the 'corrupting?'

"Hmm. Let me see. My companion, Joseph Gallo, is an investigative journalist. Ah, you know him; he's written fund-raising materials for Albert and histories of some of our benefactors. Yes, Joe Gallo. Why, we were just kids, well maybe just a bit older than Katie and Pina, when we became, uh, fast friends. It was kind of like Albert—the elite Minnetonka young men's camp."

"I am, uh, horrified! You are condoning this, Doctor? More to the point, are you admitting your own…questionable behavior? You do realize this has serious legal implications. This is shocking."

"Yes. Last year, that girl, Millicent Evers and the Exeter fellow, caught in the act. We dealt with that on the Board? And the young woman is back here now, no? Good thing the word pregnancy or termination was never used. Think of it—our reputation—"

"Perhaps, you have not heard me, Doctor." Craney raised her voice, "I am speaking of *your* reputation and what I am about to do with it. I can call the Trustees and the Board Members now. Not to mention the Police Commissioner." Miss Craney snorted.

I looked at Katie. Her mouth was open. She seemed to forget to breathe.

For several moments, not a peep came from inside Craney's office either.

"Yes," said Doc in a low, halting voice, followed by another hollow silence.

Then, judging from the sound, Miss Craney had slammed her hand down on her desk.

"You do not take my allegations seriously? I can

end this whole discussion here with one phone call to the right people."

"I do see your point," Doc said in a soft voice.

"And then, there's the matter of your license."

"Miss Craney, what would you have me do?" Doc sighed heavily.

It didn't sound like he was playacting any longer, more as if he had given up the fight.

Moments later, we heard Craney pick up the clunky phone receiver and start dialing.

I pulled Katie to me and held her while she sobbed into my chest. Things weren't supposed to go this way. Could Doc really be arrested for being homosexual?

A dry clack told us Craney had hung up the phone.

"Yes. What to do, Dr. McGuilvry? Hmm, let me see." Craney was almost humming. "Money, we were talking about money, weren't we?"

"I am sorry, Miss Craney, are you asking about my money?"

"Now that you mention it..." Craney's voice trailed off.

"Wretch!" Katie whispered, "Blackmail?"

I quickly covered her mouth. I was afraid Craney would hear us in the stark silence following her last comment.

I sat there, chilled to the bone. Craney was evil itself. She would actually blackmail Doc...or...

In a flash, I remembered the article about the homosexual Boy Scout leader in The Daily News on the plane to Andover. Doc would be arrested. Splashed across the front pages. Because of me...

Nah, nah...not after all he'd done for me—and all Craney had done to me.

"*No!*" A loud no poured out of my mouth and echoed the length of the hallway. Again, I let go another booming, "No!" No one was going to do that to Doc or me.

I was on my feet. Katie reached up to pull me down. I twisted away from her, spitting out, "No more!"

Katie made one last grab for my wrist, thrusting something into my hand.

"Use it," she said.

Upon hearing my yells, Craney threw open her door. She yanked me into her office.

"How dare you!" Craney bellowed.

My gaze darted from her crimson face and bloodshot eyes to the object in my hand. Craney's journal.

I had no time to tease out how Katie had gotten her hands on this green suede book, Craney's birthday present to me.

I held it up; the journal's presence was as much a surprise to me as it was a shock to Craney.

"Give me that!" Craney screeched.

Doc was on his feet by my side. I froze. I flicked my eyes. I saw Doc's eyes on me. I blinked. I saw Craney's hands wildly clutch at the journal. Her eyes flashed venom.

I pulled way back and raised my hand, a human stop sign. I opened the book, and in a robotic voice started to read, our two names, "Mary Margaret Craney and Pina Mazzini, embossed together." I continued reading, "To our dreams." I stopped short after the opening lines of the poem We'll Go No More a Roving.

Miss Craney collapsed in her chair, hand to her chest. With a jerk of his head, Doc motioned for me to leave. The last thing I saw was Doc taking Craney's pulse.

I found my way to the door despite my semi-paralyzed state. Katie pulled me the rest of the way out.

"Phew! You're safe. I was afraid she'd smack you," Katie said, stroking my face.

"I, uh, I don't believe I did that…"

"You did. There'll be hell to pay later. " Katie chuckled.

"I did, didn't I?" I started to put it all together as my blood thawed. "Hot damn! If I'm going to be expelled, I might as well go out in a blaze of glory. But Katie, the journal, how'd you do—"

"Shush, later. We've got to hear the rest," Katie said. "Craney's no longer speechless."

"Feeling better, Miss Craney?" Doc asked.

"Yes, yes. The audacity of youth these days…Her behavior…untenable but you can't…excuse me, Dr. McGuilvry; I must take a break. Please stay."

Craney must have left the room. Katie raised her eyebrows. We had no idea what would happen next, but we didn't dare budge.

I was still recouping from my unexpected actions. My body tingled and shook as if an animal sprung from a trap, totally alive in the here-and-now.

We heard a door shut. Craney was back.

"There have to be consequences, Doctor. We don't need a scandal, do we?" Craney babbled.

"Funny, Miss Craney, I was just thinking that. I will speak to Pina about that curious outburst and that interesting book."

"I can explain. I truly can."

"No need, Miss Craney," said Doc, sounding like a parent embarrassed by a child's annoying behavior.

"May I?" asked Craney.

We heard Craney pour something. Katie's dad exclaimed, "1949, an excellent VSOP."

Ha! Craney had resorted to booze. And was Doc apologizing for me? This confused me.

"Yes," continued Doc. "Earlier we had been speaking about my Pulitzer-winning companion, Joe Gallo. He has been doing research on private institutions and their staffs. He would like to shine a light on some brilliant lecturers who have disappeared and bring those individuals out of the shadows."

"Ah, yes. That's admirable. And this relates to Albert and our troubled Pina?"

Craney's voice seemed to regain some strength and volume.

"He would like to interview you, you as a role model for these gifted young women."

"Well, well, of course," said Craney. "What would he like to focus on?"

By now, Katie and I were even more confused. We weren't sure where Doc was going, but we hoped he was stringing Craney along.

"Joe Gallo believes you could provide missing information about a Miss Emily Whitfield, a much beloved English instructor here in your first year as Head Mistress."

We heard nothing but Doc's voice for almost two minutes. We had been hanging on his every word. Maybe he had delivered the coup de grace. But then...

"I am sorry. I uh...think the cognac has gone to my head. Hmm. Emily. I don't recall an Emily, English Instructor, you say? I could check the records. You say your friend—"

"Companion. He believes she vanished. Would any staff know?"

Craney almost choked when Doc said, "Like Mademoiselle, who has also left?"

Katie poked me and made the sign for another point scored by her father.

"I'll tell you what, Miss Craney," Doc continued. "You give me a sense of your calendar, and I'll have Joe up here immediately. And concerning staff vacancies, I would like to propose at the next Board meeting that we rehire Mademoiselle Lesage and Miss Emily Whitfield. We absolutely cannot afford to let such youthful, inspiring talent go elsewhere—or underground."

"But…but I thought you said Miss Whitfield was nowhere to be found."

Craney's voice was also disappearing. It was hard to hear the sigh at the end of her sentence.

"I did, didn't I? But Joe is an expert investigative journalist and could locate Dorotea and Alda along with Miss Whitfield. Joe's father, a member of the Italian Brotherhood, La Cosa Nostra, has many tools at his disposal for locating a Baciadalupo. I refer only to Fifi Gallo's legal connections."

"Dr. McGuilvry, give me a minute."

We heard Craney scrape her chair back. "Doctor, you've mentioned many interesting things this morning. It is late. As I said, there must be consequences."

"Excuse me, Miss Craney, if I am being dense, consequences of my connections, consequences of Joe's articles being published, because, of course, there will be."

"Consequences for Pina's behavior!"

"Which one is that? Are you punishing her and my daughter for their friendship or Pina for being without means and Italian? Oh, yes, and that journal?"

"Please don't insult my intelligence."

"On the contrary. I am appealing to the very intelligent being in you. I predict all the disappearances will reappear and facts and people will come out of the woodwork."

"Please, Doctor…"

Doc seemed to be tying it all up. I certainly hoped so. I really had to pee and to die laughing. Katie looked as if she would burst. And had Katie told Doc I was recording all of Craney's crap in the journal she gave me?

"You're right, Miss Craney. It is late. I'm going to join Mrs. Mazzini for lunch. How charming that she stayed to have lunch with the girls and me! Oh, I believe she is also awaiting your reflections. I ask that you not keep her waiting."

"Yes. Of course."

"I look forward to our next Board meeting. I'll be expecting your call about setting up an interview with Joe."

"Certainly, Doctor."

"Miss Craney, one more thing. I failed to mention, I'll be withdrawing my daughter along with Pina, should you so decide."

When Doc exited, Katie and I latched onto him. The three of us made a triumphant recessional down the hall, our arms linked in Doc's. He commented that I deserved the Oscar.

Chapter Fifty-three

Appetizers and Lunch

Doc had told us to meet him before our lunch with my mother. He wanted to read us the riot act about being…I still didn't know what to call us other than two girls in love. "Lesbians" sounded old. "Homosexuals" were British men who got thrown in jail.

Katie and I were waiting for him in the smaller dining room of the Inn where he also had a room. We noticed my mother hurrying down the stairs.

"Girls, oh good, you're here," she said, catching her breath. She hugged us in a stiff embrace. "Miss Craney has sent for me."

"Mom, you'll be fine. Oh, did you see Dr. McGuilvry?" I asked.

"I just bumped into him in the reading room. He told me a bit." My mother smiled.

We both held my mom's hand, and she turned to go.

As my mother disappeared, Doc appeared and sat down at the table.

"Well, my little chickadees, what do you think?"

"Dad, I think you deserve an Oscar," laughed Katie.

"Maybe so, but you do realize that if she had proof—hell, she doesn't really need it—she could chase you out of here today. Just the mere suspicion. You're lucky she's so devious. She's surely preyed on girls before and has most likely left a trail like your journal. It should be easy to dig up more dirt on her. Oh, and Pina, that performance…"

"I didn't plan it." I gritted my teeth.

"I realize that," said Doc.

"You have to admit, Dad, it was brilliant." Katie chortled.

"Not the way I normally do business, but…" Doc scratched his head, and continued, "Yes, bravo, Pina! We, I mean you, could have pushed Miss Craney closer to the edge with the journal, but I was truly concerned with her health at that point."

"Yeah, Katie, when did you swipe my journal? C'mon, did the two of you plan this?" I still didn't understand where my courage came from, but it sure felt good.

"I'll never tell," Katie said.

"By the way, I will need that journal. Joe will know what to do with it," said Doc, beginning to frown. "But, as I had started to say, you cannot, absolutely not flaunt—"

"Flaunt?" screeched Katie.

"Yes, flaunt how enamored you are with one another. Goo-goo eyes give you away."

"Dad! You're telling us to hide?" asked Katie.

"I'm telling you, there's a time and a place. If something's not safe, I don't give a good galdarned what, I'm going to prevent you from doing it. Right now that includes looking into each other's eyes in public. And if you can't bring a boy into your bed, it's not okay for them to see a girl in your bed."

"Hmm. I heard you say, 'For them to *see*,'" I said.

"Pina, am I clear? I'm not asking you to be nuns, just discreet."

Katie had started to fold her hands over her chest in a Madonna-like pose. My mother rushed in, cheeks ablaze, almost singing, "Jesus, Mary, and Joseph!"

Once seated, my mother caught her breath as we pumped her for info.

"Wait just a minute," she said. "Finally, I can breathe. Miss Craney, she actually patted my hand and served me tea and cookies."

"Mommy!"

"She's put off her decision until after the Board meeting in January," said my mother.

"Huh? You mean I get to stay until January?" I blurted out.

"Only if you want to," said Doc. "I'm going to make a motion at the January Board meeting to rehire Mademoiselle and Miss Whitfield, the teacher who mysteriously disappeared. I'm pretty sure we'll find her."

"Now, I don't understand," said my mother.

"Giusy, there are other stories about Miss Craney preying on young women and getting rid of them if they didn't comply. Miss Whitfield's return could cause a scandal for Miss Craney."

"So, she's waiting to see if you can produce Miss Whitfield," said Katie.

"I believe so. But the mere mention…" said Doc.

"Ah, I see," laughed my mother. "You beat her at her own game."

"Yes. He's a real card." Katie laughed as she leaned over to kiss her dad.

Doc continued, "Giusy, Joe will publish an article about Miss Whitfield, who will miraculously receive a

'Teacher of the Year Award' from whatever institution employs her now. Also, I believe Joe and his dad will track down Dorotea and Alda. And now with Pina's journal…"

"Jesus, Mary, and Joseph!" My mother took out her hankie again.

Doc winked. "They might help, too."

Doc seemed quite optimistic as he wished all of us "good bye."

We thanked him profusely, my mother offering to say Novenas for his favorite cause.

Katie and I hung around his neck. "*Careful!*" He said, "Walls have ears."

My mother had to pack, but before she did, she presented us with little packages. "Open them, one for each of you."

She pushed the larger one in my direction. I unwrapped the yellow tissue paper to uncover an owl finger puppet. It was soft, and I could move its wings and rotate its head. I turned it in Katie's direction to see her unwrap an owlet, which she put under my wings.

I cried, "I really love you, Mom. I know I don't show it, but I do." I hiccoughed. "I'll make you proud, I promise."

Katie was hugging my mom and sobbing as well. My mom was on her second hankie. "I love you, my girls." She waved goodbye.

Chapter Fifty-four

Pajama Party

We were returning to campus after the departure of Doc and my mother. The weekend had left us intact but different, older, and yet, lighter in a way. The snow felt equally cleansing.

"Now remember what your father said." I shook my finger at Katie. "You'd better walk ten feet away from me."

"Doofus!" Katie replied. "I just want to hold onto you, your arm, your pinky. Ach."

"I hate this, but I think he's right. They could string us up just for being us." I frowned.

"Well, for being us, in public," Katie added.

"It's still us!" I shook my head. "Not fair."

"But hey, are you forgetting you're not expelled?"

"Yet," I said.

"And you won't have to have Craney's paws on you."

"Yuck!"

"And your mom didn't disown you."

"Thank God."

"Pina. C'mon. That took real guts to stand up to Craney. According to my father, you literally knocked her off her feet."

"Yeah, I guess, but I am relieved. I am so relieved, most by my mother's reaction. Not just relieved..." I started to choke back tears. "I mean she really loves me...she's okay with me. And I'm okay with me!"

"Yeah. She was super. And you, too." Katie beamed.

I dried my tears on my sleeve and went someplace in my head as I tried to single out the feel of one crystal of snow. The light glistened through it still, even now close to dusk.

Katie smiled her biggest smile at me. She also took advantage of my dreaminess to rub a soft, wet snowball in my face. "I couldn't resist. I wanted so badly to kiss you, I needed to cool things off."

"Witch! I'll get you."

We ran the last two blocks to Albert and spent the next ten minutes stomping off our boots and coats, as well as smearing each other with wet mittens.

Our rooms felt empty without Dorotea and Alda, and we wanted this weekend of reprieve to continue. Next week would entail new, final school projects to be completed by Thanksgiving.

"What do we have?" I asked Katie, showing her the chocolate chip cookies and salami from my mom.

"My father brought me Italian cookies and nougat from Italy. And we still have Dorotea's tea and landjaeger. Let's have a party and invite those girls who wished us good luck the other day."

"You think they'd come?" I asked.

"Of course! We're just too cool," said Katie.

"Uh oh, do you have more snowballs?" I pushed a pillow into Katie's midriff, and we wound up hugging each other for a long time. I pulled away softly and touched her cheek.

"You really are my best friend."

She covered my hand with hers and whispered,

"I know."

"So let's go start a party," I said.

Armed with our goodies, we were about to open Katie's door when Jocelyn and Emily and two other girls appeared, blocking the doorway. They seemed to be younger, thinner collegiate versions of Santa Claus in November, minus the beard and the red suit. Actually, two were attired in red sweaters, and they all carried bundles.

Jocelyn was the spokesman. "Hi," she said. "We need normal after a weekend of our mothers."

"I asked my mother for Wise potato chips, and what did I get? A year's supply of gourmet, imported British Oil Chips. You've got to help me eat them," Emily announced.

"Oh, is it okay? We kind of invited ourselves and some friends, Elizabeth Montgomery and Christa Van Buren." Jocelyn propelled each girl forward into Katie's room.

I poked Katie, who finally extended her hand and invited them in.

They all dropped their packages of chocolate and chips and cheese and fruit on the desks, complaining of their mothers' strange taste in snacks.

Christa started asking me about the visits Katie and I had received, as she poured us all some sparkling cider.

"Did both your mothers come?"

"Just mine. Katie lost her mom," I said.

"Oh God, I wish I hadn't found mine in the crowd on the golf course." Christa rolled her eyes.

"No," I said quietly. "Katie's mom disappeared."

"Oh...oh. I'm a total jerk. Where is she, Katie, I mean?"

My heart seemed to skip a beat as I watched my Katie talking and outshining the other girls. I pointed her out to Christa.

"Do you think she heard me? I really…I didn't mean to…God, I'm just like my mother." Christa said.

"You're fine. I take it your mom's…" I didn't know how to finish my sentence.

"A total jerk. Une veritable *snob*! Right, Jocelyn?"

"What, Christa? Oh, your mom? Not as bad as mine. You all have to hear this. My mom and I wound up getting a hot chocolate in the crummy cafe, you know, Eunice's. It's just that it was so cold, we couldn't wait to get to the Inn. My mother announced in a loud voice that they had only hand washed the cheap cups. I almost died." Jocelyn pretended to do a Victorian swoon.

"Katie, c'mere," I said. "This is Christa."

"Hi Christa," said Katie.

"Hi Katie. I'm really sorry about your mom. I uh…"

"It's okay, but thanks. You're in our science class, right?" said Katie.

"Yeah. Didn't you just love those esters?" Christa took a whiff of the imaginary smell in the air. "Oh right. I saw you two cut out half-way through the class that day."

"God, is everybody spying on us?" I asked before hearing how paranoid I sounded. I looked at Katie.

She sized up the situation quickly and announced in a loud voice, "Miss Craney should be awarded the 'Spook of the Year' award."

The crunching of chips and slurps of cider stopped. There was a collective outburst of "What?"

Katie explained, "Well, I think you know Craney's

been watching Pina."

Emily yelled, "Spying on is more like it."

"Right," Katie continued. "Well, they call spies 'spooks'."

"You have to admit," said Elizabeth, "she's also just plain spooky!"

"So," I told Christa. "I'm a bit weird when someone says they've been watching me."

Katie winked at me and whispered, "Nice recovery."

I answered, "Not bad, yourself."

We decided to hang Craney in effigy with a black sock stuffed and tied around the ankle. We added a monocle on it with white poster paint. Then the ceremony began. We bowed down in front of "Her Spookiness" and pulled imaginary spy cloaks over our faces as we passed by.

They grilled me on where I had hidden Dorotea and Alda and pretended to use a spyglass to search in my ears and up my sleeve. I hadn't laughed so hard in a long time.

Emily said she had seen my mother. I started to freeze.

"She reminded me of Eleanor Roosevelt," Emily said.

I gawked. "Really?"

"Yes. She seemed to smile right from the heart," Emily said.

"Not my mother," said Elizabeth. "She couldn't fake 'heart' if it meant her death by heart seizure."

Jocelyn winced and asked how my mother was reacting to my potential expulsion.

"Mrs. Mazzini may have single-handedly undone Craney," piped up Katie, winking at me. "And Pina made Craney's hair curl! We'll tell you all about it when there's more time."

"Craney is postponing her decision until January." I joked, "To see if I can produce Dorotea and Alda."

Christa laughed. "It'll give you time to dig up Dorotea and Alda from wherever it is you stashed them!"

We all pitched in to clean up. I noticed Emily doing a lot of teasing and dancing around the other girls, tickling and hanging on Jocelyn—*a lot*. Maybe she, too, was uh, that way?

I stayed with Katie a while after they left, both Katie and I grinning big, stupid grins and feeling normal.

"Wow!" Katie said. "We can be one of the girls. Or did you hate them, Pina?"

"No. They were neat."

"Sure? They're rich." Katie smirked.

"D'ya hear what they said about their mothers? They're not snobs just because their folks are," I said.

"Hmm." Katie pushed up her nose.

"Hey, Katie. It really felt good."

"What?" Katie was playing dumb on purpose.

"To be liked. Like they want to be friends," I said.

"Uh huh!" Katie grinned.

"You think Emily and Jocelyn are...?"

"Nah. Those girls just do that. It's just out of friendship," Katie said.

"Well, we're friends," I said.

"Duh."

"I mean could we grab each other's arm? No one's accusing them of being lesbos."

"Pina! Cool it. Time for bed. C'mon, we both

need a gigantic hug after this weekend."

After a long, long hug, I toddled off to my room. I fell into a deep sleep and dreamt of angels floating on a lake in Maine. Katie and I were small and fat, Italian-style Cherubim. My mother, more like a grown up Seraphim, was paddling a canoe over to us, and Doc was Michael the Archangel navigating the canoe. They lifted us up and sailed us over to an island filled with lots and lots of sweet girl angels eating gourmet potato communion wafers.

Chapter Fifty-five

First Day of Normal

A fresh carpet of snow paved the way between buildings. Everything seemed new. Everyone friendly and normal.

I didn't quite know what normal was, but it felt like it had started last night. Katie told me my eyes were seeing differently.

I had lingered over breakfast where another four girls joined Jocelyn, Emily, Christa, and Elizabeth at our table.

Word about the standoff between our parents and Craney had spread. We had earned a reputation for being cool. Because of our parents? Because we hanged Craney in effigy?

What about the details? Did they have a clue why Craney wanted me? I corrected my thoughts—why she wanted to throw me out? No one treated me like a leper. Well, I wasn't a leper, just a lesbo or a les-bi-an?

I shook myself back to Albert and the patch of ice that had almost caused my downfall. I was approaching my French class. *Sacre bleu!* I forgot that Mademoiselle Lesage was gone, but I knew we were going to get our mid-term projects today.

I pondered the Eiffel Tower and Mont Saint-Michel when I heard Craney's familiar hoarse cackle. Every muscle, every ligament, every joint refused to operate my body.

She stood in the doorway, staring at me, saying, *"Entrez, s'il vous plait."*

I squeezed my eyes tight. Just practice mind over matter, I told myself. I managed to move forward with a jaunty thrust to my chin. I nodded my head and moved to the desk closest to the door.

Craney smiled. "Mademoiselle Mazzini, bon jour."

My lips formed, "Bon jour, Maitresse."

With that, the Maitresse turned to the class and explained in passable French that she would assign projects. She sighed, and in faltering French mumbled something about Mademoiselle Lesage's family feeling better so that she would be returning. The class gave up a booming, "Bravo!"

Miss Craney was actually ignoring me. I wondered if I had already spent two months at Albert. Maybe I was in a time warp. Had anything really preceded these moments here and now? Nothing, absolutely nothing rang false here. This was not the same Albert I had been experiencing up until now.

I almost sighed to myself. I felt my muscles and my skin loosen and stretch out in relaxed elongation, a kind of Dali-like smear. This was new.

Miss Craney was calling girls by name and giving them packets with instructions for their projects. I heard her poor pronunciation of Gare Saint-Lazare, Tour Eiffel, and Montmartre, followed by *oui* and *merci.*

I waited for my name. Would I receive *enfer,* hell, or were my days in hell truly over? As other girls filed out of the class, I sat among the last few left.

In fact, I was the last. I held my breath. Surely, this

was where Craney planned to get me. I sat within three feet of the door; it remained open. I would scream. I would push her down and cut and run!

"Mademoiselle Mazzini," said Craney. She extended her bony arm covered in ecru silk and thrust the manila envelope at me. "*Les Catacombes, Les Catacombes de Paris.*"

The catacombs. Was there really such a place in Paris? Weird. At least it wasn't hell. Underground, but not hell.

I realized I had been standing still, holding the packet. Craney's cough drew me from my stupor. I was free to go. She smiled a normal smile as I left.

Katie was coming from the opposite direction. As our paths crossed, I grabbed her by the arm best friend style and asked her to sit with me for a few seconds before our next class. I waved the catacomb packet at her.

"What's that?" she asked.

"My French project. I just want you here while I open it. Might be weird."

Katie squinted at the lettering on the front. "Catacombes?"

"Yup," I said, tearing the packet apart. Names, dates, and the letters RIP on small slips of paper flew out, scattering at our feet.

"Graves?" asked Katie. "I thought the catacombs were in Rome?"

"Guess there are catacombs all over. Shoot. Help me pick these up."

"The corpses?" Katie laughed.

We sat with all the dead people on our laps while girls walked by laughing and jostling each other. Somehow, I felt we owed the dead some solemnity.

Katie poked me. "C'mon. What do you have to do? Read that sheet."

"I have to make a model based on these photos and descriptions. Yuck! Look at all the bones. And write a history of how they came to rest here under Paris. Wait. Oh jeez. I have to record a walking tour from the perspective of one of the dead." I continued to read.

"No?" Katie had grabbed the instructions and read the names of the other cemeteries where the bones had come from.

"Oh man. I don't believe it. There are bones here from the French Revolution." I slipped everything in my binder.

"Fun," said Katie, giving me a sisterly pat on the arm.

"I hate to say this," I started.

"Then don't," Katie added.

We both burst out, "Craney?"

The weird thing was that we were laughing, doubling over laughing our fool heads off.

"I can do this; I mean it."

"I want to make the bones," said Katie.

"Let's throw a bone-making mãché party!"

"What a gas!" Katie said. "Hey, gotta split."

"Hey, hey. Too cool, huh? See ya."

Chapter Fifty-six

The Postman Always Rings Twice

My classes went by quickly, and I loved the projects my instructors had assigned. In English, I chose to write a fairy tale about Albert, and in science, to create my version of Canoe cologne. In history, I would write an abridged history of the year I was born, and in math, I would construct a scale model of the Albert's Memorial Gate. Best of all, girls wanted to partner up with me.

It was a neat day, as if I were breaking in new hiking boots and they felt right from the start. No blisters, no chaff.

I almost didn't want to read the newspaper or watch the news. I was afraid the other boot would fall.

There was a letter in my glass-windowed brass mailbox. I was so nervous about its origin and its message, I forgot my combination. I asked the student volunteer behind the counter to give it to me.

"Hey Pina, it's from your mom," said the girl named Harriet. "Nice handwriting."

I didn't even think she knew my name.

"Thanks," I said.

Hmm. My mother. This could be the kiss of death. I debated whether to wait until I saw Katie to read it.

I really was chicken. How could I believe my mother would take things so calmly? This day didn't feel like all the ones that came before. My mother's behavior over the weekend belonged to a different mother, not the mother I knew.

Maybe she thought I was a changeling too. Maybe she was saying, "Change, change back."

I really was the same person I had always been. I just hadn't had a clue who or what I was. Neither did my mother. But she also didn't know I worried about Civil Rights, Jews, and poverty, and that I thought our family's daily conversation about the price of tea in China was obnoxious.

Imagining this typical Mazzini table talk, I thought I'd barf. In my anger, I had ripped apart the envelope. I watched the special art postage stamp float to the ground.

"Dear Honey" popped out at me. I figured I better sit down for the rest. My mother had a unique way of starting out with terms of endearment only to guillotine me with gnashing words a sentence or two later.

Settled on the bench in the campus post office, I covered myself with my stadium coat and unfolded the thin blue sheets.

"I was so sad to leave on Monday." I was about to crumple the letter when I spotted the words, *so proud.* That gave me the courage to fold up the entire letter and get my coat on to return to the dorm. This letter merited a more intimate setting.

Despite the ice, I hurried back to my room. This letter held promise. I wanted to be as authentic as I could when I read my mother's words "from the heart." What was it Emily had said? Oh yeah, that my mother smiled right from the heart.

I flopped onto my bed and read:

"I was so happy to be a part of your life this past weekend. You let me into your world there at Albert, your world with Katie.

"I am so proud of you and how you weren't disrespectful to that awful woman, Miss Craney. She should be ashamed of herself. Your father and I gave you good values—I could certainly see that—and so did Dr. McGuilvry, by the way.

"You are absolutely correct, though. Honey, I didn't want this life for you. It will make things harder for you. There will be people who reject you. But I wish you love, richness, and beauty, and I think you have that.

"Some mothers on the bus had noticed you. They admired how you took me to the bus, how you took care of me. Their daughters hadn't.

"Dr. McGuilvry is also quite taken with you. He is such a charming man. No wonder Katie is so lovely. He's already called me to tell me he's working on things.

"Daddy sends his love. I was chatting with him about Aunt Athena. I told him I thought you had inherited a lot of Mazzini genes. He laughed, saying that of course you had his mother's and his grandmother's disposition and gifts. But then, he lifted his silly eyebrows and asked if I knew anything about Aunt Athena, any new news.

"I told him I wondered if you and she were alike. He chuckled and said you were his buddy. 'Like Athena when she was young?' I asked. You know, your father is fifteen years older than she, so he taught her sports and protected her when kids picked on her and called her a tomboy.

"Your father actually phoned her. I didn't hear what he said, but he passed the phone to me. Athena was full of life and so excited that you're doing well (except for Miss Craney, but I'm saying novenas, don't you worry). She would love to visit you and in the meantime, invited you and Katie to her bungalow in Carmel, New York. You'd have to take a bus and change in Danbury, Connecticut. Now, if you do go, make sure to help out.

"She intends to write but sends her love for now. She wants you to know she has never hidden who she is and has earned a comfortable living and the respect of her peers. She envies you, she said, since she has not had a special person in her life for a while.

"So, honey, I just wanted to tell you how proud you make us. Whatever Dr. McGuilvry can work out is fine. If he can't, we will manage quite well. Athena will help and you know Katie will always be in our lives.

"Thank you sweetheart for letting me in.

"I love you, Mommy"

I could hardly read the last lines as my tears were pouring down. The blue-black ink had washed to turquoise; I had to find a blotter to damn up the waterworks.

Katie entered my room to see me bleary-eyed, hair matted, racing to rip out a blotter from my desk drawer.

"What happened?" she asked, running over to me.

I hugged her and smiled through the tears. "You've got to read this. It's poetry!"

Katie sat in silence, reading and sobbing. She placed her hand on my arm and patted the spot next to her on the bed.

"We're so lucky. We really are," she said.

We held hands in silence. No more words were necessary.

Chapter Fifty-seven

Normal is as Normal Does

As we moved closer to Thanksgiving, things at Albert became more and more routine or, as I was learning, normal. The normal ice and sleet of mid-November was upon us. Normal class lectures and partnering up on projects took place. Normal girls shared normal treats sent in normal care packages from normal homes.

Katie and I were in her room working on some papier-mâché bones for my French catacomb project, trying not to slop too much on the floor. An occasional splash and plop were the only sounds; we weren't talkative, and the snow outdoors created a soundproofed vacuum in the room.

We heard a slight tapping and checked the window to see if a bird had gotten stuck on the icy sill. Katie wiped her hands and went to the door.

I turned around to see a much thinner Dorotea, her hands held together in a prayer-like gesture. The crystals of ice pinging against the windowpane barely broke the silence.

Dorotea put her index finger to her mouth and entered one slow step after the other. We helped her with her coat and took her bag. Finally, the numbness wore off, and we three embraced in silent tears.

Dorotea led us over to the bed. We could barely hear her say, "I am so sorry. I was *ganz verrucht,* truly crazy, *deprimiert.*"

"Shush," said Katie, wiping Dorotea's tears.

"Are you all right?" I said out loud, but my head was noisy with questions about where she had come from, who knew she was here, was she safe?

"*Nein.* I know I am not good with you, Pina. Can you forgive me, ever?" She burst into tears again, pounding her fist, muttering, *"Dummkopf!* I was so green with envy, so..."

"Jealous?" Katie said.

"*Javohl!* I was no good, nowhere. No one had time for me. All the girls think I am Brunhilde. I just wished to die."

"The pills?" asked Katie. "All those pills you used to sneak into your music box?"

"*Ach!*" Dorotea just sobbed.

I leaned over and put my arms around her shoulders. The sight of her blotchy, puffy face, tear-stained and drawn, upset me more than I thought.

"I do forgive you. Don't cry," I said, feeling totally dumb and useless. "Dorotea, how can we help?"

"I must to explain. Craney...she made me...tell her things about you."

"It's okay," I said. "We know she's crazy."

"I thought I must to go away—she will hurt Pina, but...she made me believe you, Pina, wished to harm me. I could not think what to do. So I run and run."

"Where?" Katie asked. "You were supposed to go to your aunt's."

"I know Alda played joke about my aunt's. I had fear of her too and her father's friend. I run away, take car ride with guy. I try to take too many pills; I go to hospital, but my aunt, she knew."

"Oh shoot, Dorotea, I am so sorry," I said as the

lines of the room started to blur, and I felt like I was being funneled deep into my eyes and the center of my brain. I realized Craney had lied about the whole thing.

I heard Dorotea as if through a glass held against a wall. *"Nein.* I—how you say—spill beans on you out to Craney." Then, she told us that she had nightmares where Craney was Dr. Faustus lusting after our souls. She dreamt that Craney tortured me into selling our souls to her.

I was almost in tears when Dorotea said she could not bear to live with herself and had to die.

Both Katie and I put our arms around her. We sat like that in silence for a good while. I still had so many questions, but they could wait. The important thing was Dorotea. How could I help her? How to take away all that hate? The hate she turned on herself?

"Dorotea, listen, 'D,' can we call you 'D?' You're good, warm, and friendly. You share your food with us. We locked you out. We were not friendly." I was desperate to help her feel wanted.

"Ah ja. You call me 'D.' I like that, a nigname."

"Nickname," Katie said, stifling a giggle.

"Did Alda's father hurt you?" I dared.

"No. His men had a fight. Some man, big, hairy, ugly had a gun. He point the gun at me. Alda's father say, 'Get her fuck out.' I think he mean to have sex with me."

"Oh lord," I said. "No, D, no one was supposed to see those bad men, but no one was going to rape you."

"Alda was always so sexy, I think everyone have sex on mind," confessed Dorotea.

"And us?" asked Katie.

"No, you two don't want to have anything to do with me."

"Huh?" I said. "But you told Craney I was a lesbian."

"Ja. She tell me to write that note. I just say you are being a 'boytom.'"

"Tomboy, D." I laughed. "D, I'm not laughing at you; it just sounds funny when someone turns the words around."

Katie got a twinkle in her eye. "D, we are really so glad you're back. You think you still have some Schnapps?"

"*Naturlich!*" Dorotea submerged herself amidst lederhosen and dirndls in her closet and emerged with a bottle of kirsch.

We toasted Dorotea's return and helped her prepare her story for Craney, whom she hadn't contacted yet.

"You tell Craney you were in the hospital. No boyfriend, nothing else. You will call your mother in Germany now and tell her to say she was so upset with you in the hospital, she forgot to call school. Ja?"

I dictated Dorotea's plan of action. We couldn't yet let on to Craney that we knew she had lied, claiming Dorotea's aunt didn't know where Dorotea was.

Dorotea asked what Craney had done with my soul. I gave her the short version so she wouldn't feel so bad. Besides a new bout of convulsive sobbing, Dorotea's response was, "But she, Craney, she is sick in the head, yes?"

"Yes, Katie's father and his friend, Joe, might be able to prove that." I crossed my fingers.

"*Gott sei dank!*" Dorotea made the sign of the cross.

"Right," I said. "Listen, D, I really feel bad that we left you out. I've been so afraid that kids would reject me. I know how it feels to be different. Sorry I hurt you."

Dorotea gave me a big, slurpy kiss on the cheek. She poured us all another kirsch and hugged Katie within an inch of her life.

"We will be friends, yes? Yes!" said Dorotea.

I felt toasty warm with the kirsch and Dorotea's joy at being accepted. I was trying hard not to be angry with myself for having been so mean to her.

As if she could read my thoughts, Dorotea approached me and shook me by the shoulder.

"You know, I did act like an *arschloch*."

Katie frowned. I mouthed, "Asshole."

We all laughed as Katie repeated *"arschloch"* with a terrible accent.

Dorotea laughed and laughed. "I go see the monster Craney tomorrow about the hospital. Then, I say I do not know nothing about Pina. I was jealous. *Das war alles!*"

"Yeah!" I said.

⁂

"Phew," I said to Katie as she walked me back to my room with the papier-mãché.

"Yeah," Katie agreed. "That solves one problem."

"Kat…she tried to commit suicide? I feel so bad."

After five minutes of silence, both of us staring at papier-mãché bones for the catacombs project, Katie said, "I am glad she's back."

And so, things continued to go back to normal. We wouldn't even hold our breath while Dorotea went to see Craney.

The next morning, Katie and I escorted Dorotea to breakfast and introduced her to Jocelyn, Emily, Elizabeth, and Christa. Her foreign mannerisms and accent must have refined themselves overnight for the gang to appreciate! The girls actually oohed and aahed over Dorotea's fictitious story of her two-week Oktoberfest adventure back in Germany.

We all played with a *schneefrau,* our German snowlady on our way to French class. I explained Mademoiselle's equally mysterious disappearance to Dorotea and reassured her she would return shortly.

Miss Craney spotted Dorotea immediately. Her face froze, followed by a thaw in my direction and a feeble smile. She then proceeded to Dorotea's desk and snapped *"Suivez-moi!"* Craney all but yanked her from her desk.

I showed Dorotea my crossed fingers. I marveled at my calm, and even refrained from listening at the door.

Dorotea returned at the very end of the class bearing a manila envelope with her final French project. Dorotea had to construct Les Egouts de Paris out of papier-mãché. By assigning us these particular Parisian attractions, Craney had relegated both Dorotea and myself to the netherworld, me to the catacombs, Dorotea to the sewers.

At lunch, Dorotea told me she tore up the note reading, "Pina is a lez be friends" during the meeting where Craney confirmed the hospital story. Dorotea raved about how welcoming Katie and I had been. Dorotea said, "I almost spit up when Craney said that she was glad you, Pina, and Katie and I were on the same foot!"

"Getting off on the right foot, dear D." I giggled back at her.

Dorotea put her finger to her temple. A broad smile tiptoed across her face. She lowered her voice, leaning into Katie and me.

"We get back at Fraulein Craney, yes?" Dorotea said.

"You mean get even?" I asked.

"*Javohl!*" Dorotea rubbed her hands together.

Katie jumped right in, "I can get some of the other girls to help too."

"Hmm. What if we found Craney's diary or letters to Miss Whitfield?" I said. I started to lick my chops and mused, "We could break in—"

"You wish," said Katie.

"No, Katie. I can do this. Wait! I absolutely have to do this. I will break into her office if it's the last thing I do. I'll prove Craney's evil." I emphasized my words by pretending to wring Craney's neck.

"It may just be the last thing you do but not alone, you won't," Katie said.

"*Ja, gut.* I know where secret files are. Craney had my letter there. *Und der schlussel*, yes, I know where it is too."

"The key?" I was ecstatic. "Okay, I'm going to do this." I was already on my feet.

Katie already seemed to be setting alarms and schedules in her head. She kept checking her watch.

"Psst!" Katie called over to Christa, Jocelyn, Elizabeth, and Emily at the other end of the table. She pulled them aside.

"Sitz." Dorotea pulled me back to my seat. "Tonight," she whispered.

"Yeah! First, we make sure Craney stays out of her office." Then, I called down to Katie, "Katie, can you and the gang stage a distraction to get Craney out of her office?"

By the looks of it, Katie had the plan worked out: the girls would stage a snowball fight outside Craney's office. Craney would come out, and they would graciously invite her to join in the fun, followed by hot chocolate and baked goodies from Jocelyn's mom in the dorm. Katie was beaming. "That will give us a full hour for the heist," she said.

Dorotea clapped her hands and giggled. "*Gute, gute, gute*! And you know where she keeps the key, Pina? In her Modess box!"

"Yuck!" I said. "With her sanitary napkins?"

Dorotea set the time for seven and made all of us synchronize our watches.

I knew this was crazy, but I really had to dig deep and find that one thing that would really clear us all and teach Craney not to mess with me or anyone else!

"Katie," I wiped all kidding from my face and voice, "I will get the goods on Craney and help write that article with Joe one way or another!"

"Okay, Pina…You did say you wanted to go out in a blaze of glory." Katie laughed, but I knew she took me seriously.

꙳ ꙳ ꙳ ꙳

At seven, we separated into two groups. The snowballers stationed themselves in the unplowed area outside Craney's windows. They started taking aim at the shutters nearest to the window with the light.

Katie, Dorotea, and I waited until they had

lobbed a few close to the pane, and we saw Craney exit the building, bundled against the weather.

We heard the gang deflect Craney's attempts at scolding with giggling and flattery. They danced around her, saying they had seen her play tennis and were very impressed with her muscular forehand. When Craney actually bent down to make a snowball, we snuck into the building.

Dorotea pulled a special German hairpin from her braids and opened Craney's door. She immediately went for the Modess box and shook out the key to the files.

"Now, I will show you the underground files," she said. With one swift stroke, she moved Craney's massive chair and flipped up the rug from underneath. Bits of Craney's dried skin and fingernails flicked to the floor. There was the trapdoor with the secret files.

"I'll take the file marked staff," said Katie.

I grabbed the 1954 box. Dorotea used the key to open the files and started to tackle the poetry file.

Katie got the first hit. "Miss Whitfield's reviews are stellar. Miss Craney commented, 'Miss Whitfield's enthusiasm for her subject is contagious. If I were a student, I would take every one of her classes.'"

"I bet," I said.

Dorotea found Shakespearean sonnets and poems by Lovelace and Suckling addressed to *E. W.* But not pay dirt.

I checked my watch. Only fifteen minutes left. Then, bingo! I found gold. A letter.

"Hey guys, listen!" I said, starting to read the letter:

"My dearest Emily,
I lie here alone, pining for you. You have not come

to me. Last night when you pushed me out of your room, I feared your cries would alert others. You force me to take desperate measures. You will come to me tomorrow or I will see to it that you leave my sight for good.

MMCraney"

"Oh wow!" I said. "There's something attached to the back of this: a letter from Craney firing Ms. Whitfield for 'reckless endangerment of a minor' and 'moral depravity.'"

Katie and Dorotea let out a discreet cheer.

"Nice work, team. Grab those papers, stuff your bras with them, and let's split." My face was one big smile.

Dorotea locked up. We slithered noiselessly, stuffed bras notwithstanding, along the walls to the exit and then up the back stairs to our dorm.

We could hear the hot chocolate party at the other end of the hall. In a few minutes, we would have our own version, a tea and schnapps party, in Katie's and Dorotea's room.

And tomorrow, I would decide how to get these papers to Joe Gallo.

Chapter Fifty-eight

Vin Santo

I was up early. I made sure to stash the papers away in my box of Tampax, but I hadn't yet figured out how to get them to Joe.

Lunch was normal for the second day in a row, only now we had another member, Dorotea, in our gang. Conversation was dumb, mostly about the lumpy Shepherd's Pie, and Dr. Eisenberg's awful dress and her nylons—they contained two runs apiece. And an occasional cryptic reference to last night's fun.

Katie leaned over closer to me, pretending to tie her shoelace. She grazed my elbow and whispered, "You okay?"

I bent down to get my napkin and answered, "I really do want to stay at Albert."

The softness of her eyes offered me the caress her hands couldn't. "I know," she said.

We had been joking for a while when the girls' abrupt silence made me turn around. Joe Gallo was standing behind Katie and me.

Joe looked as young mand as cute as any of the guys on American Bandstand. He was just waiting to surprise us, quietly standing there, wearing bucks, a green heather Shetland, and lush tan cords. To top it off, he had a crewcut!

After freeing himself from our hugs, he

introduced himself as Katie's dad's close friend. Katie said, "He's really like a dad to me. Like Pina's mom is. A mom, I mean." Katie still didn't know exactly what to say about Joe.

The girls gave somewhat tentative smiles. I saw one girl whisper. The answer came in hushed tones, "No, her dad's alive."

When Dorotea introduced herself, Joe burst out in a broad grin. "*Gott sei dank!*"

We didn't know the German God was so popular, but lots of us were thanking him these days.

Dorotea asked, "You are so happy to make my acquaint, why?"

Joe winked. "You're not missing. You are a sight for sore eyes."

Dorotea winced. "I make your eyes hurt?"

Katie leaned over and tugged on Dorotea's jacket. "No, he's glad to see you, just like us!"

Joe asked us before I could ask him. We needed to speak in private. We sat at a distant table. Katie was squirming a bit. I think she was afraid to say we broke into Craney's office. I figured Joe, as an investigative journalist, might not be too angry.

"Joe," I said. I looked around before producing the manila bundle from my satchel.

"What's this?" he asked.

"Please! Not here, don't open it here," I said.

My face was hot. Katie looked uneasy. Joe narrowed his gaze at me.

"I can't just let you do all the work," I looked at Joe. "This whole problem was my doing; I had to help undo it." I whispered, "Here's the dirt on Craney and Whitfield."

"You didn't?" Joe grinned. "The journal you gave

to Doc was already big stuff. This will put the article over the top!"

It was clear Joe knew I had stolen the contents of the folder. His eyes darted from me to the bundle. He gave a soft chuckle and clapped me on the back. Then, he made me promise no further inside jobs, and explained the main purpose of his visit today.

"I want to rattle Miss Craney's cage. I thought I'd ask her in person for a spot on her calendar since she hasn't returned my phone calls. In the meantime, I want to take in the atmosphere for the article I'm writing. "

"Up-turned noses?" Katie asked.

"Actually, your friends there didn't seem all that affected. Hey you." Joe poked me. "You're awfully quiet for an investigative reporter."

"Will it work, Joe? Will it get Craney off our backs forever?" I chewed on my lip.

"That's what I'm trusting our story, *yours* and mine, will do. Right now, this is step one, 'rattle the cage.' After I meet with Miss Craney, I'll let you know about steps two and three. Mind you, your information will put the icing on the cake."

"Hot dog!" I said.

"This about the Whitfield scandal or…?" asked Katie.

"Well, it will only be a bigger scandal if Craney resists the efforts of my pen," said Joe.

"Right. The one that's mightier than the sword," I said.

"Heck," said Joe. "I might even rattle some sabers, whatever it takes."

Joe chucked me under the chin and smiled his gorgeous smile.

"Craney won't be able to resist his charm," I said to Katie.

"Hope she falls for it—hard!" smirked Katie.

"Ladies, I'll catch you later. I've got a message and a package for you. Hope I also have some good news. Come give Uncle Joe a hug."

While his good looks and manners might charm Craney, his writing would cause her to straighten up and fly right. He had exposed corruption and payola in various institutions.

I realized with a huge grin that Joe had said *"our"* story!

He wasn't going to discuss the Emily Whitfield story with Craney today, but the mere mention of scheduling a time for it would cause Craney great grief. According to our new friends, not many people had resisted her advances, and the few who did suffered the brutal consequences. Mine might still await me like the hangman's lonely noose.

We saw Joe stop halfway through the loggia. His smile would light up even the shadiest nooks and their denizens. The light accentuated, in particular, the paleness of Craney lurking about. Not only did she appear ashen, but also her face blanched a lighter shade of gray when she saw Joe.

We saw Joe shake her hand and take out his appointment book. Craney's hand flew to her forehead as if in doubt that her weeks contained seven days. Her index finger switched positions from her mouth to her forehead. She grimaced and shook her head. The potential interview seemed ill fated.

Joe smiled and shrugged. Craney left in such haste, she forgot her briefcase. Papers flew out of her hand, some hovering mid-air. They seemed the tail of

Craney's kite-like flight down the loggia.

Joe joined us again in the refectory. All smiles. "She's flustered all right. Just wait until the articles come out."

"Have you found Miss Whitfield?" asked Katie, jumping up and down.

"Just a few more T's to cross and I's to dot." Joe formed those letters in the air with his finger.

"Oh, wait!" Joe stopped his spelling and started to dig around in his briefcase. He removed an overwrapped brown package.

"Quick, put it in your satchel, Katie. It's a gift from my father, Fifi. He also sends kisses, the real kind, and the chocolate ones too." Joe produced another package, clearly the typical blue and silver packaging of Ferrara chocolate kisses with fortunes inside their wrappers.

"Fifi's working on locating the other folks, your Alda Baciadalupo. Seems they move around a lot." Joe's cough suggested things it wasn't safe to say.

"Oh. I miss them," I said.

"Send kisses—real ones—back," said Katie.

"The first package," said Joe. "Is contraband."

"Yeah." I giggled.

"Fifi knows how much you like it. Seems you two and a certain Italian friend had quite a liking for biscotti and Vin Santo. *E vero*?"

"Wha?" I squinted at Joe. "What are you really saying?"

"Nothing. It's my father. He said he had a very dear friend whose daughter always used to ask for a sip."

"Uh oh!" Katie's eyes darted around. I could see she was trying to read between Joe's lines.

"My father added that it would be a shame if you could never share it again."

"Joe, c'mon," I said.

"Top secret." Joe put his finger to his mouth and winked.

"Don't joke if it's Alda…" I started to say.

"Shush. Do not say it!" Joe's taut face indicated his sudden seriousness. "But, if you want, you could write a note to my dad with an enclosure for his long-lost friend's daughter."

Katie took one look at me and suggested she and Joe go for a walk. I was on the verge of tears. I wasn't quite sure why, but I needed some time to think and to write a letter.

I had two hours until science. Enough time for what? All I knew was that Alda was alive and okay. And for that, I was grateful. Where or how was irrelevant.

I remembered Alda saying, "My father's friend in Maine." I had thought of Fifi, who wanted the Feds to relocate him to rural Maine, but I figured it was just a stretch of my imagination. Maybe the Feds had relocated all of them together. Maybe I wasn't really stretching.

How could I have accused Alda of making Dorotea disappear? Of trying to mastermind a Mafia execution of Craney? I did actually claim she had no morals.

Shoot. What kind of friend was I? I could almost hear her say, "You and Katie are the closest things I've had to friends."

She would have done anything to make us happy. She-it!

I knew what I had to do.

❧❧❧❧

"Dear Fifi!
Baci, baci, baci! *Grazie*! We love you.
Pina and Katie
PS If you know a girl named Alda, please give this letter to her.

My other letter started:
"Alda, *ciccia*!
"We miss you. I miss you, and I am soooo sorry. I was always blaming you like some amoral mafiosa toots. Just didn't know what to believe, but I know I hurt you. Forgive me, huh?

"I have so much to tell you, but I'll wait until I see you. I will, won't I? Maybe I won't be expelled. Maybe you'll be back just like Dorotea came back. And I feel bad about her too. I was such a turd.

"Your friend, Pina

"PS I really, really want to stay here at Albert. Would you ever come back?"

I finished my letter, a torrent of tears cascading down my face. I could almost hear the plop plop as they hit the desk. I was happy; I had Katie, I had friends, I had fun. I had to stay at Albert. I just had to.

Chapter Fifty-nine

All the News That's Fit to Print

Katie, Dorotea, and I busied ourselves with our final projects, all due before Thanksgiving break. We made papier-mâché bones for my French catacombs, as well as turdlets for Dorotea's French sewer project. We also made merry with our newfound friends. Our sterling reputation as outlaws and our supply of schnapps helped. We were careful to hide the latter.

My hands would graze Katie's occasionally, and our eyes would linger on each other a bit too long. Yet, it felt as if we'd taken a vow of chastity, in addition to our unspoken vow of silence. We didn't talk about "it" or anything much, for that matter. Perhaps we were holding our breath until Thanksgiving break. (Doc and Joe had invited my family to their home outside of Boston for the Thanksgiving weekend.) Maybe we sensed we were living on borrowed time until we had the final word from Craney.

I was thrilled my parents had agreed to the invitation. My father, who normally would have had a conniption at the thought of winter driving to a stranger's house for the holiday—he knew Doc and Joe and even liked the boys—apparently jumped at the opportunity to see Boston. Thrilled, yes, but I still had to talk to my father face to face about my problem.

Another reason to hold my breath.

In the midst of all the breath-holding, Katie seemed like "Little Mary Sunshine." She hummed on her way to class and whistled while doing reports. When she did touch me, it was often to pinch me on the cheek, urging me to look on the bright side. Once when she actually came all the way into my room, she held me by the shoulders and looked me in the eyes to say, "It *will* work out."

Even Dorotea was nifty. Her English was improving. We were "in step" together not "stepping out" or "stepping it up," and "what's up?" didn't mean the sky. She was delighted to be our friend and invited by Katie's dad to spend Thanksgiving with us.

Dorotea saw me pouting one day as I left the room she and Katie shared. She followed me on tiptoes back to my room. I was just about to slam the door when she gently touched my hand to stop me.

"May I?" she said.

I grumbled, "Yeah."

She led me to the edge of my bed and sat me down, still holding my hand. "*Warum?*" she said.

"Why what, D?" I was not in the mood.

"You are sad about Katie." She lowered her head to catch my eye. Her gaze went deep and tender. "Pina, Pina, you are such a *dummmkopf*! Sorry, but it is true."

I pulled away and snapped back, "*Ruhig!*"

"No. I will not shut up!" Dorotea stood staring back down at me. "Yes, you, dummy, she loves you! So you shut up!"

"Huh?" My voice had all but disappeared.

"I hear Katie's dreams in the middle of the night. Always, 'Pina this, Pina that.' Or 'No! Don't leave!' Dummy, you, Pina. She is so afraid you will leave."

My tears told the rest of the story. I was scared too. Dorotea hugged me and used the sweetest German terms of endearment. I was "*liebling* Pina" and "*schaetzle*." I felt truly comforted by her. Of course, a glass of Eierlikor enhanced Dorotea's soothing. She knew I had a weakness for German eggnog.

A week had passed since Joe's surprise visit. I didn't expect miracles, but I was beginning to doubt even he could produce the holy grail of articles exposing Craney. In the meantime, my mother had called. She was quite the doll-like Chatty Cathy, oohing and aahing, asking about Thanksgiving less than two weeks away.

"I'm dying to see Dr. McGuilvry's home," she said.

"I've seen pictures," I said. "It's old, straight out of my history book."

"Did his friend Joe help decorate? I bet he's got some taste." She was almost smacking her lips.

After her questions about the decorating skills of two homosexual men, my mother switched the topic to my Aunt Athena. She would send brochures about Barnard Prep in New York if I were interested. Since she was a notable Barnard College alumna, Athena said I would be a shoe-in. I agreed to check my mailbox frequently and hurried my mother off the phone.

Our almost daily jaunts to Albert's postal room to claim care packages had been eliminated due to ice and below freezing temperatures. This morning, however, Katie found a phone message from Doc that Jocelyn had taken late the night before. He wanted Katie to know a special pre-Thanksgiving gift was on its way.

Bundled beyond recognition against the near zero temperature, Katie and I actually walked side by side, almost touching, to retrieve our mail. Through layers of wool and cotton I said, "I miss this closeness. I miss you."

"What?" Katie attempted to slide her earmuff off.

"I miss you, dammit," I said.

"Dammit?"

I ripped the scarf away from my mouth. "I mean, do I have the plague?"

"Oh, Pina…" Katie squeezed her eyes shut. "Don't make me cry. My eyes will freeze." She laughed, but her chest rising through the padding said she was crying inside. "I am so scared. Scared of losing you. Scared of hurt."

I stole staccato glances. I pulled her scarf down and kissed her lips. One brief, chaste kiss. "Don't cry. Don't cry," I pleaded. "I can't cry anymore, and you're right. Our eyes will freeze shut. C'mon."

I pulled her along. Again, our voices were muffled. "I do love you," Katie said.

When we arrived at the school post office, we had to push our way in. Apparently, everyone was expecting packages. Once inside, we saw that no one was paying attention to the glass plated brass mailboxes. Katie pulled herself up to her full five foot, six inches to peer over the swarm of girls buzzing in the corner. Individuals squirmed to inch closer to the bulletin board that usually announced class cancellations, concerts, and earth-shattering news from world papers or The Albert Buzz, our school rag.

"Bravos" were rising from the masses along with giggles and ill-quoted lines of poetry.

The rest of the words were blotted out by the

humming of the chain of Albert girls flowing out of the office like an exuberant river, streaming down the hall out into the Circle. Through the window, we saw the single-file march round into an unbroken circle. We saw mouths open in an inaudible cheer followed by an eruption of books thrown up in unison.

Katie and I rushed over to the bulletin board and saw what someone had typed and posted unofficially; it lacked the official seal of Head Mistress Craney's office.

Typed in bold lettering on cream-colored vellum, the crispness of the announcement stood out dead center against the bland, pit-marked cork of the empty bulletin board. Its title in capital letters read,

"*Miss Emily Whitefield Outstanding Teacher of the Year.*"

Katie and I jumped up and down, slapping each other playfully.

"Joe did it. You two really did it."

Katie read the announcement that must have been mailed to parents.

"In an unprecedented gesture, members of the Advisory Board and the Board of Directors of the Albert Academy have chosen to acknowledge former instructor Miss Emily Whitfield's outstanding service and rousing inspiration to the young women of the Albert Community. The Board owes a debt of gratitude to the Albert girls who scoured the archives of Albert as well as the faculty rosters of various institutions to reveal the whereabouts of this mysterious and dedicated *artiste*. Mysterious both for her curious withdrawal from public life and for the depths from which she draws her inspiration. Miss Whitfield has written a novel and a history dedicated to the Academy, her former students, and the Village."

"Katie, just give me the gist. I need a break."

"Oh God, Pina, They're putting on a reception for her on December tenth and comparing it to the television program "This is Your Life." Oh, you've got to hear this:

"The Albert Board will ask Miss Whitfield to speak at its gifted lecturer series early in the New Year."

"But, no mention of how Craney seduced and defiled her and ran her out of town? Funny how that's missing." Katie smirked.

Chapter Sixty

The Real News

Holy crow!" I whispered to Katie, who had her hand plastered to her forehead.

"My father and Joe did it; they tracked her down!" Katie sported the biggest grin I've ever seen. "Let's go join the celebration," she guffawed.

"Wait, Katie. They're celebrating Emily Whitfield, right? The announcement doesn't say Craney's goose is cooked. Maybe that's not what their march is all about." I shivered with a new worry.

"Does it matter, Pin?"

"I gotta think. Open your mailbox to get your father's package in the meantime. Check mine too."

I slumped against the wall as a new group of girls read the announcement. I wasn't convinced that I was out of the frying pan. Craney might have me burn in the fires of hell just out of revenge.

Katie clacked her mailbox shut and thrust a newspaper article at me. "Scandal among American Elite, Gifted Teacher Removed," from the newspaper *The Guardian. This* was the gift her father promised!

"Pina, look!"

I stared at the newspaper in a state of shock. Numb. Was this real?

Katie shook the newspaper in my face, saying, "Don't you get it?"

"Okay, got it," I mumbled. "What if Craney wants revenge?"

"Dammit, Pina. I've got to knock some sense into your head. We've won, you boob!"

"Thanks for the compliment," I said.

"We've got to go read every single word of this back at the dorm, but first…" Katie pulled on the sleeve of one of the older girls whooping it up. "What's up?" she asked.

"Don't you know? She was the best." The older, sophisticated girl threw a haughty glance around. "Craney axed her; she'll get what's coming to her."

"Who?" said Katie.

The girl sneered. "Use your head. Craney's been found out. Heads are going to fly. Bye-bye. Toodles. I have some serious celebrating to do."

"Quit moping, Pina!" Katie grabbed me. "You heard her."

"Whose head is going to fly? And who's going bye-bye?"

"You can't tell shit from shinola. Oops! Pina, I'm sorry. Let's go," said Katie, her look softening.

We ran back to the dorm and settled in with the article. Before we could begin the article, we spotted the words, "Copy sent to Miss Craney" in Doc's handwriting.

I screeched, "Uh oh." when the door flew open and Dorotea strode in singing, "Ding-dong, the wicked witch is dead!"

We stared at her, amazed at her mastery of this song, which seemed so American. The swiftness with which the news had spread also stunned us.

"Rumor has it," said Dorotea, who loved this expression, "That Craney is, how you say, washed up?

Ja, da gibt's ein Gott!"

Katie said, "What?"

I chimed in, "She says there is a God!"

"Holiday! We rebel!" Dorotea beamed. "I am a rebel!"

Dorotea broke out the Schnapps, poured three glasses, and pounced on the bed. We clinked our glasses, and Katie cleared her throat to read:

"Scandal among American Elite"

"Attorneys for the Albert Academy, a prestigious New England institution for the instruction of young girls from several of America's oldest families, ready themselves for an imminent lawsuit to be filed on behalf of a gifted instructor, Miss Emily Whitfield. Her removal from the Albert Academy and subsequent blackballing formed part of a systematic and thorough character assassination by the Head Mistress of the Academy, Miss Mary Margaret Craney."

Katie started to summarize the stilted language and then cited:

"Instructors have often wielded their influence in a compelling manner. While the image of the youngster harking to the side of a beloved teacher for guidance and inspiration is legendary, the heinous representation of the administrator preying upon the innocent shocks and repulses."

Katie took a deep breath. "Oh, you've gotta hear this."

"Such was the case of Head Mistress, Miss Mary Margaret Craney, rebuffed in her unwelcome attentions to young instructor, Miss Emily Whitfield. Subsequently, the Head Mistress was recalcitrant in her efforts to have this instructor banned from public and private institutions and took it upon herself to cast doubt in the minds of Head Mistresses of other institutions as to Miss Whitfield's stability and to indict her on issues of moral turpitude."

"Jesus, give me another shot," I said to Dorotea.

"Hats off to Joe!" yelled Katie and Dorotea.

Dorotea added, "But…but what about Pina?"

"Wait," said Katie. "Look, Pina, quick look at Joe's acknowledgements."

"The small print?" I said.

"Yup!"

"Hot damn! It says, 'I thank P.M. for valor under pressure and for her collaboration on this piece.' That's me! Whoopee!"

"Yeah. Hats off to P.M.," shrieked Katie and Dorotea.

⚜ ⚜ ⚜ ⚜

By now, we were on our third shot when it occurred to me to ask Dorotea what she meant by the "rebellion."

"The students are protesting," said Dorotea, who knew all about protests from watching the Tibet and Alabama Civil Rights demonstrations on TV. And with a huge grin, she added, "About time—me too!"

"Hurray!" yelled Katie.

"Katie, please," I said. "We have to call your dad, right now. Craney's going to be on the warpath."

Katie was slurring her words and laughing, slapping us upside the shoulders. Dorotea, who also said she had to thank Doc for inviting her to Thanksgiving, was dancing around singing, "God bless America" with the thickest German accent.

And me? I was beginning to believe Craney would

never have her way with me. I laughed and laughed and laughed.

❧❧❧❧

Walking from the dorm to an outdoor phone booth—all the school phones were tied up—we were freezing our buttocks off, but the booze helped. They might find us frozen to death, but we would die with smiles on our faces.

We reached the phone booth a bit more sober. Katie dialed her father's number while we steamed up the booth with our laughter.

"Hey, Dad. It's me."

Katie listened, and then her eyes bugged out of her head.

"Holy cow! When?" asked Katie. Then, to us she said, "They're going to remove Craney."

"And the Board is calling back Mademoiselle Lesage *and* they want to hire Miss Whitfield as Head Mistress!" Katie repeated her father's words.

We let go a huge, "Yahoo!"

I stopped cold. "Katie, don't hang up. Gimme the phone, please. Right now!" I grabbed the phone and said, "Doc, thank you, thank you. But I have to know. Could she possibly refuse to leave?"

"First off, Pina, thank *you*! And if needs be, we will see that she is removed with police escort."

Katie and Dorotea were jumping up and down. I finally started to cheer. Snowflakes covered our smiling faces as we all linked arms to charge back to campus.

Chapter Sixty-one

Open Door Policy

Katie, Dorotea, and I didn't waste any time getting home. We did an ecstatic sashay all the way back, convinced that Craney was dead in the water. Just the same, Katie and Dorotea helped me pick a chair and position it under the doorknob. They tested it and even pretended to break in. Secure!

I said, "Better safe—"

"Yeah, yeah," said Katie.

"You know, I laugh, Pina, but I understand how sick Craney is." Dorotea patted my hand in a big-sisterly way. "She really was out to get you from the start!"

We played a dumb game of Scrabble, allowing curses and German words. Obviously, we were cheating. We even borrowed words from the Kirschwasser bottle. This helped broaden our German vocabulary; it also helped quiet any remaining nerves to the point where we fell asleep fully clothed.

When we awoke, Katie and I were all for cleaning up immediately. Dorotea, who had been winning, begged us to continue the Scrabble game to the very end. I played my last seven lucky letters to form the word "scheiss" in German. Katie yelled, "Sh...t!" at my good fortune, and Dorotea innocently claimed that Katie's translation was unnecessary. Needless to say, I won the game with my extra fifty points.

"Yikes!" was our simultaneous outcry to the knock on the door. Reality had just set in again. We looked at each other blankly before Katie asked who it was.

More pounding, followed by Jocelyn's voice yelling, "Quick, quick. You must come, *now*!"

Katie removed the chair and threw open the door. Jocelyn and Emily were roaring with bubbly laughter.

"Get your coats. You're coming with us!" Jocelyn commanded.

"Good or bad," I asked sheepishly.

"Dummkopf." Dorotea slapped me on the back. "They laugh."

"Tell us already." said Katie.

"No, no. It has to be seen to be believed," said Emily.

Katie and Dorotea carried me along at breakneck speed. We followed Jocelyn and Emily to Craney's office.

"Shoot. Put me down," I screamed. "What the heck?"

"It's safe, Pina. I swear," said Jocelyn, who ran to my side and pushed me into Craney's office. "It's just the way we found it."

"*Empty.*" said Katie.

"Oh sweet Jesus," I swore. "Craney's...uh... gone?" I jumped on a chair and sang out, "She's gone. The witch is gone!"

Dorotea yodeled, "Ding-dong, the wicked witch is gone."

Emily explained, "We came to find out what was going on and found everything empty: open drawers, books missing, academic gown gone, tea pot smashed.

And then this!"

"My journal," I said, staring at an exact replica of the one Craney had given me on my birthday. I flipped through the worn pages. There were dates and cryptic comments like "gown found" and "play delivered" and "peep hole in place."

On the last page, I found a poem entitled "My whimsical sprite, Pina." It had been crossed out so vehemently that the page was almost shredded. Thank God I wouldn't have to read it. The next to last page contained a poem Craney had sent me, "Why so pale and wan fond lover."

I started to wretch. Katie ran over, wrenching the book from my hands. She and Dorotea sped to the fireplace and put lighted matches to its edges. I screamed, "No" and managed to pull it out intact. "Evidence, my dears. And for that book I'm going to write with Joe."

We laughed, we cried, we cheered. We threw open the drapes allowing a brilliant almost-Thanksgiving sun to flood the once-dreary quarters. Snow crystals twinkled, and notes of "chestnuts roasting on an open fire" floated over from the radio Dorotea had just turned on.

Katie picked up the phone to tell her father about Craney's disappearance. She hung up beaming and ran over to hug Dorotea and me.

"You, my dear," Katie said to Dorotea. "You are going to be touring Boston with my father and Joe today and of course, dining with us tomorrow."

"I am so thankful! Fantastisch! I get to see history in America and eat a turkey."

"You're leaving today, Katie?" I asked.

"No. You, my sweet, you and I are driving

together with your parents to make sure they don't get lost." Katie winked at me and pushed my lips back up into a smile.

Everyone laughed. Jocelyn and Emily said their parents would also be picking them up today. We all hugged and started back to the dorm.

I hummed and skipped for the first time in two months, cocky with the knowledge that I held in my pocket proof positive, the journal, in black and white, of Craney's perversion. I patted my pocket occasionally, reveling in the security provided by its touch and the arms of Katie and Dorotea laced through mine.

Chapter Sixty-two

Another Open Door

I went back to my room to do some serious breathing and left Dorotea and Katie to clean up their room and help Dorotea pack. They would come and get me when Doc and Joe arrived. I also had some serious thinking to do.

Crashed on my bed, I allowed myself to cry for all the unspoken fears. I realized that at times, I had been pretty dramatic, but that was only the half of what I had been feeling. All the Greek tragedies had played themselves out in my chest and bowels. My Italian pride had only allowed me to cry "help" when my physical and mental being felt too small to contain all that pathos.

It really was time to switch to comedies. I thought I'd read Aristophanes. I liked frogs—I would read that play—and the thought of all those women in *Lysistrata* refusing to have sex with their husbands until they stopped the wars—that was definitely neat.

Maybe the most important thing I had to cry about was not finding my voice sooner, not yelling, "No." I could be loud; that wasn't the problem. I didn't think people would believe me. Today, for sure, I would tell my parents that there's a price to be paid for being too respectful towards authority figures.

Wow! I am so lucky my mother believed me!

Yeah, and I've got to believe Katie when she says I can ask her for anything. That's a hard one. As if I deserve it…Hmm. Something new to try.

⚛⚛⚛⚛

"Coming?" Katie crept into my room.

"Wish I was…" I had been having a pleasurable daydream when she entered.

"You little piglet, you." Katie tickled me, pulling me off the bed. "C'mon, my dad and Joe are here."

There was no end of the hugs and thanks we had for Doc and Joe. Joe winked and joked about his mighty pen and about my skills as a safecracker. Doc confessed to questionable behavior too: somewhat slippery convocations of the Boards in Craney's absence.

I fished out Craney's version of *the* journal and slipped it into Joe's hands. "If you need any more documentation."

Dorotea embraced us with tears in her eyes. "I am so thankful, especially that you have taught me friendship."

"See you tomorrow, D. We can even do the wishbone with you," said Katie.

"Not papier-mâché bones, D, a real turkey bone to make wishes on." I explained the tradition to erase the big question mark on Dorotea's face.

"I want our friendship to go on and on and on," she said.

"*Javohl!*" I answered.

Katie and I watched Doc's Lincoln drive off. I turned to Katie and whispered, "Come home with me?"

Katie's soft, open look took me back to our plane ride to Andover. Then our eyes reflected back to each other all the energy and expectations we had entrusted to Albert: our room awaiting us, free, rampant expression of feelings, easy sailing and adulation by the flock of girls and the shepherding staff.

Well, that didn't happen, but that moment of hope and belief and of holding our breath—that moment was here again, now.

I opened the door to my room and with reverent fingers removed Katie's coat. She stared into my eyes and brushed her lips across them. "So so long…" she whispered.

"I was scared we didn't have anything left, no feelings, no touch," I breathed out slowly.

"Shush," said Katie.

Katie led me to the bed and unbuttoned my shirt. She kissed my neck and shoulders and cupped my breast.

I shivered with all those pent up feelings. I wrapped my legs around her and slid along her long body to fit into the right grooves together. I felt her tongue in my mouth, the key that opened all my yearnings and readiness for her, all of her.

I pressed her to me and felt her dampness ooze into mine. Our bodies found their rhythm, slow and easy; we were a stream flowing lazily, softly swelling up at bends, dipping into valleys.

"You fill me up," I whispered.

Katie brushed my lips, sighing. "Whole and holy."

I brought her fingers to my lips and then to my heart.

We were still that way at sunset. A reddish sun lit up the whole horizon, followed by a special huge moon surrounded by a pale red aura.

"Did you lock the door with a chair?" Katie asked.

I laughed and laughed. "No," I confessed. "Everybody could have walked in."

"Maybe they did!" She mussed my hair into my eyes and my mouth. She had to kiss my lips to extract the three strands caught there.

"We will have to lock doors, you know," I said.

"Not at my father's," said Katie with a twinkle in her eye.

Her eyes softened. A tear threatened to swell. Katie sniffled "We really do have a lot to be thankful for."

"Each other, our folks, how this worked out," I said.

"I'm so glad you and I will be coming back here and Dorotea too!"

"Hey, but let's have Thanksgiving first! Tell me, did you get a hint from Joe about Alda?" I asked.

"Well, duh! Something about sharing the Vin Santo? Pina, I gotta tell you. Joe made me promise not to say anything about relocation and visits—"

"Really...at Thanksgiving?" I pulled a surprised face.

"Here, you'll definitely want to read this now." Katie laughed as she handed me a note with handwriting I recognized so well.

"See you real soon, maybe here, maybe there," spiraled all over the small square, larger than life just like Alda.

Katie had a dreamy look on her face, and she started doing that hair-twirling thing. "But something else is happening, something about us."

"Something is happening *to* us," I said. "It's like you're the same, Katie, but you're not. Know what I mean?"

"Yeah. Like we're different somehow."

"Do I have a big 'L' on my forehead?" I teased.

"Turkey! No. I started to say maybe more mature, but now I'm not so sure!" Katie pushed me off the bed. "You may be a turkey, and tomorrow is turkey day, but we've got to get some food now."

Chapter Sixty-three

Thanksgiving Break

Katie and I awoke early to a shawl-like fog draping down the hills. It felt like vacation. We shifted about slowly in the bed, blankets coddling us. We made instant cocoa with our heater.

"Mmm. I feel lazy," Katie said.

I yawned. "You have plenty of time to loll about. I'm going to have to chat with my father before we leave."

"Right, well, send your mom up when they arrive. She can help me pack."

"Good idea. This is my final fear for the day, maybe for the year," I said.

"That would be something." Katie smirked.

"Hey!"

"Joking, sweetie." She yawned and chuckled at the same time. "What'll you tell him?"

"Don't know. Besides, my mother must have told him the basics. She told him about Athena."

"Yeah. I'll help if you want."

"Thanks, but let me do this one. Hey, there's their car pulling up," I said, glancing out the window.

"Break a leg! You know, your figurative leg, sweetie."

My parents had arrived. I was a bit nervous, but I bounded down the stairs to meet them.

"Hey Mommy and Daddy." I kissed my mother, who immediately said, "And Katie?"

"Upstairs. Go help her pack, Mommy."

My mother disappeared as if by plan.

"Hi, Daddy." I leaned in the window opened for his cigarette smoke.

"Hi, toots!" He pulled the unfiltered Raleigh from his lips and kissed me.

"You want to sit in the parlor?" I asked.

"How about you show me that pond?" My father had his arm around my shoulder as we walked down the gravel path leading to the stocked pond. "You have to bring me fishing here sometime. Nice brown trout." He squatted on a stump and lit up another Raleigh. "I heard the good news that you're staying."

"Wow! News gets around. Sure, we could even ice fish."

"Too cold for my blood. Doc called your mother yesterday. He said you helped to solve an important case."

"Did he?"

"You know, toots…"

Uh oh, I thought, here it comes. I'd have to hear it sooner or later.

"You do know, don't you…" I faltered.

Dammit, spit it out.

"I am so proud of you. Being up here, showing all those fancy pants you can hold your own."

I fought back the tears and said in a quiet voice, "Thank you, Daddy."

"Yup. You certainly hold your own. That's a

Mazzini for you. Your aunt, boy she was a tough one. Capotosta, a real thick head. But look at where it got her."

"Yeah. Mommy said you taught her everything she knows," I teased.

"Wait one minute, smarty pants."

"Daddy, I love you."

"Come here, toots. You're okay in my book. Just don't embarrass your mother. You know she wants people to think she's the Queen of England."

"Daddy." I slapped him on the wrist.

"Before you go up to get your things, I wish you could have spoken up sooner. Authority or no, nobody's going to blackmail my family! *Putana!*" My father spit out tobacco along with the curse.

"Daddy!"

"Now go and don't tell your mother I've been teaching you Italian curses."

❧❧❧❧

Katie and my mom had packed my bag and were descending the front steps of Smythe, the same steps where Katie and I first saw the cloaked figure of Craney point in silence to our dorm.

Katie ran to my father and hugged him. He tipped his fedora and blushed.

The trunk was packed; the car was inching away along the ice-crunchy gravel. My mother immediately handed a bag of homemade chocolate chip cookies to Katie and me.

We sat munching in the backseat, both of us sporting stupid grins that leaked crumbs and brown smears all over our chins. We reached up to my parents, putting our hands on their shoulders to say, "Happy Thanksgiving."

Katie and I sank all the way back, deep into the overstuffed Nash Rambler seats. We pressed our heads into the cushions and turned to look, that look, at each other. We mouthed, "I love you," and in quiet voices said, "Happy Thanksgiving, Katie" and again, "Happy Thanksgiving, Pina!"

About the Author

Dolores grew up in Ozone Park, Queens, New York, where from the age of three she ventured away from this home on her own. While this first solo mission landed her in a nearby cathedral, her further ventures brought her to great physical and psychic distances from Ozone Park.

In addition to teaching foreign languages, and selling antiques, Dolores worked as a psychotherapist with children, teens, and couples and published reference books on lesbians and psychotherapy and child custody.

Dolores lives in Portland, OR and Borrego Springs, CA with her wife, Terrie, and Murphy, the rescue poodle, and Xander, the lynx point critic. She enjoys hiking and gardening with Terrie and Murphy and birding with Xander, from the safety of his indoor perch.

Other books by Sapphire Books Publishing

The Dreamcatcher - ISBN - 978-1-943353-67-5

High school is rarely easy, especially for a tall, somewhat gangly Native American girl. Add a sprinkle of shyness, a dash of athletic prowess, an above-average IQ, and some bizarre history that places her in the guardianship of her aunt. Then normal high school life is only an illusion.

Kai Tiva faces an uphill struggle until she runs into Riley Beth James, the extroverted class cutie, at the principal's office. Riley shows up for a newspaper interview, while Kai is summoned for punching out a classmate.

Riley is the attractive girl-next-door-type whom everyone likes. Though a fairly good student, an emerging choral star, and wildly popular, she knows she'll never live up to her older sister. She makes up for it with bravery, kindness, and a brash can-do attitude.

Their odd matchup is strengthened by curiosity, compassion, humor, and all the drama of typical teenage life. But their experiences go beyond the normal teen angst; theirs is compounded by a curious attraction to each other, and an emerging, insidious danger related to mysterious death of Kai's father.

Their emerging friendship is tested as they navigate this risky challenge. But the powerful bond forged between them has existed through past lives. The outcome this time will affect the next generation of Kai's people.

In the Direction of the Sun - ISBN - 978-1-943353-65-1

"The emotions flying between the two women who tell their story here is as dramatic as the Appalachian Trail and as tumultuous as the Atlantic Ocean. These natural elements are a perfect backdrop for the revelations of love which both repel and engage them."
    – Jewelle Gomez, author, The Gilda Stories

Steady and smart, Alex McKenzie is settled into a comfortable life in her beloved hometown of Stockbridge, MA. Everything Alex thought she knew about life and about herself changes the moment Cate Conrad blows into town like a warm breeze. Alex falls head over heels in love with the free-spirited artist and sailor but there's one problem: Cate's complicated past makes it impossible for her to open her heart completely and so she does what she's always done—she runs away. Devastated, Alex tries to heal her heart by literally walking away from her life to hike the famed Appalachian Trail while Cate takes to the water. The unexpected turn of events shows Cate and Alex how fragile life is and how love is the all that really matters.

Lavender Dreams - ISBN - 978-1-943353-59-0

When Sarah Chase got on the ferry to Bainbridge Island, she left her lover, her job, and her past behind. She didn't know that in the course of one day she would meet a woman who might be the girl of her dreams, change her career path, create a new family, and find herself in a fairytale mansion with two of the quirkiest little old ladies imaginable.

Razor's Edge (American Yakuza) – ISBN – 978-1-943353-81-1

Luce Potter lives by a code of honor. Push her and she shoves back, harder. There's only one problem: Luce has just found out that revenge is a knife that cuts both ways. Now that her lover Brooke has survived the attack on her life, Luce has only one thing on her mind, and his name is Frank. Unfortunately, someone walks into her life that she didn't see coming.

Brooke Erickson has survived an attack so brutal it's left a permanent scar on her soul. All she wants to do now is go home and finish recuperating with her lover, Luce Potter, by her side. An unexpected event puts Brooke at the head of the Yakuza family. Can she command the respect necessary to lead it through the crisis?

Luce and Brooke's worlds are upending. Can each do what's necessary to survive and return to a new normal?

Meet Me in The Middle – ISBN – 978-1-943353-63-7

Veterinarian Aislin O'Shea runs a busy clinic. She wasn't looking for a relationship. She'd already had the perfect one. She certainly wasn't attracted to fancy pants executive, Ms. Zane Whitman - she wasn't her type.

Zane Whitman had it all. Stellar career, wealth, exclusive social circle, and models vying for her attention. Impulsive, emotionally charged Aislin was not her type.

Two women from the opposite side of the tracks.

Neither one expects meddling from an unexpected source on the Other side.
Neither one knows the train is coming.

Over There – ISBN – 978-1-943353-55-7

A gripping romance spanning two continents...

Ruth Carroway is twenty years old and has lived in the shadow of her older brother, Frank, for as long as she can remember. Independent and head-strong, she can't wait to escape the confines of her small hometown in Indiana. On December 7, 1941, the events a world away at Pearl Harbor set into a motion a series of changes in Ruth's life that she never could have imagined.

With Frank at war, but still the center of his family's attention, Ruth itches to do something, anything. Moving out, she soon finds herself rooming with Lillian, a young newlywed whose husband is also at the front. Ruth blossoms when she realizes that, not only is she "one of those girls," it appears Lillian is as well. The war seems non-existent for the two women in the throes of new love until a sudden turn in events becomes the catalyst for Ruth's decision to volunteer for nursing duty.

Landing in war-torn London, Ruth is forced to grow up quickly as she is thrown into the chaos and brutality of World War II. Along the way, she meets Helene, a sexy, enigmatic French nurse, eager to introduce Ruth to the ways of the world, and Tess, an all-business English

nurse who she finds herself drawn to immediately.
Ruth is no longer the same small town girl from
Evansville, Indiana and she is now faced with
impossible choices.

Will she make the right ones?

www.ingramcontent.com/pod-product-compliance
Lightning Source LLC
Chambersburg PA
CBHW030540190726
48283CB00006B/1949